"I was a jerk this morning and I'm sorry," he said gruffly.

"Let's just forget it, okay?" Her tone was abrupt.

Walker gazed at her, wishing he could find the words. "In spite of how I acted, I didn't take what happened this morning lightly, Riley. I want you to know that."

She turned to face him, anger flaring in her eyes. "It wasn't how you acted, Walker. I knew what you were doing. It's how you come so close, then always pull back. You keep fighting me, and I don't even know why."

A muscle in his jaw twitched. "I should have stayed away from you."

Riley held his gaze, her voice shaking with emotion. "And what in hell is that supposed to mean?"

He stared at her, his expression unyielding. "It means that I'm bad news. It means that I don't want to mess up your life."

Dear Reader,

As usual, this month's Silhouette Intimate Moments lineup is a strong one, but there are two books that deserve special mention. First off, Nora Roberts completes her exciting "Calhoun Women" series with *Suzanna's Surrender,* the story of the fourth Calhoun sister and her successful search for love. You won't want to miss this book; Nora Roberts fans all around the world are eagerly collecting this new series from an author whose name is synonymous with the best reading in romance fiction today.

Another author of note is Judith Duncan. Her name may already be familiar to some of you, in which case you know that *A Risk Worth Taking,* her debut for Intimate Moments, promises reading pleasure well beyond the ordinary. For those of you who aren't familiar with her previous work, let me say only that the power of her writing and the depth of the emotions she captures on paper will astound you. This is a book that will haunt your memory long after you've turned the last page.

But I can't let these two special events keep me from drawing your attention to the other two books we're offering this month. Paula Detmer Riggs is an award-winner and a veteran of the bestseller lists, and *Silent Impact* is a perfect example of the deeply emotional style that is her hallmark. And let Marilyn Tracy introduce you to two characters who truly are *Too Good to Forget.* Memory—or the lack of it—can play strange tricks; in this case, those tricks lead to marriage!

In coming months, look for more of your favorite authors— Emilie Richards, Marilyn Pappano, Kathleen Eagle and Heather Graham Pozzessere—to name only a few—writing more of your favorite books.

Enjoy!

Leslie Wainger
Senior Editor and Editorial Coordinator

JUDITH DUNCAN

A Risk Worth Taking

SILHOUETTE·INTIMATE·MOMENTS®

Published by Silhouette Books New York

America's Publisher of Contemporary Romance

SILHOUETTE BOOKS
300 East 42nd St., New York, N.Y. 10017

A RISK WORTH TAKING

ISBN: 0-373-07400-X

First Silhouette Books printing September 1991

Printed in the U.S.A.

JUDITH DUNCAN

is married and lives, along with two of her five children and her husband, in Calgary, Alberta, Canada. A staunch supporter of anyone wishing to become a published writer, she has lectured at several workshops for Alberta's Department of Culture and participated in conventions in both British Columbia and Oregon. After having served a term as second vice president for the Canadian Authors' Association, she is currently working with the Alberta Romance Writers' Association, which she helped to found.

This book is dedicated to the
Alberta Romance Writers' Association.
Thanks, guys, for always being there.

Chapter 1

A country and western you-done-me-wrong song blared from the battered jukebox in the corner, the music adding to the din of a boisterous Friday-night crowd. Peanut shells littered the floor, empty beer glasses cluttered the table, and the smoke was as thick as a three-alarm fire. All the place needed was some horseshoes nailed over the bar, sawdust on the floor, a stack of bales in the corner, and it would be a perfect setting for Hick Town, U.S.A. Only this wasn't the good old U.S. of A.; this was Canada. Walton, Alberta, to be exact, and the Silverado Saloon.

Walker Manley gave the crowded bar one derisive glance, then downed another beer, wondering how in hell he got talked into this. He watched the foam settle to the bottom of the glass. Actually he knew how he got talked into this. Because of a stupid whim. Because the big cheese at Priscella Cosmetics wanted to check out a country bar, because George Nicholson could charm the socks off Attila the Hun, and because one quick beer before heading back to Calgary hadn't seemed like such a bad idea. But it was.

But if the saloon was a bad idea, the town was even worse. It was a godforsaken place buried like a bleached bone in the cattle country southwest of Calgary. And after the week he'd put in here, on the last leg of an assignment that had gone berserk, he'd seen enough cattle country to last him a lifetime. He felt like a fatality waiting to happen. He hadn't eaten since breakfast, he needed a shower, every bone in his body ached, and here he was, sitting in this hokey honky-tonk bar in the middle of nowhere with the Anvil Chorus pounding in his head. Walker felt as if his eyeballs had been dredged in dirt as he stared dispassionately across the table at his agent. For the hundredth time in his career, Walker felt like throttling the man.

As if reading his client's mind, Michael grinned and raised his glass in a salute, his newly acquired western drawl barely audible above the noise. "What's the matter with you? You look meaner than a junkyard dog."

Walker picked out the remaining full glass from the cluster of empties on the table, acute irritation in his voice. "Go to hell."

Michael Aston Bonner III chuckled and leaned back in his chair, stretching his long legs out in front of him. "Anybody ever tell you what an ungrateful SOB you are?"

"Frequently."

There was a glint of knowing humor in the other man's eyes as he studied Walker across the small table. "This is not some two-bit job we're discussing here," he explained calmly. "There isn't another photographer around who wouldn't drive over his grandmother to get this account. And I think you're damned lucky that Nicholson flew all the way up here to talk to you personally. So he wanted to hang around to see the final day of your shoot—it wasn't a big deal. What *is* a big deal is that he's prepared to give you full creative license for this campaign, and you know damned well an opportunity like this comes around about once every hundred years."

Walker slouched down in his chair, a stubborn set to his jaw. "I don't see why it couldn't have waited until I got back to New York. Or at least until I got back to Calgary tonight. Hell, we're stuck out here in the middle of nowhere, and I'm supposed to make a rational decision."

Having had years of experience with his short-tempered client, Michael presented a front of well-practiced tolerance. "Look, Walker, you don't put someone like him off. He wanted to talk to you, and he wanted to talk to you now. I wasn't about to give him some half-baked excuse why he shouldn't come."

Walker sighed and took another long draft of beer, letting his gaze drift around the crowded room. Talk about being up to your armpits in cowboys. There were enough tooled cowboy boots, Stetsons and Wrangler jeans in the place to launch a whole chain of country and western stores. And somebody had certainly cornered the market on flashy silver belt buckles. Most of the noisy crowd were authentic, though—right off a horse—but the rest were clearly urban cowboys and Hopalong Cassidy wanna-be's. A cynical smile tugged at his mouth. There was no accounting for taste.

He shook his head. He couldn't believe he was in a cowboy bar stuck somewhere in the backwoods of Alberta, talking about the biggest account of his life with the head of the fastest growing cosmetics firm in the U.S. No wonder he had such a hell of a headache. If he'd had a brain left in his head, he would have gone back to Calgary with the rest of the crew when they'd wrapped up. But no, he'd let Michael talk him into this ridiculousness. And all because Nicholson fancied himself a good old country boy. Another warped smile appeared. The good old country boy likely hadn't been within forty feet of a pile of horse manure in his entire life.

Michael interrupted his musings. "You make me nervous as hell when you smile like that. Reminds me of a whacked-out psycho in third grade who used to pull the wings off flies."

That wormed a genuine grin out of Walker, and he slouched lower in his chair as he met his agent's gaze, a wry expression carved around his mouth. "Ignore it. These past few weeks haven't exactly been the high point of my life."

Michael signaled for another round, then fixed his gaze on Walker. "Major problems, I take it."

Walker exhaled wearily as he set his glass back on the table. "Not major, just endless."

The agent's expression was deceptively bland. "Haven't we had this conversation before?"

Walker shot him a tart look. "Is this where you say, 'I told you so'?"

Michael cocked his eyebrows and grinned. "Damned if I know. Is it?"

There was a hint of amusement in Walker's eyes as he held his agent's gaze. "You'd think after a few thousand times I'd learn, wouldn't you?"

Rocking back in his chair, Michael shrugged, dredging up his western drawl again. "As my granddaddy used to say, doing business as a favor never makes for favorable business."

"God forbid." Finding his tongue slightly too thick for his mouth, Walker took another drink from his glass. Hell, one more beer and he'd be out cold on the floor, which wasn't all that unappealing, except for the peanut shells. He was so damned exhausted, he could sleep on a pile of rocks.

He picked up his glass, studying the bubbles rising to the top, once again kicking himself for getting roped into this last project. But he had owed a favor to a friend, and when she had approached him, he couldn't say no. She was launching a new Canadian teen magazine, and she had somehow managed to work a promotional deal with one of the big modelling agencies in New York. The magazine was to sponsor a cross-country competition, and the New York agency would sign on the winner. All he was supposed to do was photograph the ten provincial finalists. It hadn't seemed like a big deal at the time. Michael had tried to talk him out of it, but Walker had ignored his advice. But if he had known then what he knew now, he would have drowned himself in the muddy Hudson first.

The Great Canadian Model Competition. Which had rapidly turned into the Great Canadian Muddle Competition. Initially it was supposed to cover a four-week period and twenty locations across the country. That had stretched into five weeks, then into six, and he was beginning to wonder if this was really hell, and he was condemned to an eternity of traipsing around after a bunch of beautiful, bubble-brained teenagers. Over the past six weeks he had gritted his teeth and coped with overbearing stage mothers, mopped up rivers of hysterical tears, faced everything from paranoia to petulance, and tracked down enough lost and misplaced luggage to fill a Boeing 747 airplane. He would have had a better time in a psychiatric ward.

"Do you want to talk about the Priscella line, or are you just going to sit there and sulk and get quietly drunk?"

With a concerted effort, Walker made himself focus on the man sitting across the table from him. "Drunk sounds fine."

Michael chuckled. "Well, try to look intelligent. Nicholson's on his way back from the john."

Walker laboriously directed his attention to the man crossing the small space that served as the dance floor. Poor bastard. There he was, one of the shrewdest businessmen around, trying to turn his wife's millions into billions, and all he really wanted to do was ride off into the sunset. Walker's face creased in an intoxicated grin. Maybe he should buy him a cowboy hat, a horse and aim him out of town. George Nicholson and happy trails.

Mopping his forehead, George Nicholson sat down next to Michael, a satisfied look on his face. "This is the life. Fresh air, real people and good draft beer."

The intoxicated grin remained plastered on Walker's face. "I read that Roy Rogers had his horse stuffed," he interjected irreverently. Michael shot him a look warning him to keep his mouth shut. Walker shrugged and kept on grinning. The headache was gone, replaced by a fuzzy spaced-out feeling, and he studiously fixed his gaze on the foam in his glass. Great stuff, beer.

There was movement at his elbow, and a female hand picked up the empty glasses, wiped the black Formica tabletop, then unloaded another tray of beer. It was a great hand—beautiful, even—with long tapered fingers and perfectly shaped nails. Through the fuzz in his head, Walker decided it was the best hand he'd ever seen. And he, the black-sheep genius of fashion photography, should know. He'd photographed enough of them.

With enormous effort, he raised his head to check out what kind of body was attached to the hand. His gaze slid up a long length of blue-jean-clad leg to a lushly rounded set of hips and an absurdly small waist. Trying very hard to bring the blurry shape into focus, he continued his perusal, his gaze arrested by a blue T-shirt that clung in all the right places, the deep vee revealing a hint of cleavage that was just short of phenomenal. He felt his smile broaden. There was a body that should raise old George's blood pressure a point or two.

Amused by his own thoughts, he propped his head against the back of the chair and studiously concentrated on the face attached to the body. An impression of wide hazel eyes and thick coffee-colored hair clipped back in a banana comb registered in his sodden brain, and, further amused by his sharp wit, he slurred out, "Has anyone ever told you what a great ass you have?"

The wide hazel eyes turned on him in a censuring look, as though she was dealing with a cute but obnoxious child. "I'll bet your mama doesn't know you talk like that."

Michael grinned as he tossed a bill on her tray to pay for the round, his tone apologetic. "Don't mind him. He's from New York and doesn't know any better."

Gorgeous Hands placed the change on the table, amusement in her voice. "Don't worry about it. Someday he'll get the hang of being a grown-up."

George let out a loud guffaw and stuck a sizable tip in an empty glass. Walker's brow knotted in concentration as he tried to decipher both George's amusement and the actual intent of her retort. Unable to hold on to such a complicated sequence of thoughts, he shrugged and reached for another glass as he watched her walk away. His dulled senses belatedly processed impressions, and he was suddenly acutely aware of her, aware of the subtle scent that lingered. Only it wasn't a scent from any perfume. It was the fragrance of sunshine and sensuality, and it was alarmingly potent. Clamping down on the effect it had on him, he took another long drink, deciding beer-induced paralysis wasn't such a bad idea.

"What do you think, Walker? How do you feel about working with Carol Armitage again?"

Walker dragged his attention back to his agent, who was looking surprisingly blurred around the edges. "What?"

"George wants to sign up Carol Armitage for this promotion." He gave his client a narrow look, then pointedly prompted Walker's train of thought. "For the new line of hair-care products Priscella Cosmetics is launching."

"I'd rather drink straight lye first."

George rested his arms on the table, his expression earnest. "She's the hottest model in North America right now. She's a great attention getter."

"So's a pit full of vipers."

"If we could get her for our spokesperson, it'd be quite a coup."

Walker straightened up, forcing himself to concentrate on the business at hand. "Have you ever heard her talk? She has a voice that would strip armor plate off a tank." Very carefully he set his glass on the table, then folded his arms across his chest, determined to present a logical and sober front. His words were only slightly slurred. "She's going to cost you megabucks, she'll never sign an exclusive, and she'll insist on everything from her personal makeup artist to her own masseuse. You'll need a fleet of buses to haul around her private entourage. It's enough to drive you damned well crazy." His voice was thicker as he added an afterthought. "And on top of that, she's a pain in the butt."

George shook his head. "Maybe, but she is gorgeous."

Walker bridled. "She is *not* gorgeous. With the right makeup, the right lighting, the right colors, she *appears* gorgeous. Her face is going on her, and she knows it. That's why she'll only work with a few photographers." He snorted and picked up his glass. "You couldn't pay me enough money to work with her again."

"Then who do you suggest as an alternative?"

"You could drag somebody in off the street, and she would still be a more honest representative than Carol Armitage. Hell, I could make an absolute dog look as good as she does."

Michael interceded, trying to haul his client in before he got in over his head. "Well, that's a bit of an exaggeration, but I do agree with you about Carol."

Walker nailed his agent with bleary-eyed stubbornness. "It isn't an exaggeration. I could take any female George hauled in off the street and make her look just as good as Carol Armitage."

Michael's exasperation began to show. "Don't be so damned arrogant. You're good, but you aren't a fairy godmother. This whole campaign is beginning to sound like some bizarre scene out of *Alice in Wonderland*. George is dumping his whole advertising protocol to give you creative license. You're turning your nose up at a face that's known worldwide. You can't take some damned unknown off the street just for the hell of it."

Drunkenly indignant, Walker forced himself upright in the chair. "I'll bet you five thousand bucks I could."

"Not a chance."

Walker bristled. "Put your money on the table, Bonner, and I'll prove it to you."

Michael, who wasn't quite sober either, was getting equally riled. "Hell, man, you couldn't do it for twice that amount."

"I could."

"You could not. If that was the case, every kid with stars in her eyes could make it to the big time."

"That's right."

"You're dead on your feet, you haven't eaten all day, and you've had too damned much to drink, and you're talking drivel."

"If you're so sure, put your money on the table."

George Nicholson leaned forward, a look of keen speculation in his eyes, obviously caught up in the idea of using a nobody, an *anybody*, for his company's promotion. "If we run with this idea, we'd have to have some contingency plans. Which would mean you'd have to produce a layout within a given time."

Michael groaned. "I thought Walker was the only one who spit on convention. But Lord Almighty, I'm dealing with two outlaws."

George ignored him. "How much time would you need?"

Walker struggled to bring the older man's face into focus. "Four weeks. I could give you what you want in four weeks." He waggled his finger at George. "But she can't be bald and weigh three hundred pounds."

George Nicholson thrived on taking risks, and he had made a pile of money doing just that. "Agreed. She'll have to be presentable and available."

Walker's agent could see a major catastrophe looming on the horizon, and he tried to cut them off at the pass. "Look, this is a harebrained idea if I ever heard one—"

George interjected, his zeal running rampant, "No, it's a hell of an idea. A woman every potential buyer can identify with—someone ordinary and natural." His tone took on new fervor. "In fact, it's damned genius!"

Michael groaned and slid down in his chair. "I can't believe this. Use some common sense, for God's sake. You're talking about spending thousands and thousands of dollars on a shot in the dark."

"Oh, hell, Michael!" snorted George. "Have some backbone. Just think. This is *My Fair Lady* in real life."

That nettled Michael, who had downed two more beer without realizing it, and he rose to the bait. "Fine," he shot back. "Fine! *My Fair Lady* was the figment of somebody's imagination. *This* is the figment of somebody's imagination. It's a dumb idea, you two are both crazy, and damn it, I'll bet you five thousand dollars it can't be done."

There was a sly gleam in Walker's eyes. "You said I couldn't do it for twice that amount."

"Okay!" Michael nearly shouted. "Okay! Twice the amount. Ten thousand dollars says you cannot pull this stupid stunt off."

George rubbed his hands in glee. "There you go, Walker. You've got him backed into a corner."

Having suddenly acquired Walker's headache, Michael nailed George with a disgruntled look. "So now that you've got us at each other's throats, how are *you* going to deal with it? Who the hell are you going to pull out of the hat?"

"Excuse me, fellas, but it's last call. Would you like another round before the bar closes?"

All heads turned, and Walker was once again confronted with a long length of blue-jean-clad legs, a lushly rounded set of hips and an absurdly small waist. The same awareness settled in his gut, and his pulse took off. He forced himself to take another drink.

There was a brief silence as George stared up at the woman waiting for an answer, his eyes narrowed in speculation. Suddenly he grinned, a delighted twinkle in his eyes. He folded his arms and rocked back in his chair, smugness written all over him. "Another round, my dear. Another round."

* * *

Walker leaned against the side of the shower, cold water sluicing over him, his head pounding with a Class A hangover. He tried to decide if he should have a long talk with the toilet and get it over with, or whether he should simply blow his brains out and end it all. He hadn't tied one on like this in years, and he was sure as hell paying for it now. It was a dumb stunt to begin with, downing God knows how many beer when he hadn't eaten all day. It was a wonder he hadn't passed out cold. Keeping all movement to a minimum so his head wouldn't explode, he turned off the faucet and wiped the beads of water off his face. Sudden death was sounding better and better.

He dragged the towel off the Plexiglas door and made a weak attempt to dry himself, but that gave him an acute case of motion sickness, and he closed his eyes and rested his head against the tiled wall. And to think this agony was self-inflicted.

Trying to keep from setting off a bombing run in his head, he steeled himself and stepped out of the shower stall. The mirror above the sink was fogged with steam, throwing his face into blurry indistinctness. That only made things worse. Needing to see the full extent of the damages, he made a halfhearted swipe at the condensation on the mirror. It was not a pretty sight. His ashen, haggard face was in shocking contrast to his dark spiky-wet hair and twenty-four-hour stubble. He looked like something out of a horror movie. His eyes were so dull that their usual deep blue color looked like mold, and the whites were so bloodshot they resembled road maps. To nicely round out the I'm-going-to-die feeling, his mouth tasted as if something had decomposed in it.

He briefly considered going back to bed, but he knew the room would start revolving the minute he lay down, and just the thought gave him another acute bout of motion sickness. With grim determination, he pulled on a pair of pants and picked up a shirt, then headed toward the sitting room of the hotel suite.

Michael Bonner was sprawled on the sofa, groaning softly and holding his head.

If Walker hadn't felt like Dracula's revenge, he would have laughed. "Nice to see you're having such a good time," he said dryly.

Emitting another low groan, Michael opened his eyes, squinting against the bright light of morning. He took one look at his client and closed his eyes again. "Hell, you mean I'm not dead?"

Amusement almost surfaced again. "You aren't even on the critical list."

Michael swore and pulled a cushion over his head.

Slipping into his shirt, Walker resolutely fixed his attention on the fridge built into the cabinet along one wall, then headed for it. Tomato juice. Dear Lord, let there be a can of tomato juice. Half expecting the excruciating pounding in his brain to blow the top off his skull, he bent down and opened the door. The sudden rush of pain was the equivalent of having a piano dropped on his head, and he nearly went blind from it. His prayer answered, he picked up two single-serving cans of tomato juice, then cautiously straightened up. He cast a bloodshot glance at Michael. "Juice?"

The response was another muffled groan.

Deciding he had discovered a new meaning for the phrase, "the living dead," Walker crossed the room and eased himself down in the easy chair adjacent to the sofa, then cracked open one can. He took a long drink, then closed his eyes and weakly rested his head against the back of the chair, waiting for his stomach to either accept or reject. It was iffy for a moment, but it decided to accept. Grateful for the lull, Walker released his breath and opened his eyes. "I feel like there's a tank parked on my head."

Michael pushed the cushion onto the floor and fixed his client with a beady-eyed stare. "It's not a tank. It's your ego."

Deciding the loud pounding in his head had priority over a verbal go-around, Walker declined to take the bait.

Michael winced, turning an odd shade of green as he bit the bullet and struggled into a sitting position. "I must admit, though, you sure in hell make life interesting."

Absorbed by his own internal torment, Walker declined that comment as well and downed another large portion of tomato juice.

His agent's expression became suddenly intent. "Do you have *any* recollection of what you did last night?"

Wondering if his stomach was going to go into full revolt after all, Walker stared at Michael with glazed eyes. "Right now I don't care."

The other man returned the stare, a combination of humor, incredulity and admiration glinting in his eyes. "No wonder I'm on the verge of ulcers all the time." He slouched down in the overstuffed sofa, a wry grin hovering around his mouth. "But as much as I hate to admit it, that's what I like about you. You spit on convention."

Walker gave him a disinterested look. "Is this conversation leading up to something, or are you just feeling chatty?"

Michael's grin broadened. "How does ten thousand dollars grab you?"

That figure rang a distant bell, and Walker's brow knotted in concentration as he tried to recover some fuzzy recollection through the sludge in his brain.

Michael watched him, waiting for the lights to go on. But nothing happened. A quizzical look appeared in his eyes, then a glint of comprehension when he realized Walker didn't have a clue what he was talking about. He took ruthless pleasure in filling in the gaps. "You dug a nice deep hole for yourself last night, Walker, my son, my son. In your somewhat drunken, cocky stupor, you tooted your own horn rather loudly. You convinced George you were such a hotshot with a camera that you could take some Little Miss Nobody off the street and turn her into the next Carol

Armitage. I said you were crazy. You told me to shut up and put my money where my mouth was. We went back and forth like that for a bit, then our good friend George decided it would be good sport to play both ends against the middle. The outcome was a ten-thousand-dollar bet between a drunken you and an only slightly-more-sober me—duly witnessed and encouraged by George, I might add. The terms are that Mr. Nicholson selects the candidate and location, and you get to wave your magic wand and turn her into Cinderella." He folded his arms across his chest, his expression indicating he was relishing every minute of this. "And," he added mercilessly, "you have four weeks to do it in." Michael had the gall to smirk. "Which was set by you, I might add."

It took a minute for the full implication to register; then fragments of recollections began to connect. His memory fully reinstated, Walker swore and rammed his head against the back of the chair. The jolt set off a symphony of kettledrums in his head, and he winced and swore again.

Michael's fiendish satisfaction reached an all-time high. "So, hotshot, how does it feel to have cast yourself in the roll of Henry Higgins?"

Walker's voice sounded like it came from the bowels of the earth. "Get me out of it."

The agent grinned broadly. "Not a chance. This could be the easiest money I've ever made."

Walker looked like a man going down for the third time. "I'll *give* you ten thousand dollars to get me out of it."

Enjoying himself immensely, Michael studied his client, trying to decide whether to let him off the hook or not.

Walker's tone was hoarse and desperate. "You've got to get me out of it. Then get me out of this hotel, out of this city, out of this bloody country, before I lose all my marbles."

After long consideration, Michael finally relented. "I'll talk to George. Nothing's been signed yet, so there shouldn't be a problem."

Wishing he'd never been born, Walker shifted his head and closed his eyes. "Why do I keep doing this to myself?"

"I don't know. Maybe it's because you were a slow child."

Walker's mouth lifted just a little. There was a brief silence, then he spoke again. "God, I'm never going to have another drink as long as I live."

"You said that the last time."

"This is the last time."

"Sure it is." Michael studied a spot on the carpet for a second, then carefully got to his feet. "Is there any more juice in the fridge?"

Walker extended the unopened can in his direction, his tone morguelike. "Who knows?"

Michael took the can from him, popped the top and was in the process of downing the whole can when there was a knock on the door. The agent glanced at Walker. "Did you order something from room service?"

Walker gave his agent a baleful look. "Are you kidding? My stomach's on the verge of mutiny. It's likely good old kick-'em-while-they're-down George."

Moving as though he expected parts of his body to fall off, Michael went to the alcove, unlocked the dead bolt and pulled open the door.

George Nicholson was standing there, showered, shaved and in obvious high spirits. "Good morning, Michael. Is that client of yours presentable?"

Michael gave the older man a wry smile. "Walker's never presentable." He opened the door and motioned him in.

The king of cosmetics stepped into the room, beaming from ear to ear. "Well, Walker. How are you this morning?"

"I'm not a happy camper."

Chuckling, George went to stand before the window, his hands clasped behind his back. "Well, I'm sorry to hear that. But I have some good news that ought to cheer you up.

I've decided to keep you here. The country around here is perfect for the campaign.''

Stay here? Walker stared at him. Stay here? For another four weeks? Here? He'd rather eat live worms.

George continued, supremely pleased with himself, oblivious to the fact that Walker had turned an unbecoming shade of gray. "And I just signed up our new Priscella girl. I drove out to Walton this morning and hired the barmaid at the Silverado Saloon."

He deserved this, Walker thought glumly. Of all the dumb-assed stunts he'd pulled, this was the dumbest. Stuck four more weeks in no-man's-land. With a hayseed to boot. It was enough to turn his brain to porridge. Slouching down, he closed his eyes and rested his head against the seat of the car, letting the movement of the vehicle disconnect his thoughts. He tried to tune out the discussion from the front seat between George and Michael, but bits and pieces of conversation managed to snag in his unwilling mind. Enough registered for him to know that Michael had made sure Walker would have full artistic control, that there would be no artistic director hovering around and driving him crazy. Nor would there be a bunch of neurotics from advertising flitting around, driving *everyone* crazy. Walker Manley would be calling the shots, and even though he had earned a reputation as a hotshot renegade in the industry, that was still unheard of.

Enough had also registered for him to know that Miss Hayseed was being paid a moderate daily modeling fee for the four-week period, with a substantial lump-sum payment if her shots were actually used. A small smile appeared. No wonder George was so damned pleased with himself. He wouldn't have been able to sign Carol Armitage for twenty times that amount. And to add a little zing to his life, the king of cosmetics was going to let the maverick photographer with the big mouth turn the barmaid from the Silverado into something wonderful. It sounded like something right out of The Three Stooges. And he, Walker Manley, was supposed to be ecstatic. It was a slice, especially when he couldn't even remember what she looked like. What it was, Walker thought darkly, was insanity at its very best.

Michael spoke from the front seat. "You're looking like a piranha again."

Walker opened his eyes and met his agent's gaze framed in the rearview mirror. "Then don't go in the water."

The laugh lines around Michael's eyes creased. "Happy trails to you, too."

The corner of Walker's mouth lifted in a reluctant smile. Shifting his head, he looked out the window at the passing landscape. They were southwest of Calgary, traveling through mile after mile of barren rolling hills. This was ranching country—desolate, unending and empty, even in summer. It unearthed the same kind of emptiness in him, an aloneness that affected him far more than he liked to admit. The endlessness isolated him, making him sharply aware of how insignificant he really was.

Wanting to avoid that kind of disturbing reflection, he closed his eyes again, concentrating on the sound of tires on the oiled surface. Three days ago, he would have sworn over his own dead body that he'd never step foot in Walton again, let alone the Ranchman's Hotel and the Silverado Saloon. But he'd done himself in. Three nights ago he'd got bombed out of his mind and shot off his big mouth—and figuratively shot himself in the foot, as well. But it was too late to dig himself out of this mess. George, ever the country boy, had insisted on dragging them out to meet Miss Hayseed Incorporated. Walker, ever the boy from New York, would rather have had all his toenails ripped out.

He glumly wondered how come George hadn't run Priscella Cosmetics into the ground long ago. He never did anything in the prescribed manner. This campaign was a perfect example. That George was personally involved with it at all was amazing enough, but that he was involved to the degree he was, was downright startling. Mr. Nicholson was running on sheer whim, without any input from an advertising agency, without any discussion with his corporate executives, without any forethought. It was as though this was nothing more than a Saturday night crapshoot. Only someone like George would have taken him seriously when he was falling-down drunk. Only a maniac eccentric like George would have hired some backwoods barmaid for a megabuck campaign.

George intruded on his glum wallowing. "I've decided to keep this little project under wraps until you get what you want here, Walker. I'd like to have a substantial portfolio of photographs to show to our advertising people when I tell them about your idea."

Walker opened his eyes and stared gloomily at the back of the executive's head. His idea. The Silverado Saloon was becoming less and less appealing by the minute.

The street in front of the hotel was nearly deserted, except for a couple of mud-splattered pickup trucks, and an aged car pockmarked with rust. The hot June breeze sent dried leaves and bits of garbage scurrying before it, and shadows shrank against the buildings, retreating from the relentless glare of the sun.

The bar, too, was nearly deserted. Two wizened old cowboys in battered straw Stetsons slouched over a table by the door, the sunlight from the window angling across them, grooving the creases in their leathery faces with deep shadows. One took a drag on the stub of a roll-your-own cigarette pinched between his gnarled, calloused fingers, his eyes squinting as the smoke rose, swirling and separating in the rays of light. There was something gripping and poignant, something haunting, in their weathered profiles, and Walker paused, a familiar twist stirring in his gut. He saw life etched in every line, every wrinkle—a life endured with stoic dignity. He would have so' his soul for a camera right then.

Affected by the hardship and depth of character he had seen in those two faces, Walker avoided Michael's gaze as he sat down at the table his agent had selected.

Leaning back in the chair, Michael stretched out his long legs as he studied him. "Are you in a snit, or is something else bothering you?" he asked quietly.

Still avoiding eye contact, Walker didn't answer as he straightened the small stand-up beverage list on the table. Michael watched him for a moment, then turned to look at George, who was leaning against the bar, talking to the man who stood behind it. He glanced back at his client. "Don't sweat it, Walker. If this ends up being an absolute bust, we can always bail out."

Walker finally met his gaze, a rueful grin appearing. "And spoil George's fun?" His eyes grew solemn, and he looked away, exhaling heavily. "No, I got us into this mess. I'll get us out." Sinking lower into the chair, he laced his hands across his chest, wondering what it was about this damned country that got to him the way it did. Maybe he was like a rat let out of its maze for the first time, and all that endless space was driving him crazy.

George's voice sounded behind him. "Boys, I'd like you to meet Miss Riley McCormick, our new Priscella girl."

Walker expelled a sigh of resignation, then reluctantly followed Michael's lead and stood up. Bracing himself for the worst, he turned to confront the source of his ultimate undoing.

Up until then, any distinct recollection of her had been buried in fog. But the minute he looked at her, one particular recollection focused clearly in his mind, and a glimmer of amusement surfaced. She did have a great ass. He blocked off that lapse, forcing his mind to register other facts. She was about four inches shorter than he was, five foot six or seven. When she raised her eyes to look at him, he noticed how long and thick her eyelashes were.

- But it was the full force of her eyes that locked his brain in neutral. Steady and unsmiling, they were an odd shade of hazel flecked with brown and gold, and her gaze challenged him with a directness, a mesmerizing intensity, that seemed to swallow him up. Something furry unfolded in his abdomen. A man could get lost in eyes like those.

The weight of George's hand on his shoulder snapped him back to reality, and Walker quickly closed down his expression. "This is Walker Manley. Walker's the photographer you'll be working with."

She stared at him, amusement and recognition dancing in her eyes. "Ah, *you're* the photographer," she said, her tone indicating that that explained everything. She held out her hand, the gleam intensifying. "I hope you're focusing a little higher today, Mr. Manley."

For one startled instant Walker thought he was going to do something adolescent, like blush. Him and his big mouth. Something in him balked at making physical contact, but common courtesy overrode the sensation, and he took the hand she'd extended toward him. He released his hold almost immediately. His voice was as expressionless as his face. "Welcome aboard, Riley."

Feeling as though her presence crowded his personal space, he braced his legs and leaned back against the wrought iron railing enclosing the dance floor, then folded his arms in front of him. George was looking like the cat that ate the canary; Walker was feeling as though someone had just hung an albatross around his neck. Which meant, he thought with a wry twist of his mouth, that this whole mess was for the birds.

George finished introducing Riley to Michael, then waved her into a seat. "I'm glad you could talk to us this afternoon, Riley. I thought it would give us a chance to answer any questions you might have."

Walker pulled out the chair that was farthest away from her and sat down. Rocking back until it rested against the railing, he again folded his arms across his chest, knowing exactly what to expect. Now it would start, the Just-Discovered, I'm-So-Exicted Syndrome. The breathless questions and the Miss America routine. He'd seen it a hundred times before.

Resting her hands in her lap, she hesitated, then met George's gaze, her expression sober. There was the same husky catch in her voice. "I've never done anything like this before, Mr. Nicholson. I don't have a clue what to expect—or what's expected of me."

Walker was situated at a wide enough angle that he could see her hands clasped in her lap, and his eyes narrowed slightly. Her fingers were tightly interlaced, and she was rubbing one thumb nervously against the back of the other. Angling his head slightly, he turned his attention back to her face. He tuned out the conversation around the table as his gaze became more critical. She wore no makeup, and her complexion was clear and lightly tanned. He couldn't tell much about her hair, because she had it pulled back in a banana comb again, but it appeared to be naturally curly, healthy and fairly long. Her bone structure was excellent, with even, well-proportioned features, perfect teeth, nice ears, good neck and shoulders. She didn't have the cool, classical beauty that people automatically looked for in potential models, but there was something there, something that would photograph well. A vitality, a sensuality. He abruptly shut down that train of thought and refocused on the possibilities. Yes, he could do something with this face, as long as she didn't freeze up in front of a camera.

"I've seen the same expression on my father's face when he's trying to decide whether he should keep an old mare or sell her for dog meat."

Walker's preoccupied squint vanished as his gaze connected with hers. She was watching him, a touch of humor in her eyes.

His expression relaxed into a near smile. "Then rest assured," he said, deliberately maintaining eye contact, "you are not in the same category as dog meat."

Her mouth twitched just a little. "Well, that's a comfort. For a minute I thought I was headed for Rover's dish."

Her answer amused him, but the fact that it amused him irritated the hell out of him, and he shifted his gaze. Damn, but he was turning into a contrary SOB in his old age.

As if reading the expression on his client's face, Michael jumped in to fill the gap. "Riley, you realize this arrangement is unusual. George is trying something very different with this idea."

She turned her attention to him and answered with that same unnerving directness. "I think the point you're trying to make is that Mr. Nicholson has bought himself a pig in a poke."

George Nicholson leaned back in his chair and steepled his hands across his chest, a razor-sharp gleam in his eyes. He glanced from Michael to Walker, then back to Michael, waiting to see how these two city boys would handle this straight-talking girl from the country.

For the first time in the twenty years Walker had known him, he saw Michael Bonner squirm.

Obviously caught off guard by her candor, Michael grinned sheepishly. "You relate heavily to livestock, don't you?"

Laughter broke from Riley McCormick with such a full, rich spontaneity it seemed to fill up the whole room, and the sparkle in her eyes was like watching the Fourth of July. It was so genuine and so contagious, it even wrung a smile out of Walker.

Noticeably relaxing, she sighed, expelling the last of her amusement. "I'm a true-blue country girl, and I'm afraid it shows more than I realize."

George looked unduly pleased with himself. "Don't apologize, my dear. I find it utterly charming."

He would, Walker thought with dark humor, annoyed with himself for feeling so unaccountably testy.

She glanced at George, her expression sobering, her tone without censure as she said quietly, "I never apologize for who I am, Mr. Nicholson."

Her answer hit a nerve, and Walker looked away. Part of the problem, he admitted with some degree of honesty, was that his big-city arrogance and preconceived notions about her were being shot to hell before his very eyes, and that made him very uncomfortable. And as much as he hated to admit it, he found himself warming to her, country or not. But for some perverse reason, which he was not about to dissect, he didn't *want* to like her. And that was irrational, even for him. Maybe the past six weeks had truly scrambled his brains.

He mulled over his contrariness, deciding through some sort of illogical process of elimination, which didn't even make sense to him, that the problem was that he had been sitting around for the past three days with nothing to do. Once he was working, once his energies were focused again, he would quit feeling so damned edgy.

"What do you think, Walker?"

Walker dragged his attention back to the table and gave George a blank look.

George cocked his eyebrow in a knowing expression, then turned to make an explanation to his new Priscella girl. "Walker always tunes out when we talk business. I suspect it offends his sensibilities."

Riley McCormick fixed her gaze on Walker, an unnerving half smile hovering around her mouth as she studied him. Walker had the nasty feeling she could see far more than he liked with those damned eyes of hers, and he turned away. He focused on George. "What did you want to know?"

"Well, I think we've cleared up all the loose ends as far as the company's concerned. Riley understands that we expect her to use all our hair-care products for the duration. A shipment will be arriving tomorrow, along with some of our makeup people. And Della, of course. That's about it, as far as Priscella Cosmetics is concerned. So all we need to do is nail down your shooting schedule and what your plans are."

His plans. Great. *His* plans. How in hell could he be expected to plan for anything when he had no idea how she was going to come across on film? Humor flickered. Which took him back to the livestock scene and buying pigs in pokes. He turned his head and caught her watching him, a smile tugging at her mouth. And he knew damned well she knew exactly what he was thinking.

Letting his chair rock forward, he rested his arms on the table. Collecting his thoughts, he toyed with the beverage menu. Not sure how many of the details Michael had passed on to George, he directed his comments to George. "We have a studio and darkroom lined up in Calgary, and we have a fashion coordinator and a couple of boutiques on-line—and Della has arranged for a local hairstylist who's supposed to be hot." He shrugged in a dismissive manner. "That's about it." He glanced at Riley. "Since George has given me full creative license on this shoot, I'd like to spend a couple of days in the studio with you before we get into the heavy stuff. It'll give you a chance to get used to the routine of working in front of a camera. And it'll give me a chance to see how you photograph."

"When would you want me to start?"

"Tomorrow, if possible."

Walker watched her, waiting for the expected excitement to surface, but all he could detect was a glimmer of apprehension. It was almost as though she wasn't too keen on this whole idea, and that made him wonder. The word "model" usually put stars in the eyes of someone new to the industry, along with visions of sugarplums. He saw no evidence of that. But what he did see made him uneasy. Very uneasy.

Chapter 2

The high-powered lights glared off the pale blue backdrop, the fans doing little to dispel the heat trapped in the small studio. Sweat trickled down Walker's back, and tension knotted the muscles across his shoulders as he stood with his hands on his hips, trying to contain his mounting frustration. Two hours, and already he was ready to toss in the towel.

Nothing was going right. Not one damned thing. It had never entered his head that the studio wouldn't have air-conditioning, but that was only the beginning. The backdrops were all wrong, the shutter on one camera had jammed, and one of the crew had knocked over one of his best tripod lamps.

And as far as Miss Riley McCormick was concerned, he might as well be trying to wring animation out of petrified wood. Damn it, why couldn't she just relax a little? It wasn't as if he'd lost his patience. Patience was a must in this business. There were a thousand tricks a photographer used to get the required responses out of a model, everything from coaxing to blatant flattery, but no matter what he did, she just sat there like a post, with that stiff smile plastered on her face. His own energy level was running on empty from trying to project some life into her, and right now he had an almost uncontrollable urge to shake her.

Walker waited for the hairstylist to finish with her hair, then he stepped onto the set. Della, the Priscella consultant, started touching up Riley's makeup, and he shook his head and motioned her away. He tried to keep the edge of exasperation out of his voice when he spoke. "Look, Riley, this isn't a big deal. It's just a practice run. All we want you to do is relax and go through some of the motions Della showed you. It won't be long before you'll get the hang of it."

She expelled her breath as she tipped her head back and rubbed her neck. "I didn't think it would be so hard."

"It won't be hard once you relax a little."

She shot him a wry glance. "That's easy for you to say. You're not the one sitting here feeling like an idiot."

He studied her, considering if an outside location might work better. But he rejected that idea almost immediately. An outside shoot would draw the usual curious onlookers, and that would probably make it worse. If it could get any worse.

He stuck his hands in his back pockets and stared at the floor, looking for some shred of inspiration. Maybe she would lighten up if he gave her some sense of privacy, if she didn't feel as if she was performing. He thought about it a moment, then met her gaze. "Let's try something different." He turned to the crew, snapping out orders as he began rearranging the freestanding spotlights. "Kill the overhead lights, get some heavier makeup on her, and set me up with a chair that has a high back. And, David, load both Nikons with fast film."

By the time the makeup people were finished with Riley, he had the set arranged with subdued, almost mystical lighting, with the rest of the studio in almost total darkness. Intent on the effect and atmosphere he hoped to attain, he had her straddle a chair with her arms resting on the back, her head on her hands. It was a hackneyed pose at best, but they had to start somewhere.

He started her off with little adjustments. A different angle, a shift of her head, a slight change of body position, and little by little, he could see her relax. He added a fan out of camera range to get some sense of motion, at least with her hair, keeping up a steady stream of directions the entire time. He snapped off frame after frame, pushing her into almost constant movement. Once she caught the hang of that, he reached for some inner vitality. "Concentrate on something that makes you happy, think about someplace you'd like to be, think about how good a cold beer would taste right now."

He was so intent on what he was doing and what effect he was trying to achieve, it caught him off guard when she grinned at him. Unconsciously she tossed her hair, the thick silky curls falling back from her face, her eyes bright, and he felt as though he had just discovered sliced bread. "Great! That's it!" And to the absent George and the ghost of *My Fair Lady,* he shouted, "She's got it! By George! I think she's got it!"

As if no longer conscious of the people standing in the darkened background, she responded to his enthusiasm with a what-the-hell kind of attitude that brought a wellspring of animation to her face. Charged up by her response, Walker focused on the task, prompting her constantly, feeding her cues, pushing her with every ounce of energy he had. It was working! Damn it, it was working.

Walker lost track of time as he shot roll after roll of film, his assistant slapping a freshly loaded camera in his hand the instant he signaled for one. He had her up and moving around the set with her whole body, as if there was no one else in the room except the two of them.

He was vaguely aware of some murmuring behind him, but the comments slid by him. He was looking for a specific sequence of shots when he barked out, "Show me what you'd like to be doing right now. Show me." She shot him a quick look, then glanced at the rest of the crew. In perfect mime, she sank onto the chair in the position he had started her in, her arms across the back, her head resting on them. She closed her eyes, and if he hadn't known better, he would have sworn she was sound asleep.

Restraining a smile, he shot off a couple more frames, then straightened. His tone dry, he said, "I get the message. You don't have to carry it to extremes, you know."

She let her body sag; then she opened her eyes and looked at him. "Has anyone ever had enough nerve to run the words 'slave driver' by you?"

Rolling his shoulders to ease the bunched muscles, he set the camera on the trolley, motioned for the lights, then gave her a lopsided grin. "On occasion." He absently glanced at his watch and did a double take. Five o'clock? Couldn't be. It had been about two when he'd changed the lighting.

Correctly reading his thoughts, she confirmed them with a wry look. "Doesn't time fly when you're having fun?"

He stared at her, still not quite convinced. Three hours without one break. He couldn't believe the time had gone that fast. But one look at her, and he could see that it had. She was wiped out. He had to give her credit. There were few professional models who would have put up with that, who wouldn't have stomped off the set or thrown a temper tantrum.

With obvious weariness, Riley pulled her hair off her face and held it clutched at the back of her head as she closed her eyes and tipped her head back, slowly manipulating the kinks out of her shoulders. Heaving a sigh, she let go of her hair, then slowly levered herself out of the chair.

The words were out of Walker's mouth before he knew it. "How would that cold beer taste now?"

There was a spark of interest in her eyes; then her expression turned wistful. "It sounds wonderful. But I have a good hour's drive home, and if I have a drink, I'm apt to end up permanently parked in somebody's hay field."

For some stupid reason, he had been hoping she would take him up on it. He dismissed her apology with a shrug. "Maybe another time."

She grinned. "Providing, of course, that I last that long." She picked up her tote bag from one of the chairs. "Do you want me in the afternoon again?"

"Yeah, about one."

She raised her hand in farewell to the rest of the crew. "See you all tomorrow, then."

Walker sensed reluctance in her when she turned back to him, her gaze direct, yet oddly personal. "Take care, Walker."

There was something in her husky tone, in the way she looked at him, that indicated she sincerely meant it. Walker couldn't remember anyone telling him to take care and meaning it, and he watched her walk out the door, an empty feeling settling in his gut. He didn't like the feeling. He didn't like it at all.

That same feeling returned later that night when he stood in the darkroom, studying the photographs clipped to the line. He tried to maintain a cold, clinical objectivity as he studied shot after shot of her face, but objectivity eluded him. Instead of seeing angle, light and mood, he was seeing things that had nothing to do with composition. Like freshness, honesty, humor. It was all there. But what got to him more than anything was her warmth and her wholeness of spirit. That was what touched him most.

His face set in a sober expression, he pulled two prints from among the countless others and leaned against the counter as he studied them. It had been a mistake to shoot her in the lighting he had. He could see that now. It had created an aura of intimacy that came through in every picture. But it was strongest in these two. One was a shot of her still and unsmiling, looking directly into the camera, and even in black and white, her eyes had a gripping effect on him. There was a depth to them that unsettled him far more than he liked. Trying to ignore the feeling that thickened in him, he slid that shot behind the other. The second shot had the same potent quality, only more so. This one had been taken when she was feigning sleep, and it made him think of hot summer nights, of darkened rooms, of her asleep in a tumbled bed.

Swearing under his breath, he tossed the pictures on the bench and pushed himself away from the counter. The walls were moving in on him, and it was suddenly imperative that he get out of there.

Everything irritated him. Absolutely everything. The bristles on his toothbrush, the waitress in the hotel coffee shop, the newspaper box on the corner, the traffic lights, the color of the Calgary transit buses, the damned pigeons. When he'd felt like this as a kid, he'd gone down to the creek and smashed rocks. He allowed himself a self-castigating smile. The way he was acting, he needed a whole damned quarry. He gave a female pedestrian a scathing look. Where in hell had she found that dress—at a rummage sale?

He reached the corner and stopped. Okay. This was ridiculous. He was *always* testy when he was on a job. Michael gave him hell regularly for being too intense and too demanding. And just because he'd had a bad night, it didn't mean he could take it out on the whole world and everyone in it. Forcing his mind into a meditative calm, he made himself relax, trying to let go of the tension that had him wired like a spring-loaded bomb. He was going to remain cool and collected, no matter what.

That resolve lasted a whole thirty seconds after he walked into the studio. There was newspaper scattered everywhere, an empty pizza box sat on one of the chairs, and there was a trail of Coke soft drink dribbled across the floor. He could feel his irritability soar. But he managed to keep a lid on it, and he didn't say anything. This kind of clutter drove him nuts.

Della, who had worked on several other Priscella shoots with him, greeted him with a cheery smile. "Hi. You're late."

He glared at her. "Who are you, my mother?"

His testiness didn't faze her one bit. "And good afternoon to you, too, sweetcakes."

A couple of the crew grinned, but they scrambled into action when he gave them a cold look. "Where's Riley?"

Della waved toward the back corner. "Hairdresser."

"Is her makeup done?"

"Since one o'clock," she answered pointedly.

He shot his assistant a withering look. "Cameras loaded?"

"Ready and waiting."

"We'll start with the same setup we had yesterday." As the crew went to work, Walker double-checked the cameras to make sure the right film had been loaded. Without directing the order to anyone in particular, he snapped, "Let's get this show on the road."

There was an exchange of what's-bugging-him looks among the crew as they scattered like field mice.

Determined to pick up where they'd left off the day before, Walker shot with the same heavily subdued lighting, trying to give Riley time to loosen up. It went not too badly for about an hour; then things began to unravel with military precision. One floor light blew a bulb, the shutter on the damned camera jammed, and the back came off the chair. With dogged determination he continued for another half hour, then finally gave up. Riley was bored, and it showed; he was bored, and he let everyone know it.

Deciding it was now or never, he made the decision to work with a fully lighted set. Which worked for about ten minutes, then Riley started to regress. Before long she was back to her petrified wood routine, and he was ready to yank his hair out.

He finally gave up trying to coax some naturalness out of her. Slapping his camera down on the trolley, he glared at her. "Why in hell can't you relax?"

Her eyes narrowed ever so slightly, and her chin came up a notch as she turned to face him. She stared at him, her hands on her hips. "You might," she said with icy quiet, "try taking a deep breath yourself."

There wasn't so much as a murmur from the rest of the crew. Della, unfortunately, had the gall to grin. Walker turned on her. "What's with this makeup, Della? It looks like it was slapped on with a damned trowel. God, no wonder she's not smiling. She can't, with all that garbage on her face."

Della simply stared at him.

"Well, are you going to fix it or not?"

Her tone was sweetly sarcastic. "With what shall I fix it, dear Henry, dear Henry?"

"Something lighter, for God's sake."

Della tipped her head in Riley's direction, indicating with a look that she was to come with her and humor this odious child.

Walker knew he was being a jerk. If he didn't get a grip on himself, the next thing he knew, he'd be down on the floor, frothing at the mouth. With a serious effort to control his frustration, he tried to draw up the same veneer of calm he had before he entered the studio.

By the time Riley was ready to go again, he had regained some control, but it lasted only until Riley's hair started to sag in the mounting heat.

He stopped shooting and stared at the stylist. "Can't you do something with that mess on her head? It's starting to look like wet feathers."

There was fire in Riley's eyes as she stepped in front of the stylist and jammed her hands on her hips again. "It isn't his fault. I'm sweating, and it's starting to curl."

"Then stop sweating," he snapped. He felt like an idiot as soon as he said it, and that only made things worse.

"Why didn't I think of that?" she answered, her tone as sweetly sarcastic as Della's. "I'll see if I can arrange it."

He ignored her as he looked through the viewfinder. "Fine. Now move."

"How?"

"I don't care. Tap dance, if you want."

She did a shuffle, kick, shuffle across the set.

He gritted his teeth and continued to shoot. He took a couple more frames. "Now, if you can get out of your Kewpie doll mode, let's see some real action."

She went stock-still. So did the rest of the crew. She'd made it pretty clear that she wasn't the least bit cowed by him, his much-lauded reputation or his bad temper, and they waited in awestruck silence for her to explode.

She did. Kicking the chair out of her way, she came toward him, looking as if she'd like to rip his arms off. She yanked the camera out of his hand, slammed it into the trolley and let him have it. "Action! I'll give you action! I have a suggestion for you, Mr. Walker Manley. Dump your damned New York attitude, buy a case of beer, smoke a cheap cigar, chase some loose women, and for God's sake lighten up and join the human race!" Her fury virtually sizzling from her, she shoved the trolley out of her way, then headed for the exit.

The only sound in the studio was the door slamming behind her.

That scene kept resurfacing in Walker's head as he stood staring out the window of his hotel room. With one hand rammed into the back pocket of his slacks, a bottle of beer in the other, he watched dusk darken into night as the city came alive with lights.

What in hell was eating him lately? He could barely draw a civil breath. Okay, so he'd had a rough six weeks on the magazine shoot, and he knew he was a pain-in-the-butt perfectionist, but that didn't justify his behavior the past couple of days. He had always been able to regain his professional perspective as soon as a job was behind him, no matter how lousy it had been. But that ability had evaporated practically overnight, and all of a sudden he was acting like a damned mental case.

Walker took a long pull on the beer, then rested his shoulder against the window frame, his eyes darkening with self-derision. Hell, he was still playing games. He knew what was getting to him. She was getting to him—in ways he hadn't even known existed. But knowing that didn't do him one damned bit of good. Especially after what had happened today. Even if he hadn't totally blown it with her, it would have been a no-win situation. He had a maximum of four weeks here; that was it. Then he'd toddle back to New York, and she'd go back to slinging beer, and that would be the end of that. Those were the facts. Four weeks, the clock was running, and he couldn't even call for time-out.

With a cynical twist of his mouth, he turned away from the window and went over to the bed. Half a dozen photographs lay on the rumpled covers, and he reached down and picked up one, the heaviness in his chest tightening. A pair of wide, steady eyes stared back at him, and his stark, contemplative expression altered as he gazed at the glossy image. Three days. Three lousy days, and she'd managed to touch something in him that no one else ever had.

Downing the rest of the beer, he chucked the empty bottle in the garbage, then went back to stare out the window. Years of working with beautiful women all over the world, and he'd fallen flat on his face over a barmaid George had found in a saloon. If it hadn't thrown him for such a loop, it would have been almost funny. But there was nothing funny about how he was feeling. He hadn't known this kind of loneliness existed, the kind that scoured out his insides and left a deep, aching hollowness behind. But it did exist, and it wasn't going to let go. At least not tonight.

Early-morning sunlight glinted off the rearview mirror, catching Walker square in the eyes as he turned onto the narrow lilac-lined lane. Even with sunglasses on, he felt as though the brightness was sucking his eyeballs out of their sockets. He was not in great shape. He'd spent most of the night staring at the ceiling, surrounded by images of her, his insides a mess. Normally he was able to isolate his feelings, to dismember them and slot them into neat little compartments. But not this time. This time, he was on shaky ground.

Bracing his elbow on the open window, he rested the back of his hand against his mouth as he stared at the road ahead, preoccupied by his thoughts. He was tired, he was feeling like hell, and he didn't know what he hoped to gain by coming out here. Even though he'd spent the whole night hashing it over and over in his mind, he was still no closer to any answers. The only thing he was sure about was that he had to apologize for acting like such a jerk.

Granted, he'd nearly chickened out before he even got out of the city, and he'd come close to chickening out again when he pulled into Walton. But once he got that far, he was forced to make a decision. He had only three options: he could either phone first and hope she'd agree to see him; he could get directions to the McCormick ranch from somebody in town and simply show up; or he could go back to Calgary. His conscience overrode his sudden and acute case of cold feet. Eliminating the possibility of her refusing to speak to him, and counting on her inability to be rude to a visitor, he decided it was safer to just show up. But now that he was here, he was having serious misgivings. She would have every right to sic the dog on him.

The farmhouse squatted beside a row of trees in a large well-kept yard, a wide old-fashioned veranda reaching out in friendly welcome. The first word that came to mind was nostalgic—the lilacs and honeysuckles, the sheets flapping on the line. It made him think of the commercial for a phone company—the one with the farm kid leaving for college, and his dad driving him to the bus in an old beat-up truck, his mom waving from the veranda. That one always choked him up. It did what it was supposed to do; it made him want to reach out and touch somebody.

Deciding he was as close to morose as he wanted to get, he parked the rented car beside a faded red garage, tossed his sunglasses on the dash and got out. A huge black-and-tan dog, who looked as if he was closely related to a German shepherd guard dog, came galloping around from behind another outbuilding. He looked unfriendly. Very unfriendly.

Walker was suddenly back to options. He could climb in his car and stay there until someone rescued him, he could stand his ground and let the dog eat him, or he could turn tail and never come back. The first option didn't do much for his male ego, the second held no appeal at all, but if he went with the third, his conscience would eat him alive. Some choice. It looked as if he was about to die.

Braced for an attack, he decided he might as well get it over and done with. He crouched down and extended his hand, quietly calling the dog to come to him.

The dog paused, his fangs gleaming. Then, as if making up his mind that this stranger wasn't much of threat, he trotted over, his tail wagging. Walker continued to talk to him as he caught the animal's head in his hands and gave his neck a thorough scratching. The dog literally melted.

Grinning slightly, Walker ruffled his fur and stood up. He recalled Riley's comeback about ending up in the dog's dish, and he wondered if, by any chance, this was Rover.

The dog trotted beside him as he crossed the shaded yard. Walker grinned; at least he had one ally.

He tried to ignore the butterflies in his stomach as he climbed the worn cement steps. Exhaling sharply, he rapped on the metal screen door. Rover hunkered down beside him and watched him with keen eyes, and Walker absently fondled his ears. There was the sound of footsteps; then a female shape appeared in the porch, her identity obscured through the barrier of the screen door.

As she came nearer, he decided it had to be Riley's mother.

She dried her hands on the tea towel draped over her shoulder, then pushed open the door. She frowned slightly when she saw the dog sitting beside him; then she glanced back at Walker, a questioning expression in her eyes.

"Mrs. McCormick?"

She nodded. "Yes?"

He took a breath. "I'm Walker Manley, the photographer Riley's working with. I'd like to talk to her, if she's around."

Her face brightened with a warm smile as she opened the door wider. "Yes, of course. Come in. Riley's down at the barn right now, but she should be up shortly."

Some of Walker's tension eased. She was a woman in her early fifties, still very attractive, but it was her natural warmth he noticed most. That and the laugh lines around her eyes and mouth. He gave her a lopsided grin. "Thanks, but I think I'd better talk to your daughter before I get too comfortable."

There was a lively sparkle in her eyes. "Well, you'll find her down at the barn. Just follow that trail through the trees."

Walker could tell from Riley's mother's expression that she knew very well why he was there. He also sensed that Mrs. McCormick wasn't too concerned about it. "Great. Thanks a lot."

He turned to go, and the dog followed him.

Mrs. McCormick commented on it, an odd tone in her voice, as if she was enjoying a private joke. "I see you've acquired a friend."

Walker grinned. "I got his number. He thinks he's a watchdog, but he's really a piece of fluff."

Mrs. McCormick laughed. "Not usually."

Walker wasn't sure what she meant by that, but at that point, he didn't much care. His time of reckoning was at hand, and he was back to square one, with his conscience waging an out-and-out war against his inclination to get back in the car and leave.

Retrieving the keys from the ignition, he unlocked the trunk. The custom-made aluminum case that held his cameras lay in the back, but he reached across it and picked up another small cardboard case. He didn't want to admit, even to himself, how much was riding on this meeting with one Riley McCormick.

The barn door yawned open, the angle of the sun creating a shadow at the entrance. Strains of country music filtered out, along with sounds of something thunking against wood, and Walker softened his tread, pausing just outside the door.

Sunlight streamed in through the open door at the other end of the barn, framing her in the rectangle of light between two rows of box stalls. Leaning his shoulder against the splintered frame, he watched her, the knots in his stomach turning into something else.

She was humming along to the music as she worked, unaware of his presence. Obviously having just finished cleaning the stalls, she was in the process of sweeping the alleyway with a push broom. A cloud of dust rose up in front of her and settled on her boots and jeans. She was hot; the tendrils that had worked loose from her ponytail clung damply to her neck, and her not-so-clean T-shirt was marked with sweat. She was a mess. And appealing as hell.

Obscured by shadows, Walker let his weight rest against the door frame as he continued to watch her, his rigidly maintained detachment deserting him. With unexpected insight, he realized that up until now, he had very deliberately retained only disconnected images of her. Even in the bar, the night he made the lousy crack about her having a great ass, he had done it. Her hands, her figure, impressions of her face—he'd never allowed all the pieces to become a whole, and he'd been doing it ever since. Right from the beginning, the warning signs had been there.

A self-deprecating smile pulled at his mouth. This woman, without his even being aware of it, had nailed his shoes to the floor from day one. And it served him right.

Adjusting his grip on the box, he screwed up his courage and spoke. "How are you at accepting apologies?"

Her head jerked up, her movements suddenly arrested as she stared at him, her expression clearly indicating he was the last person on earth she'd expected to find in her barn. He could see her gather her wits about her, and he knew the instant her mind clicked into gear and she became conscious of the mess she was in. He expected her to make some comment, to get flustered about it, but Miss Riley McCormick had more class than that. "How long have you been standing there?" she demanded, her voice fragmented with shock.

Pushing himself away from the frame, he shrugged and started toward her. "A couple of minutes. I was debating how deadly you'd be with that broom in your hand."

She looked at the broom, then back at him, still a little dazed. "What are you doing here?"

He stopped in front of her, hesitated for a moment, then gave her a lopsided smile. "You said something about my joining a race," he said softly, "and I wondered if you'd show me how it's done."

For a split second she continued to stare at him with a blank look; then comprehension dawned. Restraining a smile, she narrowed her eyes at him. "How it's done?"

He handed her the six-pack of beer he'd brought, then fished two thin cigars out of his shirt pocket and handed them to her. The glint in his eyes intensified. "I think the directions were to dump my damned New York attitude, buy a case of beer and smoke a cheap cigar."

Still not quite with it, she glanced at the items he'd handed her, then back at him. Finally grasping what this was all about, she closed her eyes and winced, a new flush creeping up her cheeks. "God, I feel like such an idiot."

There was a twinkle in his eyes as he gazed down at her. "Jerkdom and idiocy aside, what do you say?"

Exhaling on a laugh, she opened her eyes and met his gaze, obviously trying to assimilate it all. "I think I can manage it."

He forced himself to keep his hands in his pockets as he smiled into her eyes. His voice had a husky quality to it. "That sounds positive. I thought you might tell me to go to hell."

She slanted another amused look at him, then acknowledged the chilled box. "This beer is *cold.*" She tipped her head to one side, a glint in her eyes. "How did you manage a cold six-pack at—" she glanced at her watch "—nine o'clock in the morning?"

Walker grinned. "I had a deep, meaningful discussion with the barkeep at the Silverado."

She laughed and shifted her hold on the box, letting the broom fall. "I might have known." She motioned toward the door. "Which would you prefer? Sunshine or shade."

"Which has the best view?"

"Shade." She kicked the broom to one side and started toward the far door.

Walker hadn't paid much attention to his surroundings when he walked down the path to the barn, but as they stepped outside, he faced a view that was nothing short of spectacular. The land rolled away to a wide valley scattered with scrub brush and towering clumps of spruce. Down below, a narrow, grassy-banked creek wound its way through the trees and stunted willow, its still waters shining like a silver ribbon in the brilliant sun. Off on the western horizon, the mountains rose up, gray and granite, the high jagged peaks still etched with traces of snow. The air was so clean, so clear, it was like looking through a sharply focused lens, and the colors of the countryside had that sharp edge of purity that made them almost unreal. He felt as though he had just taken his first full breath in days.

Riley selected a lush patch of grass beside the barn and sat down, crossing her legs Indian fashion as she popped up the flap on the case of beer. She pulled out two squat bottles and handed him one as he sat down beside her. She shot him a look, an unabashed twinkle in her eyes as she turned her attention back to her own bottle. "So, Mr. Manley," she said, unscrewing the cap. "As I recall, you were also told to go out and chase a few loose women. Aren't you a little off course?"

He tipped his head back and laughed. She watched him, a smile lurking at the corner of her mouth, a look of wry tolerance in her eyes. He grinned as he watched her take a swallow of beer. "Damn. I hoped I wasn't, but I guess I am."

She choked on that one, and the beer shot up her nose, and she started coughing and laughing at the same time. Leaning his full weight back against the barn, he watched her collect herself with the same look of wry tolerance she had given him. Her eyes watering, she gave him a condemning glare, her voice still croaky. "I hate it when people make me do that."

He grinned. "No one *made* you do anything." He reached out and picked up one of the cigars she'd placed on the box of beer. "Here," he said, handing one to her. "This is for you."

She closed her eyes in a grimace of distaste. "What are you trying to do, kill me?"

"Hey, you were the one who laid down the directives. I'm just following orders."

She gave him a sharp look. "Why do I have the feeling I've just been had?"

He stripped off the cellophane wrap and stuck the plastic filter between her teeth. "Like I said, I'm just following orders."

She removed it from her mouth, a who-are-you-trying-to-kid look in her eyes. "You," she said emphatically, "have never followed an order in your whole life."

He held her gaze with a challenging stare as he unwrapped his cigar and clamped it between his teeth. Without shifting his attention, he fished a book of matches out of his pocket. "Are you trying to wimp out, Ms. McCormick?" he asked, his tone smooth.

She rolled her eyes in resignation and stuck the cigar in her mouth with a gesture of defiance. "I hope I get sick all over your shoes."

Cupping his hand around the flame, he held the match for her. He grinned broadly as he watched her puff away. "Just be grateful I didn't decide to bring one of those great fat Havana things. Then you'd really have your mouth full."

She accidentally inhaled when she started to laugh, then went into spasms of coughing as the smoke hit her lungs. Figuring she'd survive, he lighted his own cigar, the smoke spiraling up as he shook out the match. By the time she recovered, her eyes were brimming with tears and she could barely speak. "You're a menace."

Walker chuckled. "Hey, this was your idea, remember?"

She managed a watery grin, her voice choked and hoarse. "I was the victim of circumstance."

"Serves you right."

"So I've found out." Giving the glowing end of her cigar a wary look, she took another cautious puff. Walker watched her, his eyes gleaming with a mixture of amusement and admiration. He liked her for that, for being a good sport.

Smoke drifted into her face, making her eyes water all the more, and she glanced at him. "You *are* trying to kill me."

Tears clung to her long lashes, turning her eyes the most phenomenal shade of green, and for what seemed like an eternity, he was lost in the color. Trying to ignore the roller coaster sensation in his chest, he clasped his hands around the bottle wedged between his thighs, his palms itching to wipe away her tears. His tone was light and teasing. "A deal's a deal."

She wiped her eyes with the side of her hand, her voice catching on a final sigh. "You probably cheat at cards, too."

He took the cigar out of his mouth and knocked off the ash, the laugh lines around his eyes crinkling. "Probably."

Riley shot him a quick look, then took a swig from her bottle.

Walker rested his head against the weathered wood as he studied her profile. "So this is what you kids from the farm do. Hang out behind the barn drinking beer and smoking."

She grinned. "Ah. So that rumor's finally reached New York."

He restrained a smile as he raised the bottle to his lips.

Riley took another cautious puff on her cigar, then raised her eyebrows in an expression of approval. "Hey, I think I could get to like this."

With a grunt, Walker plucked the cigar out of her hand and crushed the butt in the loose dirt by his hip. "Not a chance. If I'm going to lead you astray, it damned well isn't going to be over a cigar." From the slightly flustered expression on her face, he knew she wasn't going to touch that comment with a barge pole. There was a brief easy silence; then Walker spoke, his tone quiet. "Would you tell me to go to hell if I asked a personal question?"

She glanced at him, then leaned back against the barn. "Probably not."

"Why did you take this modeling job?"

She grinned. "I thought for sure you were going to ask me, 'What's a nice girl like you doing in a place like this?'"

Hooking his forearm across his upraised knee, he smiled and shrugged. "That was my next question." His gaze turned serious again as he continued to study her. "Why did you take the job?"

She looked away, her face losing its animation. She avoided his gaze when she answered him. "Because of the money."

He waited and watched, hoping she would go on.

After a short silence, she did. "It's kind of involved. My mother had a mastectomy three years ago, then had to have the other breast removed this spring. That second operation was a tough hurdle for both her and Dad. The surgery was bad enough, but she was so sick from the chemotherapy that she could barely lift her head off the pillow. So I got a leave of absence from my job as an architectural draftsman and took a job at the Silverado so I could stay at home and help out."

He continued to watch her, a solemn expression darkening his eyes. "How's she doing?"

She shrugged, deliberately avoiding his gaze. "The doctors are optimistic, and so is Mom, but it's something you can never quite put out of your mind."

"I'm sure it isn't."

She shot him a quick look, a hint of gratitude in her expression; then she looked down, plucking at the grass beside her. "It really bothered Dad that I left my job. But I knew he had enough to worry about without worrying about Mom on top of it. He helped my brother get a place of his own two years ago, so he's feeling the pressure financially."

Walker supplied his own answer. "And the kind of money you'd get from this contract would take the pressure off a little."

"Something like that."

He studied her profile a moment longer, then focused on the bottle he held in his hand, his eyes narrowing in concentration. There had to be some damned way to make this Priscella thing work. The image of her in the barn, her face flushed, her neck glistening with sweat, her hair yanked back in a messy ponytail . . . hardly the material for a big advertisement promotion—or was it?

"Walker?"

Holding on to that flicker of an idea, he turned to look at her. There was an air of disquiet about her as she lowered her gaze and began scraping at the label on the beer bottle. She didn't say anything for a moment; then she sighed and met his gaze. "Look, I know this isn't working, and it isn't your fault. I don't have what it takes, and I know it. I just want you to know I honestly will understand if you decide to pack it in."

He stared back at her, part of him listening to what she was saying, part of him still intent on the idea germinating in his mind. He was back to options again. He could stay, or he could go. It was as simple as that.

Only it wasn't as simple as that. There was a damned sight more at stake here than a stupid bet and his overinflated ego. There was one Riley McCormick—the lady who could tie his insides into square knots and make every breath feel like his first. He wasn't playing any games with himself, either. There would be no happy ending. At the end of the four weeks, he would leave here the same way he'd arrived—alone. But maybe he could cram enough into that four weeks to last him a lifetime. Or he could bail out now, while he had the chance.

She ducked her head and peered into his eyes, coaxing him with an uncertain smile. "Hey, are you still in there?"

One look at her and he felt as though he'd just inhaled a shot of pure oxygen. No damned way was he packing it in. He grinned back at her and ground out his cigar. "You, Miss McCormick, are going to be rich and famous. I just had one hell of an idea."

Chapter 3

"This is a dumb idea, Walker."

Walker stood in the doorway of the barn as he checked his light meter, then adjusted the setting on his camera. "Just shut up and keep sweeping."

Riley shot him a caustic look but did as she was told, ignoring him as she worked her way down the alleyway. Dust motes rose in the air, the light breeze from the open doors doing little to dispel the heat inside. A sheen of perspiration reappeared on her face and glistened on her neck as dust rolled up, settling on her booted feet and clinging to her jeans.

His expression fixed with concentration, Walker readjusted the focus and absently shifted the strap around his neck, the automatic advance whirling as he shot several frames. He moved constantly, searching for a better angle of light, an illusion of distance, a hint of mood, the viewfinder constantly fixed on her.

The rectangle of sunlight from the back doorway formed a bright backdrop for the long, dusky interior of the barn, boxing the solitary figure in a framework of light and shadows. Walker continued to shoot frame after frame, almost afraid to speak for fear of shattering the dramatic effect. And the effect *was* dramatic, even without the sophisticated props of a high-gloss ad. It captured an ordinary woman hard at work, yet there was an aura of mystery, of untapped sensuality, about her that was as real as the perspiration on her skin. The hot, sweat-dampened body, the fathomless eyes, the loose tendrils of hair clinging to her neck. Walker felt as though he couldn't pull enough air into his lungs, and the feeling had nothing to do with the heat.

Riley paused and glanced up at him, humor glinting in her eyes. "You'd better move, Manley, or you're going to end up with something unspeakable on your Italian loafers."

He took a step backward, altering the focus as he tried to capture the expression in her eyes. "Nice try, McCormick. But a little muck isn't going to scare me off. You're talking to a man who's stood knee-deep in a rotting swamp for four hours, trying to get *the* perfect shot."

She grinned. "Why, good for you, Walker." Stepping around him, she grabbed the shovel leaning against the wall. She scooped up the sweepings, then carried them outside.

A tautness banded his chest as Walker watched her, his awareness of her so razor-edged he could almost taste the salty moisture on her skin. Swearing under his breath, he turned back to his camera case, which was lying on a stack of bales by the door. He opened it, tossed back a piece of protective foam matting and removed a canister of film, the muscles in his jaw rigid. He didn't like the feeling—that gut-clenching awareness. He didn't like it at all. In fact, it scared the hell out of him. It left him feeling too damned exposed.

Riley came back into the barn and set the broom and shovel back in the corner, then glanced at him as she started toward the opposite end of the aisle. She motioned toward the empty camera he had in his hand. "I hope that means what I think it means."

He managed a lopsided grin. "Don't get your hopes up. One roll of film isn't even a warm-up."

She pulled a grimace of distaste as she picked up a halter from one of the pegs. "I was afraid of that."

She disappeared through the door, and Walker reloaded the camera, his expression somber. He had to keep focused on one fact: he had four weeks here. And if he couldn't keep his damned libido under control for four lousy weeks, he'd better hightail it back to New York before he was in so deep he would never be able to dig himself out. There was no way he could get involved with her, whether he wanted to or not. Except he had a sneaking suspicion that he was buried up to his neck already. And he had a sweet, self-destructive urge not to even fight it.

The sounds of hooves on the thick plank flooring echoed hollowly in the empty barn, and Walker turned and watched Riley lead a horse down the alleyway. The smell of warm horseflesh assailed his senses, and old memories stirred. He turned away, his jaw clenched as he closed his case. He'd never even thought about the McCormicks having horses. Damn it, he though he'd put that part of his life behind him. There were some things he'd never put behind him, but that was one thing he thought he had. Coming out here had been a mistake, for more reasons than one. He let his breath go and forced himself to relax.

She was tying the shank to a heavy ring mounted on the exterior of one of the stalls as he turned, and his gaze fell to the bandaged left foreleg of the animal. He indicated the wrap. "What happened?"

Riley glanced at him as she rubbed the animal's neck. "He has a bad gash just above the fetlock. I don't know whether he was tearing around and clipped himself, or if he caught it on something." She started to turn away, then turned back to stare at him. "If you're such a diehard New Yorker, how did you know it was a 'him'?"

She was quick, he had to give her that. Not too many people would have picked up on a slip like that. There was an undercurrent of dryness in his voice. "Even I know there's some basic equipment that's the same across the board," he said, his tone loaded with innuendo. "You farm kids aren't the only ones who've managed to figure that out, you know."

She cast him a chastising look, then crossed to the oat bin, an unmistakable flush creeping up her cheeks. Walker grinned broadly and rested his shoulder against the door frame, waiting to see if she would retaliate. She didn't. Instead she lifted a pail of water off the top of the bin, then picked up what looked like a wooden carryall and returned to the horse. Straightening, Walker slung the camera strap around his neck and moved to the other side of the alleyway so he could see what she was doing.

Speaking softly to the gelding, Riley slowly ran her hand down his leg, then crouched down. Walker hooked one arm on the stall door, amusement still hovering around his mouth. "You disappoint me. I thought you'd have some slicing rebuttal."

She didn't look up at him, but he could tell she was smiling. "I can hardly fight a battle of wits with someone who's unarmed."

The glint in his eyes intensified. "I never took you for a coward, McCormick."

"My Grandmother McCormick used to say there was a time to take bait and a time to leave it in the trap to rot."

Walker grinned, thinking that Grandma was one smart cookie.

Riley unwound the bandage, expertly rolling it into a compact wad. A gauze dressing was exposed, and she dropped the bandage into the first aid box, lifted out a plastic bottle and screwed off the cap. She poured a liberal amount into the water in the pail, and a strong smell of disinfectant permeated the barn. Tossing a sponge into the pail, she again stroked the horse's leg, then began to carefully saturate the gauze with the dripping sponge. The gelding dropped his head and turned it slightly, as though watching her peel away the soiled dressing, and Walker quietly changed his position. There was something very compelling about the scene—the dusky barn, a woman intent on caring for an animal, the obvious bond between horse and owner. It was reality with a sense of poignancy, and Walker knew he had a winner before he shot a single frame.

He shot several with a wide angle lens, wanting to capture the wholeness of the mood; then he took several close-ups of her hands as she cleansed the wound, covered it in thick ointment and redressed the wound. Walker tried to clamp down on the sensations those shots evoked, knowing he was balanced on a dangerous edge. One wrong move and he could take the worst fall of his life.

"You're not much help, you know."

He forced a crooked smile as she glanced up. "What do you want me to do, tap dance?"

He saw her smile as she finished tying the wrap in place. This time she passed on the tap dancing crack. "I was thinking more along the lines of hard physical labor."

Real amusement gleamed in his eyes. "I'm paid for my brains, not my brawn."

"I suppose you think that gives you the license to stand around while I work."

Sticking his hands in his pockets, he let the camera hang loose as he leaned against the wall, deliberately baiting her again. "More or less. I don't believe in equal rights for women."

Her tone was unruffled as she responded offhandedly. "I don't imagine you get many invitations to dinner, do you?"

Walker nearly laughed. He'd expected to get a rise out of her, but Grandma had taught her well. "One or two, providing I promise not to eat with my feet or drink tea out of my saucer."

He could hear laughter in her voice. "Every hostess's dream come true." She rinsed off her hands, wrung out the sponge that had been floating in the pail and tossed it into the first aid box. Patting the gelding on the shoulder, she rose and untied him. "Come on, Doc. Sunshine and green grass for you."

Walker adjusted the setting to take one last shot of her leading the horse out of the barn, his expression hardening when he realized his attention was focused on the fluid, muscled movements of the gelding. Some memories died harder than others.

He was stowing his gear in the case when Riley reentered the barn. She glanced at him, her expression changing when she saw the hard expression on his face. She studied him briefly, then spoke, her tone quiet. "Packing it in, I see."

Walker didn't look at her. "Yeah. I figure I've harassed you enough for one day."

She didn't say anything as she replaced the vet supplies on the oat bin, then came over to where he was. Sticking her hands in her back pockets, she watched him place the lens he had removed in a padded compartment. He heard her take a deep breath, as though she was steeling herself. "Walker?"

He met her gaze, his face schooled and unreadable. Her eyes were shadowed by concern as she watched him, and once again he had the unnerving feeling she could see things he wanted no one to see.

"What's wrong?"

He stared at her, her perceptiveness igniting a sudden flash of irrational anger, his determination to play fair with her overriding it. Had it been anyone else, he would have told them to go to hell. But Riley wasn't just anyone. Fighting the sudden urge to brush back the damp hair clinging to her neck, Walker managed a warped smile. "Didn't Michael warn you that I have the disposition of a junkyard dog?"

There was a hint of amusement around her mouth, but her eyes remained solemn as she held his gaze with a scrutinizing intensity. "He said you get very intense when you're working." She tipped her head to one side, her eyes narrowing in speculation. "But I wonder. Do you really have the disposition of a junkyard dog, or do you just want everyone to *think* you do?"

His expression sobered. "Don't make me into something I'm not, Riley," he said, his voice edged with a quiet warning.

"No," she answered, her husky tone igniting a response in him that made his chest hurt. "I'd never do that." She gave him a small smile, her gaze locking on his. "But don't *you* try to make yourself into something you're not, either."

Walker tried to outstare her, but finally he had to look away. She was far too close—both physically and perceptively—and he made himself concentrate on what he was doing as he tried to disconnect himself from the sensual reactions that bombarded him. He couldn't remember ever wanting to reach out and touch someone the way he wanted to touch her right then.

She picked up a large tabby cat that had wandered into the barn and wound itself around her legs. She absently stroked its head as she watched him. "You haven't had breakfast, have you?"

He shot her a sharp glance. "No."

"I didn't think so. You have a hungry look about you."

He nearly dropped the camera with that one. That kind of intuitive insight he could sure as hell do without. He avoided looking at her as he reached out and stroked the cat's chin, somehow managing to keep his tone light. "What did you have in mind? A bucket of oats, or a couple of dead mice?"

Riley grinned. "Since it's an hour and a half till lunch, I was thinking of something a little more civilized—like fresh cinnamon rolls and a cup of coffee."

She could have offered him sawdust, and it still would have had the same effect. He'd come out here, expecting her to tell him to go to hell; what he was getting was fresh cinnamon rolls and coffee. He grinned back at her. "I think I can handle that."

Riley loosened her hold on the cat, and it obligingly jumped out of her arms onto the stack of bales. As Walker closed the camera case, she collected a pair of leather work gloves wedged behind the wiring of the light switch, then picked up the opened case of beer.

As he followed her up the narrow path to the house, he tried to pigeonhole his feelings into safe little mental compartments. He tried to convince himself that the real reason he couldn't wipe the silly grin off his face was because the combination of sunshine and clean mountain air was just too wholesome for his cynical little mind. But even with that kind of self-directed irony, he knew he was lying through his teeth.

Riley waited as he set the camera case on the back seat of the car, the case of beer in her hand. As he closed the door, the dog came tearing around the corner of the house.

Her voice had a sharp tone of command. "Max. Sit!"

Max blatantly ignored her, and she made a frantic grab for his collar as he bounded by her. An unmistakable look of alarm flashed across her face, and she lunged for the dog as he pounced on Walker, nearly bowling him over as he planted his paws on his shoulders. Staggering a little, Walker looped his arms around the animal's shoulders, then grinned. "You've got a hell of a watchdog here, McCormick. It's a wonder he doesn't meet everyone at the gate with a basket of flowers."

There was a grim set to her jaw as Riley grasped the collar and yanked the dog down, an indisputable tone of authority in her voice as she snapped out a second command. "Max! Sit!"

The dog didn't ignore her this time. He sat. Walker thought the animal showed eminent good sense, especially with that expression on her face. Nobody in his right mind would challenge *that* look.

He brushed himself off and started to make some teasing comment when he saw how ashen her face was, and he realized she had been truly shaken. "Hey," he said softly. "Don't sweat it. He didn't mean any harm."

Just then Riley's mother came out of the back door. "Oh, there you are. I was coming to see if you were ready for coffee. I just put on a fresh pot."

Riley turned, her voice shaking with reaction. "I'm going to kill that damned dog. So help me."

A look of real alarm appeared on the older woman's face. "Oh, no. What did he do this time?"

"He went after Walker."

Walker figured it was up to him to defend the dog. "He didn't exactly go after me, Riley. He was just excited." He scratched the dog's neck. "Weren't you, boy?"

Max immediately sagged against his leg, his eyes closed, his tongue lolling in pure ecstasy.

Riley shot the animal a scathing look and started toward the house. "That dog's a menace," she muttered under her breath.

A peculiar look appeared in Mrs. McCormick's eyes as she scrutinized her daughter. She glanced at Walker, then back at Riley, acute amusement in her eyes. "Odd that *you* should say that, darling. Seeing as you're the one who defended him when he chased the insurance salesman down the driveway."

Walker could have sworn he saw Riley squirm, but the impression was gone as soon as it registered. He was going to have to find out the whole story about Max, the discriminating watchdog.

Mrs. McCormick looked at Max, a twinkle in her eyes. "Maxwell usually puts the run on any strange men who show up here. I was amazed he even let you out of the car this morning." Her gaze became contemplative as she studied the dog, her expression altering as she shot Walker a humor-filled quick glance. "Well, on second thought, maybe I'm not."

Walker didn't have a clue what she meant by that, but it was obvious Riley did, because she gave her mother a disgusted look and stomped up the steps.

Restraining a smile, Mrs. McCormick watched her daughter, then directed her attention back to Walker. "You don't have to humor him. He'll hang on you all day if you let him."

Max was leaning against him so heavily, Walker thought for sure the dog would fall over if he withdrew his support. Max didn't. But he gave Walker such a pitiful, soulful look, Walker felt as if he'd condemned him to life in the dog pound. Riley's mother frowned when she spotted the case of beer Riley was holding. "Where on earth did you find *that*?"

Riley correctly deciphered her mother's tone. "No, Mother. Brent and Dana aren't stashing beer in the barn." She glanced at Walker, a sparkle in her eyes. "Brent and Dana are my younger brother and sister. They're at that age where Mother stays awake at night worrying about their morals."

"I do not worry about their morals." Mrs. McCormick sent her daughter an amused glance and tapped the beer case. "Should I be worrying about yours?"

Riley shot Walker a slightly sheepish grin. "Walker brought it. He was trying to get even."

"With good reason, no doubt." She turned toward the house. "I don't know about you two, but I'm ready for a coffee break. Your father's moving cattle over on the west lease, so he won't be in."

"You'll have to cough up more than coffee, Mom. I bribed him with fresh cinnamon rolls."

Mrs. McCormick chuckled. "I suspected as much. I just finished glazing the last batch." She held the screen door open for him. "There's a sink around the corner if you want to wash up, Walker."

Riley turned and looked at him as he followed the two women into the large utility room. "Silly woman," she said with a touch of malice. "She thinks you might have actually done something to get your hands dirty."

Walker cocked his hand like a pistol, silently warning her that she was pushing her luck, but Riley cocked her finger back, deliberately mimicking him as she rounded the corner.

Throughout the easy conversation around the big oval kitchen table, Walker made a point of studying Molly McCormick. Initially he hadn't noticed any indications of her ill health, but once he had a chance to observe her up close, he could detect the telltale signs of recent chemotherapy. She was wearing a wig, and there was evidence of a recent weight loss, but what he noticed most was how she tried to camouflage how weak she was.

It didn't take him long to realize she was the type of person who would face something like cancer with equanimity and resolute optimism, at least in front of her family. No matter what her private fears might be, she would never permit those fears to touch their lives. Never in a million years. To Walker, that kind of quiet, selfless courage was worthy of near-reverent respect. It was a verbal poke from Riley that derailed his train of thought. "Do you want another cinnamon roll? Why quit at four when you can make it an even half dozen?"

He leveled a look at her, warning her that she was pushing her luck again. "How would you like me to photograph you first thing in the morning with lint stuck to your teeth?"

Her eyes narrowed in a try-it-and-you're-dead look. "You," she said, distinctly emphasizing every word, "would never draw another breath."

He gave her a slow, provoking smile. "We'll see."

Molly McCormick chuckled, and her expression lightened, as though she was enjoying some private joke. "Are you two involved in an all-out war, or just a minor skirmish?"

Leaning forward, Walker rested his arms on the table, his gaze still fixed on Riley, an expression of unmistakable deviltry in his eyes. "That depends on your daughter."

With the unblinking gaze of a poker player, Riley stared right back at him, the tilt of her chin indicating that he'd have an honest-to-God battle on his hands if he ever tried to follow through with his threat. She might as well have waved a red flag at him. There was no way on earth he could walk away from a challenge like that. He'd die trying first. His mouth lifting in an indolent grin, he held her gaze as he reframed his response. "On second thought, let's say the battle line has been drawn."

There was still an undercurrent of humor in Mrs. McCormick's firm tone. "Not in my house."

Riley laughed, breaking eye contact with Walker as she glanced at her mother. "Relax, Mom. He's just shooting arrows in the air—it's not going to deteriorate into a wrestling match."

"I should hope not. It's a wonder we have a whole piece of furniture left in the house." Molly McCormick looked at Walker, quite prepared to tell tales on her daughter. "Riley and her older brother Wayne used to get into these wild wrestling matches. They'd nearly demolish the place, then they'd laugh at me behind my back when I got annoyed."

Walker looked at Riley. "Shame on you."

"We weren't *that* bad."

"*You,*" Mrs. McCormick answered, requalifying her daughter's opinion from a mother's perspective, "were holy terrors."

Walker figured she was probably right.

Her daughter tried to change the subject. "I think it's time you had a nap."

Not wanting to overstay his welcome, Walker glanced at his watch. "And I'd better be heading back."

Riley pushed herself away from the table, then started collecting the coffee mugs. "What time do you want me at the studio?"

"I scrubbed that for today. I told Della to give the crew the day off. It'll give them a chance to see the sights and get westernized."

"Seriously?"

"Seriously."

She stopped what she was doing and studied him. "Then why don't you hang around and get westernized yourself?"

He gave her a dubious look. "Meaning what?"

"Have you ever been on a working ranch?"

He grinned. "Not in this lifetime."

"Then it's about time you were."

As far as he was concerned, getting westernized rated right up there with breathing. Not only did Riley make an excellent tour guide, but he discovered she had an easy kind of humor that had no sharp edges. Ever since he could remember, he'd loathed those sharp cosmopolitan types. But Riley wasn't like that. She was a breath of fresh air. She wasn't compelled to turn everything he said into a chess match, and he found himself laughing more than he had in years. He did not want the day to end.

But end it did, and when they returned to the house later that afternoon, he experienced such an acute attack of regret it was almost physical. He tried neutralizing it with a good dose of self-directed cynicism, telling himself he was regressing into wet-nosed adolescence, but that was about as effective as fighting a forest fire with a squirt gun. There was not one damned thing that was adolescent about how Riley McCormick made him feel.

Dust rolled in the open windows as Riley parked the battered half-ton beside the garage, and Walker collected his camera and jacket as he climbed out, his unsmiling expression partially masked by his sunglasses. The last thing he wanted to do was get in his car and leave, but somehow he was going to have to do exactly that.

He came around the back of the truck, unaware that Riley was watching him until she spoke. "You got quiet all of a sudden."

He glanced at her, forcing a crooked grin onto his face. "I think I just ran out of steam."

"Who are you trying to kid? You're not the type who runs out of steam."

The creases around his mouth deepened. "Well, I did. My boiler's dry."

"You just need a refill." Then she added slyly, "Like maybe a cold beer."

His jacket slung carelessly over his shoulder, Walker tightened his other hand around the strap of his camera, thinking it was a good thing he had sunglasses on, so she couldn't read his reactions in his eyes. "I think I'd better go. I've already managed to screw up most of your day."

She planted her hands on her hips and stared back at him. "Don't be ridiculous. I did what I had to do, and besides, my mother will be expecting you to stay for supper."

"No, I've imposed—"

She cut him off. "Don't give me that drivel." She tipped her head to one side, one of those unnerving insightful smiles pulling at her mouth. "Or are you avoiding meeting my father?"

His mouth twitched. "Maybe I should. What did you tell him about me?"

She flashed a look at him. "I told him you were arrogant, impossible and wanted your own way."

"And what did he say?"

"He said we should get along just fine."

The way she said it made Walker laugh, and every muscle in his body relaxed. "You really know how to make a guy sweat, don't you?"

She grinned and tipped her head toward the house. "That's why you need a cold beer."

The house was silent as they entered, and Riley held the screen door to keep it from slamming behind them, her voice just above a whisper. "Mom must still be sleeping."

Hooking his sunglasses in the vee of his shirt, Walker followed her into the kitchen. The mouth-watering aroma of roast beef filled the room, and he felt his stomach respond as he laid his jacket and camera on the counter by the door. Riley went straight to the fridge and got one bottle from the six-pack, glancing at the clock above the cupboard as she swung the door shut. "Do you want something to tide you over? We usually don't have supper till around six."

"I'll wait." He took the beer she handed him, then settled himself in one of the captain's chairs by the table. "Your mother said something about your father moving cattle."

"He's over at my brother's. Wayne's branding next week, so they had to move some cattle and get some corrals ready."

"How much older is Wayne than you?"

Bracing her legs, she leaned back against the cupboard and hooked her thumbs in the pockets of her jeans. "A year and a half. Brent and Dana are exactly ten years younger than Wayne and I. This is their night for swim club, so they get home late."

Walker slouched lower in the chair, a wicked gleam in his eyes. "Which still doesn't tell me how old you are."

"I didn't think it was polite to ask a woman how old she was."

His mouth lifted in a half grin. "It isn't. How old are you?"

"Twenty-six. How old are you?"

He ignored her question and took a long swallow, waiting to see what she would do.

"You're a louse, you know that?" she retaliated.

He just stared at her, deliberately tormenting her with the same half grin.

She decided to brazen him out. "Okay, if that's the way you want to be. I'll just fill in the spaces on my own. You're thirty-two, maybe thirty-three, probably live in a loft, seldom watch TV, and when you do, you watch the commercials. And you tend to be a lone wolf." She tossed in an afterthought. "And you don't like some shades of blue."

Right. On all counts. "Close, but no cigar." He could tell by the expression in her eyes that she didn't believe him for a second. He studied her for a moment, then couldn't stand it any longer. "How did you know I don't like blue?"

He caught a brief glint of satisfaction before she answered. "You never wear it, and I could tell the backdrop at the studio was driving you crazy."

He watched her through hooded eyes, not sure whether he should laugh or turn tail and run. "So what are your spaces?"

"What do you think?"

He stared at her, wishing like hell he had the insight to one-up her. As he scrutinized her, he processed all the things he knew about her, and he was surprised how many pieces fell into place. "Let's see. You could organize a three-ring circus if you had to, you don't like being closed in, and you wouldn't be caught dead in a fur coat. And you hate cooked peas."

She let out an astonished burst of laughter. "How did you know I hate peas?"

His grin broadened. "Doesn't everybody?"

She made a face at him as she opened a cupboard. "Just for that, you're going to get 'em for supper."

As she prepared the meal, Walker finished his beer and flipped through some old magazines that had been stacked on a small bookshelf by the phone, trying to ignore the edginess that was compounding in him. She was right. He was a lone wolf, and a normal family dinner was as foreign to him as life in New York was to her. Family dinners weren't a part of his life anymore—hadn't been for a very long time. The people he encountered on the job were hardly the types who got into that sort of life-style, and because everything he did revolved around his work, he had never bothered to foster any other connections. And now he was faced with a situation where he was going to feel like a damned fish out of water. What in hell could he talk to her father about? Traffic in downtown Manhattan?

The sound of a vehicle pulling into the yard intruded on his self-imposed mental exile, and he closed the magazine he'd been leafing through, wondering how he was going to look with egg all over his face.

The younger McCormicks came through the door, their gym bags emitting the faint odor of chlorine. They still had that fresh scrubbed look of people who'd spent a long time in the water.

Dana, an almost perfect carbon copy of her mother, flashed him a wide grin as she dropped her bag on the counter. "Hi. You *have* to be Walker."

Walker levered himself out of the chair, sticking his hands in the pockets of his slacks as he gave her a warped smile. "Dare I ask how you figured that out?"

There was a mischievous sparkle in her eyes. "Hey, I look at magazines you know, and those clothes came straight out of *GQ*. And Riley said you were a wicked dresser."

Looking as though she would like to stuff her sister in a hole, Riley rolled her eyes in a disgusted expression, and the laugh lines around Walker's mouth deepened. His eyes took on a wicked sparkle of their own. "And what else did she say about me?"

Unable to resist spilling the goods on her sister, Dana ignored Riley's murderous look. "She said you were a hunk."

He was not expecting that, and he felt as though he had just had the rug yanked out from under him. He glanced at Riley. A definite flush was creeping up her cheeks, and she avoided looking at him. His pulse accelerated at such a rate that he felt as if he were going into cardiac arrest. Somehow he managed to keep it together.

"Did she tell you what I said about her?" he asked, wanting to needle her just a little about the crack he'd made in the bar. She turned even redder and opened her mouth to make a rebuttal, then changed her mind. It was clear from the fire in her eyes that she would have liked to strangle them both.

Walker decided to let her off the hook. He offered his hand to her brother. "You must be Brent."

As the teenager took his outstretched hand, Walker assessed him. The boy was taller than he was, and although he had much the same coloring as his older sister, he, too, had his mother's eyes. As the teenager tightened his hand around Walker's in a firm grip, their eyes connected, and Walker was struck with the man-to-man directness in Brent's gaze. He knew he was going to like this kid; he was going to like him a lot.

There was a trace of shyness in the younger McCormick's expression. "Yeah, I am."

Walker smiled at him. "How do you put up with these two?"

Brent flashed a set of dimples any New York modeling agency would have killed for. "It takes some doing."

"I'm sure it does."

"Goodness, Riley. You shouldn't have let me sleep so long. Hello, Walker. Did she run the legs off you?"

He turned to face Mrs. McCormick, who had just entered the kitchen. "Not even close."

Molly McCormick cast her daughter a sharp look. "Not that she didn't try, I'm sure."

Riley couldn't stand it any longer. "Now that everyone's had a shot at me, I'm going to the garden to get some lettuce for supper."

It wasn't until the table was set, and Riley and Dana were getting the meal on the table, that John McCormick entered the house. Walker was seated at the end of the table, nursing another beer, when Brent and his father came into the kitchen. The rancher was a big man, his gray hair accentuated by a face that had been weathered to a permanent tan by a life spent outdoors. There was something about him—the set of his jaw, the way he carried himself, the calm expression in his eyes—that revealed the inner strength of a man content with his life. He would be slow to anger, Walker reflected, but God help the person who crossed him once he was.

Riley made the introductions, and as Walker rose to take the older man's outstretched hand, he realized John McCormick was also giving him a very thorough once-over. The fact that he had the same keen, penetrating gaze that his daughter had did nothing to ease Walker's reluctance about being there. If this man was half as astute as his daughter, Walker was in big trouble.

Riley's father grasped his hand. "Welcome to the Lazy M. I hear my daughter took you on the grand tour."

"Yes, sir, she did. All afternoon, as a matter of fact."

The deeply etched lines around his eyes creased as John McCormick restrained a smile. "No broken bones?"

Walker cast a glance at Riley, who was looking miffed again. He grinned at her. "Only mild bruising."

The older man chuckled. "I hope the same can be said for the truck."

Riley planted her hands on her hips. "Okay, you guys. Enough is enough. One more word, and Max gets the roast."

John McCormick nodded toward the table. "You'd better sit down, Walker. I think she means business."

In spite of the family's warm hospitality in including him at their table, Walker still had the uncomfortable feeling he was an interloper. Theirs wasn't so much a supper as an intimate family gathering, and that served to heighten his own displacement, his isolation. As the meal progressed, he found himself withdrawing more and more into himself, as if he was trying to make himself invisible, and that shook him. He hadn't done that for a very long time.

"You're drifting off, Manley. Can't you handle fresh air?"

Walker looked up to find Riley watching him, a smile camouflaging the disquiet in her eyes. There was something in her expression that he found oddly reassuring, as though she was physically reaching out to him. And right then, he realized how damned much he wanted these next three weeks with her. How much he wanted to bask in her wholeness of spirit. He would even open his black heart and let a little sunshine in, except it was too late for that. He strongly suspected she'd already found the way in.

Chapter 4

She stood across the rail fence from him, her hands on her hips, her posture openly challenged him. "And why not?"

Without realizing it, he mimicked her stance. "Because, damn it. I can't impose on your family like that."

"You're not imposing if you've been invited, Walker. Your moving out here makes perfect sense. You're going to be using the ranch for most of the shots, and Calgary is inconvenient—you know it is. You'd have to drive all the way out here, then all the way back every night, and you've already let the studio go. I think it's a great idea."

He sighed and braced his hands on the top rail, his head bent, trying to establish a rational tone in the debate. "Look," he said with deliberate patience, "it's not a bad idea. It's just too much of an imposition." He heard the crunch of dry grass as she moved, and he looked up as she placed her hands beside his.

"You're waltzing again, Manley," she said softly, humor in her eyes. "Are you afraid you might get countrified?"

He finally smiled, wishing she wasn't so close, wishing she was even closer. "No, I'm not afraid I'll get countrified. In fact, I'd enjoy every minute of it, but your parents have enough on their hands right now without having a stranger hanging around."

She held his gaze, amusement still lurking in her eyes. "A stranger is someone they've never met before."

"Okay. A semistranger."

"What's the matter? Aren't the accommodations classy enough for you?"

He knew she was deliberately trying to needle him. And it worked. "The accommodations," he said, trying to contain his irritation, "are just fine. But I know your mother is going to make an extra effort if I'm here, and she doesn't need that right now."

Folding her arms in front of her, Riley stared at him. "Do you know you're a very considerate man?" Before he had a chance to put in a disclaimer, she switched gears on him. "Okay, I won't dispute that about Mom, but there's also a plus side. It'll give her something else to think about other than the next session of chemo." Riley glanced away, and Walker saw her swallow hard before she spoke. "You make her laugh, Walker," she said, her voice uneven. "Right from the first day, you made her laugh, and my father would pay a king's ransom for that alone."

That caught him right in the gut, and he looked down at his hands, knowing that if he said yes, he would be setting himself up for one hell of a wrench down the road. And not just because of Riley. There was a place that was his at the McCormick table now, her father marked articles in magazines for him to read, and her mother worried about him eating right. It would be too damned easy to slip into the routine of belonging, and it was going to hurt like hell to leave as it was.

She nudged his hand. "I am winning this one, aren't I?"

He looked up at her, his face solemn. "How does your father feel about this?"

"He was the one who suggested it." She watched him, her expression equally solemn. "If you don't want to stay, that's fine, but don't say no because you think you're imposing. We wouldn't have asked you if we didn't want you here."

He managed a wry smile. "You may be sorry."

Her gaze didn't waver. "No," she answered so softly he could barely hear her, "not about that."

He didn't ask her what she *was* sorry about. He wasn't going to open any doors that were better left closed. He stuck his hands in his pockets to keep from touching her. "Okay, but I expect to help with the work while I'm here."

"We'll work your little fingers to the bone."

It would be a hell of a lot safer, he thought with dark humor, if they worked him until he dropped.

Riley climbed over the fence and started walking up the rise toward the barn. The panoramic view of the mountains rolled away behind her, silhouetting her against the blue sky, her dark, windblown hair shining in the sun. Walker followed her, stockpiling that image along with countless others.

Riley stopped, holding her hair back from her face as she waited for him. As he came abreast, she fell into step with him, her mood shifting. When she finally spoke, her tone was quiet. "You never talk about your family, Walker. How come?"

It was a jolt, coming out of the blue like that, and Walker's expression instantly shut down. His voice was taut. "We aren't exactly in the same orbit."

"Are you an only child?"

Walker struggled with a sharp stab of pain that went right through him. He forced a deep breath into his suddenly tight lungs. "No, I have a brother."

Something in his tone must have warned her, and she didn't push. And he was grateful she didn't.

They reached the crest of the hill, and Riley glanced at him, a smile on her face but a touch of concern still in her eyes. "You aren't going to back out, are you?"

He managed a grin. "No, Miss Nag, I'm not going to back out."

There was a glint of amusement in her expression. "You really hate giving in, don't you?"

He stared at her, the laugh lines around his eyes finally crinkling. "I think what we have here," he said pointedly, "is a case of the pot calling the kettle black."

She gave him a light push, laughter dancing in her eyes. "I just happen to know what's best for you, that's all."

"Sure you do."

Riley ignored his sarcasm. "Brent is home early today, so he can go with you to pack up your equipment."

The look Walker gave her was underscored with aggravation. "Lord, woman. Give me a break. I just got here."

"If I give you a break, you're going to weasel out."

She had that right. "It's nice to know you have such a high opinion of me."

She grinned. "Nice try, Manley, but you can't lay a guilt trip on me."

Nor could he pull the wool over her eyes.

Ignoring his not-so-subtle comments about her being a pushy broad, Riley had Walker and Brent in the car and on the way to Calgary before either of them could draw a deep breath. Brent didn't put up much of an argument; he would have had to fix fences otherwise. Walker's resistance was merely token; he derived a perverse kind of satisfaction out of giving her a hard time.

The first thing Walker did when he reached the city was swap his rented car for a Jeep Laredo with a removable hardtop. With the kind of locations he'd be using, he'd need a vehicle with cargo space for hauling around his equipment, as well as one that could handle the rugged terrain. The practicality of the swap was lost on Brent, though; the kid took one look at all the flashy red and chrome on the Laredo, and it was love at first sight.

By the time Walker checked out of his hotel room and they had everything loaded, it was midafternoon. Knowing

Brent would ransom his mother for a vehicle like the Jeep, Walker said to hell with the rental-car regulations and let the kid drive back to the ranch. Max, ever territorial, went into a barking frenzy when a strange vehicle pulled into the yard, then groveled in pathetic apology when Walker climbed out of the cab. Walker acknowledged the dog's remorse with a thorough scratching behind the ears, a touch of self-derision in his eyes. Even the damned dog made him feel as though he had a right to be there.

Brent had parked the Jeep beside the little clapboard bunkhouse tucked in the trees behind the garage, and the slam of the car door brought Riley and Dana out onto the back step. Riley gave Walker a perturbed stare. "You let him drive?"

With Brent still sitting in the driver's seat fiddling with the stereo, Walker had absolutely no recourse. Giving Max a final pat, he straightened and hooked his thumbs in his back pockets. "No, Max drove. Brent and I played poker in the back."

Grinning broadly, Brent climbed out of the vehicle. "What's the big deal?"

Riley drilled her brother with a no-nonsense look. "You're supposed to be twenty-one to drive a rental car."

He stared right back. "Well, I didn't know that."

"Now you do. There would have been all hell to pay if you'd been in an accident and someone had been hurt."

She might as well have punched him in the gut, Walker thought. A few words—that was all it took—and a familiar cold, hollow heaviness swallowed him up. It was stupid. He should be used to it by now; it was a feeling that had haunted him for a very long time. But every once in a while, it rose up with staggering clarity.

The muscles in his face didn't want to work as he looked at Riley, not a trace of inflection in his voice as he said, "It wasn't his fault. It was mine." Without looking at her, he picked up his duffel bag and started toward the bunkhouse.

Dana, who had been watching the exchange, grabbed Walker by the back pocket and started pulling him toward the bunkhouse. "Good old Riley. She can make a court case out of anything."

Walker forced a crooked grin and said nothing, waiting for his insides to settle. Five minutes. All he needed was five minutes and he could get it back together.

The bunkhouse was small and scrupulously clean, the lemony scent of cleaner still lingering. He dropped his duffel bag on the sofa in front of the window, taking in the layout of his new surroundings. The main room was a kitchenette and living room combined, and beyond that, the bedroom and bathroom. It was homey and bright, and the view of the mountains was postcard perfect.

"So what do you think?"

He turned to find Riley standing close behind him. He tried for dry humor. "The maid service is great."

There was no answering smile in her eyes, and his gut told him she'd seen more than he'd wanted her to. Which was impossible, because she hadn't even been looking at him. Maybe he was going soft in the head.

Brent stuck his head in the door. "We've unloaded everything into the porch. Do you want me to bring anything inside?"

"No. That's fine for now."

Riley glanced at her brother. "Dad wants you to move the horses into this pasture. And check the watering trough."

"Gotcha." He pulled the brim of his baseball hat down. "See you later, Walker." Walker heard the back door slam and was just about to say something to Riley when it slammed again and Dana came in carrying a large bag of groceries. "Here's the last of the stuff from the Jeep." She set it on the counter, then looked at her sister. "I'm going to go with Brent, okay?"

"Just be back in time to help with supper."

There was another slam as she went tearing out, yelling for Brent to wait. Tossing his jacket by his duffle bag on the sofa, Walker leaned back against the cupboard and folded his arms across his chest. He watched her, wondering what was going on in her head.

She opened the bag and started unloading the contents. "Where do you want this stuff?"

Walker reached out and clasped the top of the bag and scrunched it down, stilling her movements. "What's wrong, Riley?"

"Nothing's wrong." It was a passable attempt. There was even a touch of humor in her eyes as she met his gaze. "Housework turns me into a manic-depressive."

His mouth lifted with a smile, but his gaze remained solemn. "Even if you worked at it hard for the next hundred years, you'd still never make it to manic-depressive."

She forced a smile and started stacking the stuff she had already unloaded, deliberately not looking at him. There was an odd tremor in her voice. "I didn't mean to sound as though I was blaming you, Walker. Brent needs to understand he's responsible for his own actions."

Without thinking, without one worry about keeping his hands to himself, he caught her under the chin and turned her face, forcing her to meet his gaze. He didn't want her blaming herself, either—especially for something she'd had no part in. The contact, the feel of her, affected him profoundly, and his voice was unnaturally husky when he finally spoke. "I didn't think you were."

She closed her eyes and swallowed hard, the pulse in her neck suddenly erratic. As though caught by some immobilizing force, Walker experienced a jolt of recognition as electric tension suddenly sizzled between them, the awareness nearly unbearable in its intensity. He was so swamped by the feeling that he thought his lungs had solidified, and the only thing that kept him from caving in to impulse was his own need to protect her. Knowing he had to do something to keep from drawing her close, he grasped her wrists, her fingers curling tightly around his as he pressed their joined hands against his chest. Riley drew a deep shaky breath and rested her forehead against his chin, her body tense.

And Walker knew. The jolt of electricity had come from two sources, not just one. Feeling about her the way he did was one thing; having those feelings reciprocated in any way, shape or form was something else altogether. He closed his eyes, tightening his grip on her hands, knowing he had to defuse this time bomb that had landed in his lap.

"Man," he said, his voice so hoarse it didn't sound like his own. "You don't listen worth a damn, McCormick. I *told* you that my moving out here was a bad idea." Under the cover of raising his head, he brushed his lips against her hair, then shifted his hold on her hands.

Her breath was warm against their clasped hands as she gave a shaky laugh. Drawing another deep breath, she raised her head and looked at him, her smoky eyes lightened with a hint of amusement. "I hate that kind of smugness."

He grinned down at her. "How about dislike? Hate sounds so formidable."

She chuckled again, a soft throaty sound that made his knees want to fold; then her expression altered, becoming intent and serious. "Walker..."

He raised one finger and pressed it against her mouth, his own expression sobering. "Don't say anything now," he said, his voice gruff.

There was an edge of determination in her voice. "Then when?"

The laugh lines around his eyes deepened. "When we're forty feet apart and mad as hell at each other."

That brought a sparkle of laughter to her eyes. "You're really a big risk taker, aren't you?"

"I'm here, aren't I?"

"Yes, you are."

Walker knew he could only withstand so much temptation for so long, and he knew if he didn't get them the hell out of there, the whole situation would unravel. Trying to keep the huskiness out of his voice, he grinned at her and said, "I think we should go check the watering trough."

"Why?"

"Because it's a nice brisk walk." He released her hands, then turned toward the door. Granny McCormick knew what she was talking about, he thought with a twist of humor. There was a time to take bait, and there was a time to leave it in the trap.

It wasn't until later that night, after he had returned to his quarters, that he was forced to deal with Riley's response to their brief physical contact. The recollection of how she had reacted when he'd touched her sent his pulse rate into a frenzy, and the wrenching need he'd experienced then was just as strong now. Only now it was even worse. Now he was confronted with the stark realization that he wasn't the only one involved; she was caught in it, too. And as much as he wished it could be otherwise, he'd be out of her life in sixteen days.

Even if there was a chance for him and Riley, he still had to go back then. He had one week from the time he finished here to ramrod the Priscella layout, then he was scheduled for another major fashion shoot in New York, and from then on he was booked solid until after New Year's.

But there wasn't a chance. In the solitary confinement of his darkened bedroom, he could build whatever dreams he wanted to, but he still had to face the hard, cold facts. There was too much garbage in his past, and not a hell of a lot of hope for the future. And today reaffirmed that. Usually when he was away from New York, he experienced a kind of disconnection from the situation there. But here it was different. It was almost as though the feelings he had for Riley compounded the guilt. And no matter how much he wanted to say to hell with the consequences, he knew he would end up hurting her if he let things go beyond what had happened that afternoon. For him, it was a no-win situation. For Riley, anything more would be disaster.

But Riley would never see that. She lived in sunshine. She would never allow herself to see his dark, destructive side. She would feel she was somehow responsible for his foul moods and periods of absolute withdrawal, and he would never be able to make her understand that, in time, he would eventually destroy her. Yet after what happened today, he had to somehow let her know that this was simply a temporary phase in both their lives. He had to give her a damned good reason why he was walking out of her life in a matter of days. He had to find a way to keep her at a distance without hurting her. How, was something else altogether.

Faced with the prospect of another sleepless night, Walker knew he had to do something to disconnect his mind or he'd drive himself crazy. He got up, intent on checking out his equipment. When he turned on the light in the living room, he heard a soft whine at the back door. He knew Max was never allowed in the house, but the prospect of having some company, even if it was a dog, was too hard to resist. He let Max in, warning the animal that they'd both be in deep trouble if they got caught. Instead of doing a maintenance check, Walker taught his four-legged companion how to play dead.

Next morning Walker forced the previous night out of his mind and got down to serious business. As soon as it was light enough, he and Max, who could now play dead, cover his eyes in shame and smile, headed off to check some potential locations he had scouted earlier. Now that he had a concept in mind, he knew exactly what he was looking for.

He had shot numerous rolls of film during the past few days, and out of the hundreds of pictures he had taken of Riley, he knew there were at least a dozen that were truly exceptional. And as he shot frame after frame, he'd put together the format for the Priscella promotion. He wanted to use shots of her, like the one in the barn with the horse, that were dusky and dimly lit, that were shaded with mood and texture, shots that were anchored in real life.

He had to see those specific locations in the first morning light, then take some Polaroid test shots and see how they worked. The color film he'd already shot of Riley had been sent to a lab in New York for development, and the Polaroid shots provided the visuals he needed to assess both light and color. The locations weren't really a big problem, though. His biggest concern was Riley herself. Up until now, he had been able to attain the effect he wanted with film speed and camera setting, and she had totally ignored him as he worked. But with the next shots, he was going to have to work with the standard equipment—reflectors, portable strobe lamps and battery packs—which meant the shots were going to require a certain amount of staging. And he wasn't sure she wouldn't freeze up on him like she had in the studio.

It was going on eight when he returned to the ranch, driving up to the house through the barnyard. The school bus was just pulling away from the gate as he parked by the garage, and Max, who was sitting in the passenger seat, pricked his ears and gave a woof. Probably, Walker surmised, because he'd missed the chance to chase the big yellow thing down the lane. Walker climbed out, watching the dog jog off toward the house. He considered following him, but figured it was too early to scrounge a coffee.

He had just finished arranging all the Polaroid pictures on an adhesive matting and was hunched over the table, studying them through a magnifying glass, when there was a rap on the door.

"It's open."

John McCormick entered, his Stetson pulled low over his eyes, his large frame diminishing the space in the tiny room. "Molly said to tell you coffee's on and she's keeping breakfast warm for you."

Walker wasn't quite sure how to read Riley's father. He was a man who played his cards close to his chest, and although Walker wasn't sure if his host approved of him, he had the feeling that he didn't disapprove, either. The last thing he wanted was to take advantage of the McCormicks' hospitality. As subtly as possible, he tried to make that point clear. "I wish she wouldn't go to that extra work. I can make my meals here."

John chuckled, a glimmer of conspiracy in his eyes. "You could spare us all endless fretting if you'd humor her, son. She's certain you're on the brink of starvation as it is."

Walker grinned. "I got that impression all right."

John leaned over, studying the prints on the matting. "What are you building here?"

Walker explained his concept, and Riley's father nodded in comprehension as he studied the pictures more intently. He singled out one shot of Riley in the dingy basement doing laundry. "You want to take something like this and pair it with another picture that contrasts with it?"

"Yeah. I'd like to use outside settings like these here."

Mr. McCormick studied each picture carefully. He tapped one. "There's a prettier spot than this—get Riley to take you to the swimming hole. About half a mile upstream there's a spot where the river almost turns back on itself." He picked up the magnifying glass and squinted through it. "And there's a spot along this creek below the barn where the wild roses are in bloom right now—banks of them, with silver willow behind them. Really beautiful."

Walker shot him a surprised look. Never once had he expected this man to zero in on what he was trying to achieve. Yet he clearly had a grasp of what Walker was after, and the boy from New York got a lesson from the man who was rooted in rural Alberta on how *not* to judge a book by its cover.

John studied a few more photographs, then set the magnifying glass back on the matting. He slapped Walker on the back. "I'd better be heading off. I'm running late as it is. And you'd better go for breakfast before Molly sends a rescue party after you."

A token smile appeared, but Walker's underlying expression was serious. He hesitated a second, then finally spoke, meeting John McCormick's gaze. "If my being here gets to be a problem, I want to be told about it."

There was an edge of pointed humor in the older man's tone as the creases around his eyes deepened. "If there's ever a problem, you won't have to be told."

Riley's father couldn't have made it much plainer than that, and Walker's mouth twitched with amusement. Now he knew.

Molly was sitting at the table when Walker entered, staring out the window, her hands folded listlessly in front of her. It was clear that today was not one of her good days, but as soon as she heard him come in, Walker could see her physically collect herself and dredge up a bright smile. "Good morning, Walker. I was afraid you were going to sit out there and eat something out of a box."

Walker had a healthy respect for her brand of grit, and he sensed it was vitally important to her that no one see her with her defenses down. "Now, Molly, you make it sound as if I haven't had a decent meal in months."

"You probably survive on TV dinners and canned soup when you're at home."

Pouring himself a cup of coffee, Walker leaned back against the counter and folded his arms across his chest, cradling the mug in one hand. "I'll have you know I'm a very good cook."

Riley's mother damned his claim with a look. "Which means you can scramble eggs, make toast and heat soup."

He let out a snort of amazement. "Why, Molly McCormick, if I didn't know better, I'd say you were a female chauvinist."

There was a twinkle in her eyes as she raised her eyebrows, her expression discounting that claim as well. "Hardly. It's simply an opinion based on several years' experience." She motioned to the stove. "I put your breakfast in the oven."

He stared back at her, deliberately setting her up. "Oven?"

"The thing in the stove we're going to stick your head in if you don't stop with the Dumb Dora routine," interjected Riley as she came breezing into the kitchen.

Fixing his gaze on her, Walker took a sip of coffee, a retaliatory gleam in his eyes. "Well, good morning to you, too. What's the matter—get up on the wrong side of the bed?"

"Some of us," she said pointedly, "have been up since the crack of dawn."

"Some of us," he countered, "have already done half a day's work." He watched her, waiting for her to reply, wondering what she looked like still half-asleep, her hair tousled. He derailed that thought, recalling his warning about photographing her first thing in the morning. He decided then and there that he was honor-bound to follow through with his threat.

Riley fixed him with a suspicious look. "You're smirking. Why are you smirking?"

He simply raised his mug, watching her over the rim as he took another sip.

Her eyes narrowed, and she leveled her finger at him. "I'm on to you, Manley. I *know* when you're up to something."

Molly McCormick interceded. "She's been around too many children, Walker. And she'd developed a very suspicious streak."

"You're taking sides, Mother."

Molly looked directly at her daughter and smiled serenely. "Yes, I am. Now, come have your breakfast, Walker, and tell me what you have planned for today."

Riley retrieved Walker's breakfast from the oven, her chin stuck out as she slapped the loaded plate in front of him. "I'm telling you, he's up to something."

"Yes, dear, I know."

Riley stared at her mother for a moment, then relented with a wry grin. She filled a mug and joined them, sitting down directly across the table from Walker. She glanced up and caught him watching her, her expression altering as she stared back at him. He saw her go very still, saw the emotion darkening her eyes, saw her struggle to suppress it. It was as though she had reached out and touched him in the most intimate way, and his gut tightened, locking the air in his chest. A thick, heavy awareness immobilized him, his pulse laboring against the suffocating weight of desire that clogged his lungs and stormed through his body.

"So, what are your plans for today?"

Clenching his jaw against the sudden assault on his senses, Walker dragged his eyes away from Riley, locking his hands around his mug in a white-knuckled grip to keep from reacting. The muscles in his face hardened as he dredged up every ounce of control he had, then met Molly McCormick's gaze. "Della and the rest of the crew are coming out this afternoon, and we'll do some test shots in a couple of the locations I've picked out. George Nicholson has provided a fully equipped motor home for this phase of the shoot, so we'll be working out of that."

"The whole crew will be here?"

There was a hint of strain in Riley's voice, and he shot her a sharp glance. Sharper than he'd intended, and she stared at him with an odd look, the pulse in her throat obvious. Walker shifted his gaze, not wanting to deal with why she was looking at him the way she was. But he knew why. She'd sensed his pulling away, and she didn't understand why. For some stupid reason, he felt as though he'd just sold her out. And maybe it was because, in some way, he had. With a sudden irrational edginess climbing up every nerve end, he looked away. He wanted to get the hell out of there, away from her all-seeing eyes, but he forced himself to tackle the plate of waffles and sausage Molly had fixed for him, every mouthful settling like a rock in his stomach.

From that moment on, Walker shut down his mind. He tried to ignore the loaded-gun tenseness that made him feel like every nerve was exposed.

And to make matters worse, the afternoon shoot was a disaster. Della had studied the Polaroid test shots he'd taken, and after she talked over the concept and effect he was after, the Priscella cosmetologist set to work on her charge. She had brought several outfits for Walker to choose from, and once he'd made a selection, she'd banned him from the motor home. When Riley walked out into the yard, Walker's mood darkened even more. Della had done her job, applying her considerable know-how to create the desired effect.

And the effect was staggering. Riley's realness, her womanliness, had not been camouflaged by cosmetics but had been enhanced by subtleness and color, and she looked so damned wholesome and unspoiled, so beautiful, it made his insides knot up every time he looked at her. The only way Walker could deal with the feelings that kept bombarding him was to drive himself, and everyone else in the crew, to the limit.

They had gone to the spot by the river John had told him about, and although the setting was exactly what he was looking for, the results were not, and by midafternoon Walker was ready to pitch every single piece of equipment, along with the crew, into the river. It was not the kind of atmosphere that spawned good, let alone outstanding, pictures. And Riley wasn't helping. He could see she was trying her damnedest, but she was so tense, her expression so tight, it was as though she had turned into a block of wood. The harder she tried, the stiffer she became; and the stiffer she got, the more he snapped at her, until everyone was so tense they were all ready to jump out of their skins.

When a reflector was unanchored by a gust of wind, Walker came within an inch of pitching his camera as far as he could throw it. He turned away, his teeth locked together so hard his jaws ached, trying to get a handle on his irritation. He knew it wasn't working, he knew why, and he knew he was being a bastard, but that didn't help. The tight, almost traumatized look on Riley's face made him feel like the biggest heel alive, and every time he looked at her, he hated himself a little more. *He* was the problem, and he knew it. He walked over to the bank of the river, his camera gripped in his hand. If he had any damned sense, he would toss it in and get the hell out.

Della's angry voice sliced through the quiet. "You know, Walker, if you weren't such a genius with a camera, I'd shove you in. You're never sweetness and sunshine to work with, but today you're acting like a first-class clod."

The wind ruffled through his hair as he braced his arm against the trunk of a big old cottonwood, his face carved in an ominous expression. "Leave it, Della," he said through clenched teeth, his voice very quiet.

"Well, I'm not going to leave it. That girl is doing everything but bust a gut to please you, and she sure in hell doesn't deserve the crap you're dishing out."

He didn't look at her, his profile inflexible as he stared at the churning water. "Tell the crew to break set. We're packing it in for today."

"Walker, damn it—"

He cut her off cold. "Drop it, Della. Just get them out of here."

She paused, then spoke, a note of weary resignation in her voice. "What about tomorrow?"

"I'll call you in the morning."

He heard her sigh heavily and turn away, but she hesitated, then came back to him. Walker finally looked at her, the hardness in his face easing a little when he saw the expression of troubled concern in her eyes. He and Della went back a long way, and she was, next to Michael, the only real friend he had. He exhaled sharply, his expression altering as he stared at her. "Look, if it's any consolation, I know I'm being a miserable SOB, and I know I'm the one who's screwing up this shoot."

Della folded her arms across her chest and studied him. "Have you got a problem?" she asked quietly.

He stared back at her for a second, then looked away and heaved a sigh. "Yeah, I've got a problem."

"I see."

He knew from her subdued tone that she did.

There was another brief silence, then she asked, "Do you want me to take her home?"

Walker tipped his head back and closed his eyes, then exhaled sharply. "Yeah. That would be best. I've got to sort out my head before I talk to her."

Della patted his arm. "Maybe you'd better leave your head out of this one, Walker."

Chapter 5

Walker hiked a good ten miles that afternoon and drove another hundred, trying to discipline his feelings into isolated little compartments, but that dodge didn't work anymore. Then he spent several hours kicking himself for getting into this mess in the first place, but that didn't change anything, either. By the time he got back to the ranch, he had resigned himself to the fact that, somehow, he was going to have to smooth things out with Riley, and that scared the hell out of him. He knew, as sure as God made little green apples, that once he quit using his nasty disposition as a means of maintaining distance, it was going to be harder on him to be around her. As it was now, that was a line of defense. Once he leveled with her, that line of defense would be gone. And it was about the only one he had left.

But he had no choice. He could not, with whatever misguided sense of right and wrong he had, keep yanking her around the way he had today. He couldn't do that to someone who had the kind of emotional honesty she did.

The clouds, gathered above the jagged peaks of the mountains, trapped the last vibrant rays from the setting sun, and Walker paused as he climbed out of the Jeep, experiencing a thick tightness in his chest as he absorbed the vibrant spectacle. Colors—God, he had never seen such colors in his life. Nor had he ever seen cloud formations and sunsets like the ones he'd seen here, with the sky supreme and dominant above the landscape. It was as if the richness went right through him and saturated his soul.

Max's paw on his hip snapped him back, and he ruffled the dog's fur. "Hey, boy. I don't suppose you know where she is, do you?"

Max cocked his head to one side and answered with a quizzical woof. Walker grinned for the first time in hours and rubbed the dog's head. "Where's Riley, Max? Where is she?"

The dog squirmed in anticipation, then gave another woof and took off toward the barn. Walker slung his jacket over his shoulder and followed, the yard light casting a faint halo against the encroaching dusk.

Riley was in the barn. Through the rectangle of light made by the open door, he could see her crouched by the gelding, redressing the wounded foreleg. Standing outside in the deepening twilight, he watched her, watched the gentle firmness of her hands as she rewrapped the leg, her movements sure and swift. A feeling unfolded in him that made it nearly impossible to breathe. As she rose, she stroked the horse's neck, and every nerve in Walker's body responded to her distant caress. With his nerves jumping in his gut, he steeled himself and stepped into the splash of light angled across the ground.

Riley glanced up, her face transfixed by surprise, her expression becoming guarded when she saw who it was.

He didn't give her a chance to react. "We have to talk, Riley."

She picked up the pail and wooden carryall, then set them on the oat bin, her words clipped, her tone giving nothing away. "About what?"

"About what happened today."

Her back was to him, but he could feel her erect her defenses, and even at a distance of several feet, he could sense her reluctance. Not quite sure how to approach her, he tossed his jacket on the stack of bales by the door, then rammed his hands in the back pockets of his slacks, his expression drawn. He looked up at the shadows in the pitched roof, trying to ignore the knots in his own stomach, wishing like hell he knew what to say and how to say it. He had hurt her, and that in itself was unforgivable.

He finally forced himself to speak, his voice gruff. "The problem today wasn't you. I always get uptight as hell when I'm on a shoot, but the way I acted today was inexcusable. I'm sorry."

Keeping her back to him, Riley carefully smoothed down the horse's mane, a rigidity in her body that made Walker feel like an even bigger heel. And he knew he had to give her something more than superficial excuses. He watched her a moment, then he shifted his gaze, his face set with tension. "I've never been too concerned with what people think. When I have a job to do, I do it, and screw the consequences. But with you..." He paused, struggling to overcome the gruffness that suddenly cramped his throat. He waited for the tightness to ease, then forced himself to continue, his voice even more husky than before. "You're like sunshine, McCormick—warm and wholesome and vital. I'm impatient and moody, and temperamental as hell." A twisted smile didn't mask the lack of humor in his eyes. He shoved his hands deeper into his pockets, trying his damnedest to keep his voice steady. "The problem isn't you, Riley. It's me. And I'm sorry about this afternoon. You deserve better than that."

Her hand still on the horse's neck, Riley turned to face him, her bearing stiff and unnatural. "Are you married, Walker?"

His head shot up, and he stared at her. Her gaze was direct and level, but there was a look in her eyes that twisted at his heartstrings. He inhaled unsteadily and shook his head.

"Are you involved with someone?"

"No."

Riley stared at him a moment longer, then turned back to the horse and yanked the shank free from the metal ring. Walker watched her lead the gelding into the box stall, then turned, bracing his shoulder against the open door as he stared out into the deepening twilight. He didn't know what to say to take away the wounded expression he'd seen in her eyes. The only words that surfaced were ones he couldn't voice.

Walker wearily rubbed his hand across his face, then straightened. There was no point in sticking around. He had made her miserable enough for one day. He stepped inside to get his jacket, and he was about to pick it up when she came out of the stall. The white, tight-lipped expression on her face stopped him cold. He recognized the anger. That he could handle; it was the glimmer of tears in her eyes that did him in. He started toward her as she roughly shoved the heavy door shut, then fumbled blindly with the heavy metal bolt. The lock jammed, and Walker shoved his arm in front of her, catching her wrist just as she was about to try to ram it home with her clenched fist.

A ragged sound escaped her, and she tried to jerk her arm free, but he simply locked his own arm around her, then turned her into his embrace. Catching her by the back of the head, he cradled her tightly against him, his voice gruff and soothing against her hair. "Easy, sunshine. Easy. I'm the one you should be swinging at, not the door."

She tried to resist, but Walker's response was to pull her deeper into his hold. Another sob broke as she took a deep breath; then she went all soft and yielding in his arms. Walker hauled in a shaky breath and pressed his cheek against her temple, knowing he had just lost the battle. Whatever defenses he'd possessed had crumbled to dust the instant her body molded against his, and the surge of tenderness and longing and need nearly disabled him. He had waited his whole life for this. She was light for his darkness, calm for his storm, comfort for his pain, and he would have bargained away his soul to break out of the cold emptiness of his existence and crawl into the warmth of hers. With her, he knew he would find the kind of peace he had never known before. She had the power to make him whole again. And he would end up hurting her, as sure as he breathed. But he could let down his barriers. For the few short days he had left with her, he could at least allow himself that.

Easing a breath past the awful lump in his throat, he dragged up every shred of resolve he had. He would do his damnedest to keep her safe during the time they had together, and when it came time to leave, he would walk out of her life, leaving nothing behind but warm recollections. And he would take nothing with him, except the everlasting memory of her and hundreds of photographs that would tear him in half every time he looked at them.

His face scored with a sudden twist of pain, Walker clenched his jaw and tightened his embrace, knowing this would be the last time he ever dared hold her. He shut his eyes and tucked his head against hers, absorbing the warmth of her. God, but it felt so good to finally hold her. He would deal with the agony later; right now he wanted to savor this moment for as long as he could.

The stillness of twilight folded around them, the only sounds intruding on the silence were the odd movement from the horse in the stall and the twitter of sparrows high in the shadowed rafters. Neither of them moved for the longest time; then finally Riley stirred in his arms, and Walker knew it was time to ease away.

Brushing his mouth against her temple, he forced lightness into his voice as he murmured softly against her hair, "I didn't think you were the type to consort with the enemy."

He felt her take a deep, shaky breath; then she raised her head and met his gaze, her lashes still wetly matted. "Do you have any idea how aggravating you are?"

Keenly aware of the feel of her arms around his torso, he managed a lopsided grin. "After seeing you throw that temper tantrum, I more or less got the picture."

She narrowed her eyes at him. "It *was not* a temper tantrum."

His grin became more genuine. "You wanted to punch my face in, McCormick, and don't you dare deny it. I know blood lust when I see it."

"I'm not sure you know *anything* when you see it."

He raised one eyebrow and gave her a chiding look; then, loosening his hold, he reached behind her and pushed the stall door completely shut. "There's a lesson to be learned here. Notice, Ms. McCormick," he stated in a tutorial tone, sliding the bolt into place without any resistance. "Finesse, not force, is the key."

Riley caught him with a sharp jab in the ribs with her thumbs, and Walker let out a huff of protest, then abruptly doubled over, laughing. The sudden sparkle in her eyes was pure malice, her tone underscored with awe. "Well, I'll be damned. The manly Mr. Manley is ticklish."

Trying to talk around bits of laughter, Walker caught her hands and dragged them away from his rib cage. "Damn it, woman! Don't do that! I'm not ticklish—it's an old war wound."

Her eyes dancing with a spiteful gleam, Riley looked up at him. When she spoke, her tone indicated how impressed she was with his inventive excuse. "*Very* good, Walker. Quick, imaginative—solicits sympathy." She shook her finger at him, as though she was scolding a naughty boy. "But oh, such a big, big fib."

He grinned at her, then caught her wrist, pulling her under the shelter of his arm as he turned with her. "Your mother's right. You have been around too many kids. You do have an overdeveloped suspicious streak." Tightening his hold around her shoulders, he headed toward the open door, pausing just long enough to turn out the lights and pick up his jacket.

They started up the path, and Walker took his first full breath in hours. The weight of her arm riding on his hips sent his pulse rate into overdrive, but he put his libido in a holding pattern and savored the moment. This was good—companionable closeness, lighthearted bantering, the warmth of her hand on his hip, his hand mere inches away from the soft swell of her—no, no hands. He couldn't think about his hands. *Keep your mind out of the bedroom, Manley,* he lectured himself sternly. *If you let your mind wander like that, you're going to break out in a cold sweat.*

He tried to stuff those thoughts away in some dark corner of his mind, but it was like trying to stuff a big soft balloon into a little tin can—everything kept bulging back out. It took him a while to get the lid on it. Once he had things under control, he glanced down at her, a grin gleaming in his eyes. "Do you wanna come sit on my back porch and tell me your life story?"

Riley chuckled and shook her head in disbelief. "That's really a pathetic proposition, Manley."

"Hey, pathos is my long suit."

"Well, if it is, you'd better quit playing cards."

Max came bounding through the break in the hedge and romped against Walker's leg. Walker acknowledged him. "Hi, Max. Been out chasing women?"

The dog grinned at him and bounced around in front of them, obviously pleased with this man-to-man conversation.

On the way past the Jeep, Walker dug out a thermos of coffee; then the two of them stretched out on the back porch step. Their backs braced against the clapboard siding, they sat shoulder-to-shoulder, watching the closing spectacle of a long summer's day. The midnight blue of the darkening sky slowly absorbed the sunset colors from the western horizon, leaving the mountains in a jagged purple silhouette.

Walker drained the last of the coffee into Riley's mug, then glanced at her. He grinned, recalling his first impression of her. Man, what she did to a pair of jeans was enough to blow an average man's arteries. Squelching that thought, he folded his arms across his chest and hooked one ankle over the other. He studied the last fading rays of color for a moment, then spoke, his voice quiet. "Besides dealing with a photographer who's a raving maniac, what else is bothering you about this shoot?"

She didn't answer for a moment; then she released a heavy sigh. "Besides feeling like an idiot in front of the camera, you mean?"

The laugh lines around his eyes crinkled as he turned his head and looked at her. "Would you mind expanding on that?"

"How do you expand on idiocy?"

Walker didn't say anything, one corner of his mouth flirting with open amusement.

Riley sighed again and went on. "I know this sounds stupid, but it's having other people around. If it's just you and me, it doesn't bother me." She turned her head and looked at him, devilment in her eyes. "I figure you're so abnormal anyway, idiocy is second nature to you."

Walker gave her a shove with his shoulder, the creases around his eyes deepening. "Hell, you think this is bad? Normally there are so many experts standing around, you could fill a small auditorium with them. Art directors, fashion consultants, hairstylists, cosmetologists, color coordinators. It's a bloody three-ring circus. But old George is a maverick in the industry. He doesn't play by the rules."

"And you," she said, watching him intently, "are a maverick, too."

He grinned at her. "Yeah," he said with an undercurrent of self-satisfaction. "I'm a maverick, too."

Riley laughed that same full-bodied laugh that had drawn him that day in the Silverado, the richness of it nourishing something deep inside him. He watched her, pleased with himself for making her laugh, trying hard to ignore the warmth of her body against his. "Tell you what, we'll leave the crew with the mobile unit tomorrow, and we'll try it on our own. If it works out okay, we'll fly solo."

He could hear the relief in her voice. "If you can do that, I'll love you forever, Walker."

His expression grew sober. God, if that could only be true.

It went, as Della put it, like a hot damn. The weather was perfect, the sky was cloudless, and Riley was high on life. In the space of five hours, they shot four different locations, and every one of them went like clockwork. The crew set up each new location while Della was working on Riley in the motor home; then Riley and Walker would do the shoot alone. That night, Della took four dozen rolls of film back to the city to express to the lab in New York, and Walker knew that among those exposures there were at least eighteen that were absolutely outstanding.

The following day started out as a repeat performance. They set up the first location down by the creek, using the site with the wild roses and silver willow that John McCormick had suggested. Walker wished he could capture the fragrance on film, as well as the color. He had never smelled anything like it in his life.

But by that afternoon, Walker had forgotten that he'd sworn he wasn't going to get snarly. The heat had climbed to a near record-breaking high, the afternoon shoot wasn't going the way he wanted, his back was sunburned, the itchiness irritated by sweat. He could have joyfully bitten someone's head off.

He stood on the bank of the river, glaring at the shaded swimming hole, trying to figure out how to set up the shot. He wanted a contrast for a shot he had taken the week before when Riley had helped move a herd of cattle. It had been a scorcher of a day, and she'd been hot and sweaty, the dust from the milling cattle swirling around her and her horse. There had been trickles of perspiration along her hairline, and her shirt had clung to her in damp patches. What he wanted today was one to contrast with that—hot and dry, wet and cool—one of her in the natural pool, up to her shoulders in the cool, clear water. They had tried it without the crew, but it hadn't worked. The swimming hole was a U-shaped cut in the riverbank, with spruce and huge cottonwoods crowding the bank. It was a beautiful spot, but because of the shade and the reflection off the water, it was a nightmare to shoot. He had finally had Della bring the crew and the motor home through the pasture, and he was trying to figure out how they could set up the reflectors without getting a blinding glare off the water.

"Walker, could we get on with this? This water's cold."

Standing on the edge of the shallow cut bank, Walker stared down at Riley, who was effortlessly treading water in the deepest part of the swimming hole. Hell, what did she think he was doing, enjoying the damned scenery?

He assessed the site again. The force of the current had scooped out the rocky ledge he was standing on, exposing the roots of a huge spruce that was leaning over the water. The boughs nearly touched the water, creating a shadowed, intimate effect that was perfect, if only he could get the damned lighting right.

Exasperated, he tried to figure out a solution. He was standing in full sunlight, he could feel the sweat trickling down his back, and he was getting crankier by the second. "Tim, move that reflector and get the battery pack and the lights set up there, and let's see if we can get rid of the lousy glare. And move it, people. We have about forty minutes of this light left, then we're done for the day."

His frustration at the danger level, he fixed an assessing gaze on Riley. He wanted her shoulders bare, creating a naked effect, and they had changed the tube top she was wearing four times, trying to find a color that wouldn't show through the water. The one she had on now was almost mud-colored, the demarcation of skin and fabric barely discernible through the water. But he was still going to have to watch the angle or it would show. Damn it, nothing was working right. He snapped at her, his tone sarcastic, "Do you think you could get back in position, McCormick? We don't have all day."

Hooking her arm on the rocky outcrop he was standing on, she swept her wet hair back, a warning glint in her eyes. "Cracking the whip are we, Walker?"

The muscles in his jaw twitching, he crouched down, glaring at her. "Don't give me a hard time, okay?" he snapped. "In case you haven't noticed, this isn't a bloody picnic."

Her chin came up, and there was fire in her eyes. She stared back at him, the pulse in her neck suddenly beating in double time, her face set in a dangerous expression. "Do you know what I think?" she said a little too evenly. "I think you need to cool off." With that, she grabbed the front of his shirt and hauled him in.

Walker didn't know what hit him. One minute he was hot and sweaty on the edge of the slab; the next instant he was plunged into icy cold water, the shock knocking the wind out of him. It took an instant for him to collect his wits; then, with a powerful twist, he broke the surface, gasping for air. Riley was treading water a few feet away from him, watching him with a satisfied smirk. The entire crew was standing on the bank, cheering and whistling, obviously relishing his comeuppance. Flipping his hair back, he fixed his gaze on Riley, his eyes narrow. "That's it, woman. You're going to get yours in spades."

She smacked the water, sending a sluice of spray into his face. "Take it like a man, Manley. You had it coming."

Keeping his head above the surface, he pulled off his heavily treaded running shoes and tossed them on the bank, then did a lazy breast stroke toward her. "You're going under, lady."

Her breath breaking on laughter, she backed away from him. "Don't be a rotten loser. Besides, it did cool you off."

He moved closer, his gaze fixed on her, a grin hovering around his mouth. "You're still going down, Riley. One way or another." With unexpected speed he executed a neat surface dive that caught her off guard, and he grabbed her ankle, dragging her under.

When he finally released her, she came up sputtering and coughing, and Walker looked utterly pleased with himself. "Caught you with your mouth open, didn't I?"

Hooking her arm on the granite outcrop, she wiped the water off her face as she tried to catch her breath. She grinned at him. "Feeling better?"

He grinned back at her, the chill of the water reenergizing him. Lord, but it did feel good. Glancing at the angle of the sun through the trees, he gauged the time. A fifteen-minute break wouldn't kill him. Finally able to touch the rocky bottom, he started wading upstream to where the bank flattened out. "You guys have fifteen minutes to try out the water. Just make sure you keep that granite slab dry. I don't want it wet for the shots."

Yanking his shirt out of his jeans, he picked up his shoes and started toward the Jeep. He made it a practice to carry, among other things, a change of clothes when he was on location, for which he was grateful. As hot as it was, he didn't exactly relish the idea of spending the afternoon in sloppy wet jeans.

He had just slipped into a pair of tan cotton slacks when Riley showed up, shivering beneath the beach towel she had wrapped around her shoulders, her wet hair slicked back. "Are you in a big huff, or just sulking?"

He stared at her, his head tipped to one side. "Depends. Were you trying cool me off or drown me?"

She grinned at him. "Why, Walker, such suspicion. I was just trying to lighten up your life with a little spontaneity."

He slanted an unbelieving look at her, then turned and reached into the Jeep for a shirt. He put it on, then turned to face her, hooking his thumbs in his belt loops. He studied her a second, then grinned. "I am," he said very distinctly, "going to get even. I owe you one, sunshine. And I *always* repay my debts."

Mimicking his stance to a tee, she tipped her head to one side, pure sass gleaming in her eyes. "I don't think so, Manley. You haven't got what it takes."

"Hmm," he said, his narrow, contemplative gaze never wavering. "We'll see."

The rest of the day went like a charm. Riley didn't freeze up in front of the camera in spite of the onlookers, the crew anticipated what he wanted almost before he knew himself, and Walker got the shot he wanted in the second roll of film.

It wasn't until he was in bed, his hands laced behind his head as he considered the events of the day, that it dawned on him how damned much he *liked* her. He grinned to himself. He might like her, but he was still going to get her for dumping him into the river. That bit of cheek could not go unchallenged. He had a reputation to maintain,. And when he got even, he did it big time.

Chapter 6

The strategy was plotted. The coconspirators bribed and recruited. The stage set. And she was alone in the house. Now all he had to do was catch her.

Molly had had to go to the barn to give John a message, Brent and Dana had just left for early-morning swim club— and he owed them all. Dana had schemed with him, Brent had plotted the setup, and Molly, a twinkle in her eyes, had cautioned him that he'd have a scrap on his hands. When he'd met Molly on the path, she'd had one final warning; he was morally and financially responsible for any damages done. He had promised her a pailful of pearls, and she'd laughed and said that sounded just fine.

He'd been waiting three days for this. Riley was, without fail, already up when he got to the house in the morning. He'd finally been forced to enlist some insider help, and Dana, God bless her, had rigged Riley's clock radio the night before.

Moving on silent tread, Walker entered the house and stealthily crept up the stairs, then positioned himself in the far corner of the landing. Without making a sound, he checked his light meter, adjusted his aperture settings, then focused on Riley's door. The alarm had been reset for 7:10. Now all he had to do was wait.

The sound of the alarm alerted him, and he raised the camera, fine-tuned the focus, then geared up for the ambush. He braced himself against the wall, grinning like an idiot. She'd kill him for this.

The instant the door opened, he pressed the shutter release and said with unadulterated relish, "And a good, good morning to you, merry sunshine."

Riley froze. She had on a long T-shirt with a hole in the front and a picture of Garfield the cat emblazoned across the chest, the much-washed fabric hitting her at mid-thigh. Her eyes were bleary with sleep, there were quilt marks imprinted on her cheek, and her hair was an unruly frizzle. She was an absolute, glorious mess.

Walker knew it wasn't vanity that would set her off; it would be her absolute determination to thwart him. And because of that, he'd expected her to bolt back into the bedroom and slam the door. But he should have known better. The instant she moved, he shot one last frame, then dropped the camera in the open laundry hamper, ready to fend her off. Which was a very smart move on his part.

She seethed, "I'm going to kill you for this, Walker Manley," then took him down in a very clean, effective tackle.

Swearing at him with a fluency that made him laugh, she tried to scramble up and grab the camera, but Walker caught her around the waist and brought her down. Avoiding a headlock, he rolled with her, catching her beneath him. But Riley McCormick didn't go down without a fight. With far more strength and agility than he'd given her credit for, she shoved hard on his shoulders, bringing up her knees to heave him off. He managed to break the thrust of her legs with his own, then used his weight as an advantage. Breathing hard from trying to restrain her, he managed to grab her wrists, locking them against the floor as he straddled her hips, temporarily immobilizing her. His chest heaving, he grinned down at her, smug as hell and not even trying to hide it. "Gotcha, McCormick."

Breathing equally hard, she glared up at him, not about to give up. "You haven't got anything. The damned film isn't developed *yet*, Manley, so don't count your chickens."

He chuckled, still pleased with himself. "Ah, hell, Riley. Are you back to livestock?"

She almost laughed, but managed another glare instead. "That film is history, and you're going to be limping around here for the next week."

His grin broadened. "I don't think so."

That was the wrong thing to say, and a look of hellfire determination flared in her eyes. He felt her collect her strength, like a cat ready to spring. Making a final effort to break loose, she tried to roll with him, but Walker merely tightened his hold on her wrists and used his full weight to pin her hips to the floor.

Suddenly all thoughts of victory were driven from his head. With her stretched out beneath him, his grip handcuffing her wrists against the floor, he was physically in control, but the feelings that stampeded through him were anything but. He could feel the pulse in her wrists, the rhythm of her labored breathing, but what slammed every male hormone into high gear was the heat and hardness of her body between his thighs. His lungs suddenly refused to function, and his pulse turned thick and heavy as the edges of the room swam out of focus. She was close, so close. All he had to do was shift his legs and he would be molded intimately against her—one move, and he would know what it felt like to have her fully beneath him.

It was like hitting a wall, and they both went still, the change in mood instant and electric. For an instant their gazes locked; then Riley closed her eyes and drew a ragged breath, her body turning to silk and honey beneath his.

The only thing that registered was how damned soft and helpless she was, and Walker caved in without a single struggle. Even if his life had depended on it, he could not have rolled away from her. Emitting a rough groan, he slid his arms around her, locking her to him as he stretched out against her, wanting this more than he wanted his next breath.

Grasping his head between her hands, Riley dragged his mouth against hers, giving him right of entry on a low desperate sound. The deep, hungry kiss kicked off a storm like no other, and Walker experienced such a frenzy of emotion, his chest clogged up solid with it. If this was drowning, it was heaven, and if he never drew another breath, he didn't care. He had found the center of the universe, and the effect was cataclysmic.

Frantic to experience every inch of her body against his, he dragged her fully beneath him, his hand cupping her hips roughly against his as she twisted beneath him, parting her legs to accommodate his hips. Walker thought he was going to go out of his mind as he settled into the warm cradle of her thighs, aware that only the fabric of her T-shirt and thin cotton panties separated his hands from her naked flesh. Driven by a need that cut through what little control he had, he rocked against her, and Riley choked back a cry, her arms clutching him as she shuddered, her mouth hot and urgent beneath his. Her response unhinged him, igniting his own. He probed the moist recesses of her mouth with his tongue, a low guttural sound lodging in his chest as she drew him deeper, deeper, unleashing a hunger that made him shudder.

Her nails bit into his back, and a glimmer of rationality pierced the haze in his mind, warning him that he was a hair trigger away from being unable to stop. Dragging his mouth away, he buried his face in the tumble of hair against her neck, his breathing raw and labored, his heart slamming frantically against his ribs. Somehow he had to pull back. Somehow.

Hauling in a tortured breath, he dredged up the strength to shift his arms, his face scored by strain as he slowly lifted his head. Her eyes were clenched shut and tears slipped into her hair, and he felt such a wellspring of emotions that his own eyes smarted. With infinite tenderness, he smoothed back her hair, then closed his eyes and kissed her softly, the cramp in his throat making his jaws ache. God, but he wanted her. So much. So damned much.

Sliding his hand down her back, he locked her hips hard against his, trying to ease her unsatisfied need with a steady pressure. His fingers thrust into her hair, he cradled her head securely against the curve of his neck, all too aware of how she was trembling in his arms. In spite of how shaken he was, he realized that they would be visible to anyone coming up the stairs. And either John or Molly McCormick could return any second. He could not expose her to that kind of discovery.

Releasing the pressure in his chest on a jagged sigh, he slid one arm around her waist and, with her still clinging to him, held her head against his chest, bringing her up with him as he rocked back on his knees. Keeping her secure against him, he shifted so they were hidden in the corner of the alcove, then weakly leaned back against the wall as he pulled her across his lap. Praying like hell that no one would show up, he glanced down at her. Gently brushing back her hair, he wiped away her tears with the heel of his hand, then nestled her head securely against the curve of his shoulder. He kissed her on the forehead, his voice gruff with emotion as he whispered, "God, McCormick, you fight dirty."

Her breath caught on a soft sob, and she curled into him, her arm tightening convulsively around his neck as she pressed her face against his shirt.

Tightening his hold on her, he closed his eyes and rested his head against the wall, silently berating himself. He had royally screwed up. He had breached the safety zone. He knew he should say something cute and clever and dismissing, but he was so shaken himself that his ability to think was shot right to hell. And it didn't help, having her trembling and helpless in his arms. Knowing he had to do something to get them back on solid ground, he kissed the top of her head. "We could have a very interested audience if your parents come in," he murmured huskily against her hair. "And they're going to wonder what in hell it is we're doing up here."

Riley tucked her face against the curve of his neck, a hint of humor in her whispered reply. "So this was a setup."

Walker hugged her hard, his voice gruff. "*This* wasn't a setup. Getting a picture of you with fuzzy teeth was."

She shifted in his arms, then raised her head and looked at him, the expression in her eyes making his chest hurt. "And now?"

He grinned at her, wishing like hell he didn't have to let her go. "We're negotiating a truce."

There was humor in her eyes as she eased away from him. "I don't negotiate, Walker."

Walker felt as though he had slipped into some kind of time warp as he gazed at her, a smile lingering around his mouth. If he could make one moment of his life last forever, this would be it. Knowing he had to break the connection, he settled her on the floor beside him, then laced his fingers through hers as he tipped his head back against the wall. God, he felt as if he'd been run over by a steamroller.

Neither of them spoke for several moments, and Walker tried not to think about what had just happened between them. His pulse rate was too damned revved up as it was.

Riley's fingers tightened around his as she turned her head to look at him, her voice not quite steady when she spoke. "So what are you thinking, Walker Manley?"

The laugh lines around his eyes crinkled as he met her gaze. "I'm thinking we'd better get up before the cavalry rides in. And I'm thinking you're as cute as hell with quilt marks on your face. And I'm thinking Garfield's one lucky cat, even though he has a hole in his belly."

She almost let a smile sneak out, but she narrowed her eyes at him instead. "I think I should have drowned you when I had the chance."

He grinned, deliberately baiting her. "You and whose army?" Her answering smile was oddly distracted, her gaze just a little too intense, and Walker read the warning signs. Riley wouldn't hesitate to ask some very direct questions about what had just happened between them, and he wasn't prepared to give her any answers. Realizing the situation could get dicey at any second, he rolled to his feet, pulling her up with him. "Now, go have a shower, and I'll go tell the troops to stand down."

He expected a tart retort, something along the line that he knew what he could do with his troops. But he got silence instead. Finally she raised her head and looked at him, her eyes filled with the kind of accusing hurt that kicked off a twist of guilt. "You never let anyone get too close, do you, Walker?" she asked, her voice flat. When he didn't answer, she jerked her arm free from his grasp and brushed past him, an angry set to her profile as she went into the bathroom and slammed the door.

Walker tipped his head back and let his breath go in a rush of self-disgust. He had blown it but good. He had been cute and clever, all right. And in the process, through sheer insensitivity on his part, he had belittled what had happened between them. Wishing there was something handy to punch, he leaned over and yanked his camera out of the clothes hamper, then headed for the stairs. If there was a prize for being the biggest jerk on the face of the earth, he'd sweep the field.

It was a lousy day from every perspective. By nine o'clock that morning the sky was heavily overcast and it had started to spit rain. He canceled the shoot and, unable to face either Riley or her family, told Molly he had to go into the city and wouldn't be back until late. Then he grabbed a camera case and a squall jacket and headed down to the river. He shot roll after roll of bleak, dismal exposures, pictures of empty meadows cast in a gray drizzle, pictures of sodden rail fences stretching into the mist, pictures that were hollow and empty. When it got too wet to continue, he drove into Walton and spent the afternoon nursing a beer in the Silverado, facing some unpleasant facts about himself. He had avoided being honest with anyone, including himself, for a very long time.

When the evening crowd started rolling in, he tossed a handful of bills on the table and left. When he got back to the ranch, it was nearly eight o'clock. The overcast skies and steady drizzle had shrouded the countryside in a premature dusk, and a light from the barn winked through the trees. His face solemn, Walker stared through the misty windshield; then he exhaled heavily and climbed out of the Jeep. Yanking up the collar of his jacket, he turned toward the path, wondering if he was forever doomed to trips to the barn. He hoped like hell she was alone.

She was. Like a replay of the time before, she was just finishing redressing the slash on the gelding's foreleg when he stepped into the light.

She glanced up, her expression shutting down when she saw who it was. She did the final wrap on the bandage, fixed it in place, then collected the items lying on the floor and dropped them into the veterinary kit.

Feeling suddenly shaky, Walker stuffed his hands in his jacket pockets. "I don't blame you for being ticked off," he said gruffly. "I was a jerk this morning, and I'm sorry."

Without looking at him, she closed the lid on the jar of ointment, her tone abrupt. "Let's just forget it, okay?"

Walker gazed at her, wishing he could find the words to say what he had to say. "In spite of how I acted, I didn't take what happened this morning lightly, Riley. I want you to know that."

Pushing the box aside, she stood up, then turned to face him, anger flaring in her eyes. "It wasn't how you acted, Walker. I knew what you were doing. I was a mess, and you were trying to take the edge off. That's not what got to me.

It's how you come so close, then always pull back. You keep fighting me, and I don't even know why.''

The muscles in his jaw twitched. "I never should have moved out here. I should have stayed away from you."

Riley held his gaze, her voice shaking with emotion. "And what in hell is that supposed to mean?"

He stared at her, his expression unyielding. "It means that I'm bad news. It means that I don't want to mess up your life."

He saw her close her eyes; then she exhaled unevenly. She finally looked at him and spoke, a tinge of exasperation in her voice. "Do I get to say anything about this?"

His mouth lifted in a semblance of a smile, but the solemnness remained. He held her gaze for a moment; then he looked down, his expression heavy as he rubbed his sole against a ridge in the floor. As much as he wanted to back away from it, he knew there was only one way to deal with this, and that was head on. His voice was very strained. "I knew where my feelings were headed almost from the beginning, but I thought I could deal with that. But after this morning—" He paused, then raised his head and looked at her, his face drawn. "But after this morning, everything changed."

There was an odd intensity in her voice. "How?"

He held her gaze for a second, then looked away, his voice gruff. "Because if it hadn't been for the fact that your parents could have walked in on us, I'm not sure I could have stopped."

Walker heard the relief in her voice when she whispered, "Is that a problem?"

"I'm the problem, Riley. The situation is the problem."

There was a glimmer of unshed tears in her eyes as she came to him, her hand unsteady as she reached up and touched his face. The contact made his knees nearly buckle. He shut his eyes and covered her hand with his own, knowing he should pull it away, knowing he didn't have the strength to do it.

There was a husky catch to her voice. "Would you hold me?"

He turned his head, pressing his mouth against her palm, the storm in him nearly uncontainable. All he could do was shake his head.

He could feel the warmth radiating from her body as she laid her free hand against his jaw, framing his rigid face in a field of gentleness. "Why not?"

And he suddenly remembered what it had felt like as a kid, when he'd nearly suffocated from trying not to cry. His voice was uneven, so tortured it was barely audible. "Because if I do, I'll never be able to let go."

"Walker, look at me."

It cost him heavily to do as she asked, but he did, knowing she was going to see too much, knowing he was unable to do one damned thing about it.

Her eyes were brimming as she gazed at him, so much compassion and caring in her gaze that Walker felt as if she had physically touched him. That openness threw him into such emotional overload, he thought his heart was going to split wide open.

She smiled at him through her tears. "Would that be so bad?"

Grasping her hands tightly in his own, he pressed them against his chest as he closed his eyes and rested his forehead against hers, waiting for the awful contraction in his chest to ease. They stood like that, connected yet separated, silent yet somehow communicating, until he was finally able to speak past the painful cramp in his throat. "Yes."

As if realizing he had little left to go on, that he needed her to help him over this hurdle, she gave his hands a little shake, silently letting him know she understood. "No matter what you tell me, it isn't going to change how I feel, Walker," she said softly.

The warmth from her hands radiated up his arms and across his shoulders, slowly seeping through his tense muscles until he could finally take a breath without feeling as though his chest was going to cave in.

Untangling one hand from his grasp, Riley caressed his jaw, her touch gentle and lingering, her voice whiskey soft. "Let me put Doc in his stall, then we'll go somewhere and talk."

Walker didn't know where he was going to dig up the strength to let go of her and move away, but somehow he managed to loosen his grip on her hand. He knew if he looked at her, if he saw that warmth in her eyes, he would never be able to let go of her. Giving her hand one final squeeze, he released her and turned away, his body steeled against the overwhelming sense of loss. He went to the door and stared out, vaguely aware that it had stopped raining. He felt as though his whole life was being reduced to these few remaining days with her, and after that, there was nothing ahead except an empty black hole.

There was the sound of hooves on planking; then he heard her close the heavy stall door and bolt it. Darkness enveloped them as she shut out the light, and he turned. Her outline was barely perceptible in the fading light. Feeling as though his ribs couldn't withstand the pressure in his chest, he stretched out his hand toward her. She took it, her grip firm and sure as she laced her fingers through his. With her close beside him, they started up the narrow path.

By the time they reached the bunkhouse, every nerve in Walker's body was stretched to the limit, and as they entered through the darkened porch, he realized he'd had his jaw clenched ever since they'd left the barn.

He opened the door, releasing her hand so she could precede him. When her arm brushed his chest as she reached for the light switch, he caught her wrist, too raw to endure the harsh, exposing light. His tone was abrupt. "No lights."

She hesitated, unsure what to do; then she twisted her arm, fumbling for his hand. Her fingers wrapping around his, she turned toward the bedroom. Walker checked her short. "No, Riley. Not in there."

She faced him, lightly touching his lips. "Just this once, trust me," she whispered.

Silenced and shaken, he tried to quell the feelings that one soft caress ignited in him, his will to resist leveled by a single touch. She paused inside the bedroom and turned on a small night-light on the bureau by the door, then hooked off her boots. Without either looking at him or relinquishing her hold on his hand, she climbed onto the rumpled bed.

Walker's chest was so heavy he could barely breathe, let alone talk. "Riley, this is not a good idea."

The queen-size bed had been shoved against the wall to accommodate its size in the small room, and as she knelt in the middle of it, she looked up at him. A glint of humor appeared in her eyes as she pulled him toward her, her tone dry. "In spite of what you think, I'm not exactly prepared for any immediate changes in your game plan, Walker."

Her candor almost wrung a smile out of him, but he stayed standing, not trusting either his control or his will to resist.

Her expression altered as she stared up at him, the unspoken entreaty in her eyes creating such a longing in him, that it overrode his common sense. He saw her try to swallow, and when she spoke, her voice was very husky. "I just want to hold you for a while."

Emotions he didn't even know he possessed jammed up around his heart, and he knew nothing could be worse than not touching her at all. Stepping out of his leather loafers, he tried to steel himself as he finally yielded to the agonizing need to hold her. As he reached for her, she slipped into his arms, pulling him down beside her, and after days and nights of denial, he quit fighting himself. The feel of her against him detonated a reaction that convulsed through him, and his face contorted in a spasm of emotion, the sensory overload wringing a ragged sound from him. Locking his arms around her, he buried his face in the curve of her neck, his emotions so raw and intense that he couldn't think, couldn't breathe. All he could do was feel—the softness of her breasts against his chest, the relieving pressure of her against his groin, the strength of her embrace, the warmth of her breath against his neck. He felt as though he was enveloped by her, and he molded her even more tightly against him, wanting to absorb her, wanting to draw her inside his very soul. In the space of a heartbeat, she had become his survival.

Riley's arms tightened around him, her voice breaking with urgency as she twisted her face against him. "Hold me. Walker... don't let go."

Thrusting his fingers into her hair, he crushed her closer, his own voice hoarse as he whispered against her temple, "I won't. God, there's no way I could."

Even as tightly as he was holding her, he could feel her still trembling, and he realized her reaction had been no less staggering than his. He brushed his mouth against her forehead, then began to slowly stroke her back, offering what comfort he could. For him, he had already found his own kind of relief. He was able to block out the nearly intolerable ache of physical arousal because he had what he wanted most right now, and that was to simply hold her. The other feelings he could put on hold as long as he had her in his arms.

Her voice was husky and uneven as she whispered against his neck, "This is better than double desserts."

Surprised to find himself smiling, he hugged her tighter, too damned aware of how willingly she yielded to the pressure. Lord, he could so easily get lost in her. So easily.

Shifting against him, she rose up on one elbow, her hand pressing him onto his back as she brushed her mouth against his, caressing his lips with lazy thoroughness. Unable to maintain a coherent thought with that kind of heady enticement, he opened his mouth beneath hers, his pulse going crazy as he smoothed his hands up her back. Catching his head, Riley deepened the kiss, her body molding against his as she moved on top of him.

Fired by the solid weight of her against his pelvis, Walker tore his mouth away, his heart hammering so hard in his chest he could barely get the words out. "Riley, you're playing with dynamite."

Her fingers molded around his head, she held him still, her tongue like wet silk as she moistened his bottom lip. Tracing tormenting circles against his ear, she whispered against his mouth, "I know. Do you want me to stop?"

Hauling in a ragged breath, he clamped her hips against him, his voice hoarse. "No. But I... ah, Riley... when you move like that... Lord, don't stop." His voice caved in on a low groan as she flexed her hips, moving her weight against him with agonizing slowness. Catching her by the back of the head, he took control of the kiss, his tongue stroking hers with the same tormenting rhythm. Riley shuddered, her body going slack as he moved beneath her.

His breathing labored, he dragged his mouth away, his voice a rough whisper. "Riley... honey, if we keep this up, things are going to get out of hand real fast."

On a ragged intake of air, she slid her arms around him, a tremor coursing through her as she buried her face against his neck, her body taut with sexual tension. Walker clenched his teeth and fought down the hot need that ripped through him, knowing that if he pushed even a little, she wouldn't stop to consider the consequences. It helped, realizing that she was totally dependent on him to keep the lid on things. Her hair tangling around his fingers, he repositioned her head against him, her breath hot and moist against his skin. Clenching his jaw, he began stroking her back, too damned aware of the soft fullness of her breasts crushed against his chest.

Slowly her trembling abated and the rigidity in her body eased, and on a ragged sigh, she went lax in his arms. A fierce tenderness welled up in him, and Walker swallowed hard, determined to protect her at all costs. Exerting pressure on her head, he turned her face and kissed her softly, his mouth lingering as he comforted her with a gentle caress. Reluctantly easing away, he smoothed down her hair, his voice a husky murmur as he asked, "Are you okay?"

She tightened her hold around his neck and pressed her face tighter against his neck. She drew a deep breath. "No."

The laugh lines around his eyes crinkled as he enfolded her in a reassuring embrace. "I told you this was a bad idea."

"Don't try to weasel out, Walker," she said in a weak, rebuking tone.

Walker laughed and hugged her hard, then rolled with her until she was flat on her back. Bracing his weight on one elbow, he lay beside her, his eyes alight as he gazed down at her. "I should've locked you in the stall with Doc."

She gave him a fleeting smile; then her gaze went misty and intimate as she slowly stroked his face. Her voice had a velvety catch as she whispered, "Are *you* okay?"

He gave her a wry smile. "I'll survive."

Her gaze locked on his, she trailed her hand down his chest and across his abdomen, then moved lower to touch the thick ridge beneath the placket of his zipper. Walker jerked her hand away, gritting his teeth as he sucked in his breath. Her eyes darkened, her expression stark with remorse. "I'm sorry," she whispered. Swallowing hard, she tried to touch him again.

He tightened his hold on her wrist. He knew exactly what her game plan was. Fighting down his own response, he pressed his thumb against her mouth and slowly shook his head. "Don't even think it. It's no worse for me than it is for you."

"Liar."

Walker smiled and pulled her across him, firmly nestling her head against his shoulder. "I hate to break it to you, but that whole thing about men is a scam, sunshine."

She shifted her head on his shoulder, humor in her voice. "It's a biological fact, Walker."

"But it's still a scam. Too damned many men use it to get what they want. Guilt should never be a factor, yet if I had a dollar for every time some jerk used that line about being hot and hurting, I'd be a rich man."

She raised her head and studied him intently, an odd expression in her eyes, then she said very softly, "Are you hot and hurting, Walker?"

That was one question he was not expecting, and he wondered if she would ever be remotely predictable. His mouth lifted a fraction, and a gleam appeared in his eyes as he stared back. "Are you?"

She hadn't been expecting that, either, and a flush crept up her cheeks as she looked away, the pulse in her neck suddenly beating in double time.

He caught her face, impelling her to look at him. He lightly brushed his fingers across her cheek, his gaze sober. "I don't like leaving you tied in knots, either," he said huskily, "but I know if we take this any farther, there won't be any turning back. And that's the point. It's the two of us, Riley. Not just me, but you, too. And I wouldn't want it any other way."

She drew a shaky breath and stilled his hand against her face, her soft gaze setting off a frenzy of sensations in his chest. There was an undercurrent of bewilderment in her voice. "What is it with you? You want me to believe that you're one step above pond scum, but your principles keep popping out."

His gaze sobered, and he broke eye contact as he carefully smoothed her hair back behind her ear. Now. It had to be now. Somehow he had to make her understand that this could go nowhere. There were too many hurdles, the biggest one being that he was dead wrong for her. He was wrong; his life-style was wrong; the situation in New York was wrong. But even if he indulged in a fantasy about starting over with her away from the complications there, he couldn't. He was tied there—by the guilt that would haunt him until the day he died, by his accountability for what had happened fourteen years ago. He would destroy her as surely as he had destroyed all hope for the future. Maybe this was his ultimate punishment: to finally find someone who could be his whole life, then have to walk away. And he did have to walk away from her. He was a different person when he was back there, given to black moods and long periods of dark withdrawal. He would make her life miserable, and he knew it. He would end up causing her pain. And he couldn't live with that.

"Walker, don't go all quiet on me."

Exhaling on a long sigh, he met her gaze, then spoke, his voice solemn. "There are some things I need to make clear, Riley."

She went very still, and her own expression sobered; then she eased out of his embrace. "I'm not sure I want to hear this."

He watched her as she pulled herself free and sat up beside him, his chest tightening as she avoided his gaze. He caught her hand, his voice gruff when he said, "It's not what you think. I haven't been playing games with you, and I haven't lied to you, and believe me, I'm not using you as a convenient amusement."

He saw her swallow before she raised her head and looked at him, her eyes dark. "Then what is it?"

He didn't say anything for a moment; then he exhaled sharply. Letting go of her hand, he dragged himself up on the bed. He stuffed the pillows behind his shoulders, then leaned back against the headboard, his rib cage flush against her thigh. Hoping like hell he could find the right words, he reached up and caressed her cheek, the pressure of his hand increasing as he cupped her face. "If I didn't care about you, I wouldn't give a damn about the consequences. But I do care. One hell of a lot. And because of that, I'm not going to jerk you around. This time together is only temporary, Riley. Nothing permanent is going to come from it."

There was a hint of defiance in the way she lifted her chin. "Why not?"

He dropped his hand and looked away, the muscles in his jaw tensed. He took a deep, fortifying breath. "Believe it or not, you've seen me at my best. I'm a miserable, moody bastard, and I've spent my whole adult life running rough-shod over people.''

She gazed at him with steadfast directness, her voice catching. "I'll never believe that about you, Walker. Never. There's too much compassion in you. If you were as hard and unfeeling as you claim to be, you wouldn't have a shred of decency in you. And you are," she added with utter certainty, "a decent man."

Badly shaken by her belief in him, Walker grasped her hand, the sudden lump in his throat making it impossible for him to unclench his jaw. His voice was rough with emotion when he finally spoke. "I told you before, don't see me as something I'm not."

She held his gaze, her eyes unwavering. "And I told you before, don't make yourself into something you're not."

He stared at her, his expression taut; then he looked down at their joined hands, his gaze heavily introspective as he caressed the back of her hand with his thumb. "You see a mirage, McCormick." He continued to stroke her hand, his mouth thinning into a hard line, the muscles in his face rigid with tension. "I won't lie to you. You're the best thing that's happened to me for a very long time, but I'll be leaving here in a few days. You know that, and so do I. I'm just someone who drifted into your life for four weeks, then I'll be drifting out. That's the way it has to be."

There was a hurt, cynical edge to her tone. "Why don't you just come out and say what you mean, Walker? I'm just a little country girl, and you're a big-city boy. And we all know big-city boys like their women smooth and sophisticated."

Infuriated that she would belittle herself that way, he caught her by the chin and jerked her head around, his eyes glinting dangerously. "Don't you dare reduce it to that. And don't you ever put yourself down like that again. Not ever. If I thought for one minute that I could make you happy, you wouldn't even know what hit you. I'd have you on a plane so fast, your feet wouldn't even touch the ground. But I know damned well what would happen to you. You'd be miserable there inside a month, and I'd hate myself. And I'd hate myself even more, watching the life go out of you." He released her face and snapped, his voice seething with certainty, "And it *would* go out of you, Riley. I can guarantee it. Inside a month, you'd feel like you'd been buried alive."

She jerked her arm back, her eyes flashing. "I never asked for forever, Walker." In a swift, fluid movement, she was off the bed, fury setting her face into an expression of glorious rage. "In fact, I never asked you for anything. You treat me like some weak-minded twit who can't think for herself. I hope you and your noble attitude have a great life together. Who knows? Maybe you'll achieve sainthood for being so damned self-sacrificing."

He probably would have laughed if she hadn't made him so mad. Who in hell did she think she was dealing with here—a moral moron? He was off the bed and had her backed into the corner before she moved two feet. "Well then, Miss High and Mighty. Let's just say to hell with the consequences and get down to it."

"Don't be crude," she snapped. "You've got enough rotten qualities as it is."

She was scolding him, for God's sake, like some ten-year-old brat who got caught swearing at recess. And even as ticked off as he was, it made him want to laugh. Just barely able to squelch a grin, he stared at her, his mouth twitching. His voice shaking only a little, he met her eye to eye and said with artificial contrition, "Yes, ma'am, Miss Danderfield. I won't be crude, rude or lewd ever again."

It was like watching a torpedo go dead in the water. One minute she was mad enough to spit, the next she was staring at him as if she'd been stunned. She drew a deep, reinforcing breath. "Who," she said flatly, "is Miss Danderfield?"

His arms braced on either side of her shoulders, he gazed down at her, his expression ripe with humor. "She was my grade-three teacher—spinster, frowzy gray hair twisted high in a tight knot, a mouth like a prune. She caught me saying the *F* word in the boys' room. I had to stay after school and write out five hundred lines of 'I will not swear.' I put a frog in her desk."

She stared back at him, trying like hell to stay mad, but her mouth gave her away. Finally she shook her head. "You really are impossible, you know that?"

Walker watched her, his eyes crinkling. "Yes, ma'am. I know."

She gave him a narrow look, then gave him another one that had trouble written all over it. "I never said anything about lewd, Walker," she amended huskily. "Lewd has certain possibilities."

If Walker hadn't been so damned much in love with her already, he would have fallen like downed timber right then and there. Suddenly shaky and weak in the knees, he swallowed hard against the sudden fullness in his throat and pulled her to him. Wishing that he could simply absorb her, he wrapped his arms tightly around her. "I was just trying to make it as easy for you as I could, Riley," he said gruffly. "The last thing I want to do is make you unhappy."

Warm and willing in his arms, she slid her hand up the back of his neck, cradling his head against hers. "Don't make it too easy, Walker," she whispered. "There are some risks worth taking."

Chapter 7

He was stalling. He had been stalling for three days. Walker stared down at the contact sheets on the table, his hands on his hips, his gut in a knot. The New York lab had expressed the package, and Della had brought it out Monday afternoon. It was now Thursday, and he had used every excuse in the book to postpone the inevitable. But he had just got off the phone with Michael, and he knew his time had run out.

Dragging his hand wearily down his face, Walker fanned out a few contact sheets on the table. Countless images of Riley gazed back at him, and the knot tightened. Without even scrutinizing them, he knew he was looking at pure gold. He picked up the top sheet, and twenty-four pictures of Riley in the swimming hole came back at him. Priscella Cosmetics had enough material here to launch a campaign that could run for three solid years and blast the competition out of the water in the process. And he felt like ripping the whole damned bunch of them to shreds.

Tossing the single contact sheet onto the others, he went to the window, his face fixed in rigid lines as he stared out. He had done what George had hired him to do. Given the circumstances that got him into this in the first place, he should be wallowing in smug satisfaction. In reality he felt like hell. Professionally he had a dozen reasons to be on the first plane out of there. Personally his head was a mess. Michael had booked his airline ticket for Saturday morning, which left him with his back to the wall. He couldn't put it off any longer; he was going to have to tell Riley. And he didn't know how in hell he was going to scrape up the guts to do it.

Bracing his arm against the window frame, he stared out, his jaw clenched against the pain of separation. It wasn't just Riley he'd be leaving behind. It was the whole Mc-Cormick family, the damned dog, the sense of being a part of a whole. He had found peace of mind here, something he hadn't had in a very long time, something he'd never expected, something he'd never thought he would find again. He did not want to leave all that. But he had no choice. With the exception of two flying trips back to New York during the magazine shoot, he had been gone ten weeks. That was too long, and he knew he'd be faced with a disaster when he got back.

A sound, a light touch on his arm, dragged him back.

"What's the matter, Walker?"

Exhaling heavily, he straightened, jamming his hands in his back pockets as he turned to face her.

Ever since they'd ended up in his bedroom that night, he had quit fighting. They'd practically been joined at the hip ever since, except for this afternoon, when she had taken her mother to the doctor's. And although he'd made damned sure they hadn't gone the distance physically, he had abandoned his hands-off policy. It was a policy that didn't stand a chance around Riley McCormick, anyway. She was definitely a hands-on person. She drove him crazy.

Without thinking, he reached out and touched her cheek. "I didn't hear you come in."

Her hazel eyes held a deep shadow of concern as she stared up at him, her tone reflecting it. "Walker?"

He held her gaze for a moment, then dragged his eyes away. "I had a look at the contact sheets while you were gone."

There was a taut silence; then she turned away. "Oh." She fingered through the pile of photographs on the table without a trace of enthusiasm, then gave them a dismissing flick. "And?"

His tone was curt. "They're the best work I've ever done."

She turned finally, her face solemn, a disturbed expression in her eyes. "So you're finished," she said flatly.

He wanted to hit something. "Yeah, I'm finished."

She folded her arms as though she was suddenly cold, every trace of vitality draining out of her face. "So when are you leaving?"

"George wants me to meet with the ad people, and I have some work to do before then."

She looked at him, a sudden tension springing up between them. "When, Walker?"

The tension stretched out as he stared back at her, his gut twisting. Unable to handle the expression in her eyes when he told her, he turned back to the window. "My flight leaves at seven Saturday morning. Michael phoned while you were gone."

He heard her fumbling with the photographs, and he turned, a painful constriction tightening his chest when he saw how white she'd gone. Swearing softly, he caught her by the back of the neck, turning her face into his shoulder as he pulled her into his arms. "Don't, Riley. For God's sake, don't." He gathered her closer, his face etched with strain as he whispered raggedly against her hair, "It's not over yet."

She slipped her arms around his waist, her voice muffled when she said, "It's too soon."

His throat cramped up on him, and he tightened his hold, trying to give her what comfort he could. He stroked her back, trying like hell to inject a little brightness into what had suddenly become a very dismal situation. "Hey, lady," he whispered as he gave her a gentle shake. "We've got the rest of today and tomorrow."

He could feel her make a monumental effort not to cry, and she pressed her face against his shirt before she raised her head and looked at him. "Don't go, Walker."

With as much gentleness as he could muster, he smoothed back her hair, then cupped her face. His voice rough with regret, he met her despairing gaze. "I have to go back."

He felt her try to swallow, and her mouth trembled as she tried to smile. "I know." But in spite of her effort to hold them back, tears welled up in her eyes, and the desolation on her face completely undid him.

Exhaling on a soft curse, he grasped the back of her neck, her hair tangling around his fingers as he dragged her head back. Emotion claimed him as he covered her mouth in a bruising kiss, desperate to override the pain he'd seen in her eyes. On a soft sob, she slid her arms around his neck, molding her body urgently to his, and Walker's pulse went crazy.

It was a mistake. He knew it was a mistake the minute her mouth went warm and yielding beneath his, but it was too late to pull back. Much too late. The thought of leaving her was like a knife in his chest. A low guttural groan was dragged up from deep inside him, and he caught her buttocks, fitting her flush against his groin, certain he would explode if he didn't. She twisted against him, accommodating the fit, and every nerve in his body caught fire. She should have resisted; she should have tried to break out of his rough hold, but she didn't. She was willing in his arms, and when she explored his mouth, her tongue slick and searching against his, he thought his legs would cave in beneath him. His heart slamming against his ribs, he fought for breath and tried to grasp some thread of gentleness. Shifting his hold, he braced her head with his arm as he drank from her mouth, so much emotion breaking in him that he felt as if he were drowning.

Knowing he was going under, and going under fast, he dragged his mouth away from hers, blazing a hot trail down her neck. God, but he wanted to ride out the hunger that was driving him. He wanted to taste the softness of her breasts in his mouth; he wanted to feel her naked beneath him, and he wanted to bury himself so deep inside her, he would never find his way out. But, above all else, he wanted to keep her safe.

His chest heaving, his whole body wired with need, he held her head immobile against his neck, a hard-won restraint carving his face in harsh lines as he forced himself to ease off. He could tell by the way she trembled and clung to him that she was hot and moist and ready, and he knew that he could easily take her over the edge now—all he had to do was drop his hand and stroke her, and she would come apart. But he didn't trust himself—he was too hard, too aroused, and he was afraid if he went any farther, he would not be able to pull back.

Gentling his hold on her, he cradled her in an embrace and stroked her back, and spoke, his voice roughened with desire. "Easy, sunshine. Easy," he whispered raggedly against her ear. "You're not prepared for this, and neither am I."

Suddenly taut and desperate in his arms, she hung on to him, a tremor coursing through her as he tried to ease away. "Walker...please. Please."

Torn by the frantic need in her voice, he locked her against him as he turned with her, his hold unrelenting as he sat down on the sofa, then pulled her across his lap. His hands shook as he lifted her arms around his neck; then, exhaling jaggedly, he caught her head and tucked it roughly against his. His voice was hoarse and very strained as he whispered against her ear, "Hang on to me, Mac. Hang on, and for God's sake, don't let go." Cradling her back with one arm, he pressed his hand against her pelvis, shifting her hips; then, swallowing hard, he undid the snap of her slacks and eased down the zipper. His face contorting in an agony of control, he lifted the elastic across her abdomen, his heart slamming into overdrive as he slid his hand between her thighs.

She gave a low ragged sob and jerked against him; then, with a frantic movement, she tried to pull away. But he clenched his teeth and forced air into his aching chest, his voice gentle and strained to the limit. "Just hang on, sunshine, and don't let go. No matter what, don't let go."

If he hadn't had her to hang on to, he would never have been able to do it, but the firmness of her against his chest, the weight of her against his hard arousal, provided the buffer zone he so desperately needed. Suppressing the rough sounds lodged in his throat, he buried his face against her neck as he set up the rhythm her body craved. She cried out, clinging to him with a frantic strength as she went rigid in his arms, and he deepened his caresses, his voice ragged as he held her even tighter and whispered, "Let it happen, babe. Don't fight it."

She gave an agonized cry and twisted beneath his touch; then her body convulsed around his fingers, and spasm after spasm coursed through her as she went to pieces in his arms. Realizing her body was in sensory overload, Walker cupped her groin hard until the tremors ceased. With a shudder, she went slack in his arms, then curled around him, still trembling, her breath hot against his neck. Walker closed his eyes and slipped both arms around her in a fierce embrace, the fragrance of sunshine and sensuality filling up his mind. Lord, she was everything to him.

Exhaling on a shaky sigh, he forced his muscles to relax, and as the tension eased from him, an unexpected tenderness crept in. He was hard and aroused and he still wanted her, but he had given her what she needed, and he had kept her safe. And he felt good about that.

Drawing a deep, tight-chested breath, he nestled her closer. He had felt protective as hell about her before, but never anything like this. Holding her chin, he tenderly repositioned her head on his shoulder, his kiss soft and gentling as he slowly caressed her mouth. God, but he needed her. She was like air to him.

He smoothed back her hair as he reluctantly raised his head and gazed down at her, a gentle smile in his eyes as he wiped away her tears with his thumb. "Okay?" he murmured huskily.

Riley nodded, her eyes brimming with fresh tears. She touched his mouth and swallowed hard, then whispered, her voice weak and shaky, "You said it would be you and me together."

His hand resting on her jaw, he lifted her face slightly and kissed her again, his mouth brushing against hers as he whispered, "You know you can't believe a damned word I say."

She hugged him with a fierce kind of urgency, her breath catching on a little sob. "Oh, Walker—"

Not giving her a chance to say any more, he kissed her again, his hand still pressed against her face.

Riley released a pent-up sigh, then pulled away, her lashes wet as she gazed up at him with dark, solemn eyes. "You aren't going to let me say I love you, are you?"

He felt as though she had reached right inside him and grabbed his heart, and it was a long while before he could speak. His voice was gruff as he caressed her face. "No. I'm not. And I'm not going to let you trick *me* into saying it, either."

She stared at him for a moment; then she gave him a tremulous smile that just barely camouflaged her tears. "You've got a streak of mean, Walker Manley," she whispered brokenly.

*And you're soft and warm and loving, Riley Mc-
Cormick.* His chest plugged solid with tenderness, he
hugged her hard, then caught her face again and looked at
her, concern in his eyes. "Are you sure you're okay?" he
whispered huskily.

She smiled again, a little steadier this time, just a hint of
amusement in her eyes. "No. But you aren't going to do
anything about it, are you?"

"No," he said firmly, his eyes crinkling with amusement, "I'm not." Slouching into a more comfortable position, he put his feet up on the coffee table, then snuggled her
against him. "But I'll tell you what I am going to do. I'm
going to sit here for exactly half an hour, then we're going
to go peel potatoes."

He could feel her smile against his neck as she slipped her
arm around his chest and hugged him. "You should have
been a horse, Walker. You could win prizes for sidestepping as well as you do."

Walker considered her comment much later that night, in
the wee, small hours of the morning, when sleep completely eluded him. His hands locked behind his head, he
stared at the ceiling, the yard light taking the edge off the
darkness, nothing taking the edge off the heavy, empty
feeling that kept him awake. There was more truth in that
comment than she had realized.

He excelled at sidestepping issues. God only knew he'd
had enough practice at it. He had sidestepped the situation
with his parents, he was sidestepping involvement with her,
and if he had the strength to do it, he would sidestep his way
right out of her life. He had even sidestepped her tonight by
leaving her with her father and Brent after a late-night bil-
liard game in the basement, afraid of what might happen if
they were alone together.

The only thing he hadn't sidestepped was what was waiting for him back east. That was something he'd have to live
with for the rest of his life, and the guilt and self-loathing
that went with it had become ingrained in him. Over the past

fourteen years he had tried everything. He had tried to anesthetize those dark, destructive feelings with booze, he'd tried to keep them at bay with long, demanding hours of work, and he was still trying to exorcise them with penitence, but nothing helped. He'd spent fourteen years trying to find absolution, but there was none.

Draping his arm across his eyes, he clamped his teeth together, trying to ease the paralyzing ache in his throat, trying not to acknowledge the moisture that gathered along his lashes. God, if only he could relive that one moment in time, if only he could take back that one bit of carelessness. If only. Then he could grab on to the future Riley offered and never let go.

Needing desperately to disconnect those thoughts, he threw back the covers, grabbing his slacks as he stood up. Lord, but he needed a cigarette.

Max had been sleeping on the braided rug by the bed, and he stirred and stretched when Walker turned on the light. The dog gave an enormous yawn, then stretched again, looking up with bright-eyed expectation.

Walker gave his companion a warped grin as he slipped into a shirt. "Got a cigarette on you, Max?"

The dog wagged his tail, obviously not too concerned that Walker was about to throw away two years of smokeless living.

Walker ruffled the dog's fur on his way to the door. One of the crew had left a pack in the Jeep, and he had tried to goad himself into tossing it out, knowing damned well it rated a ten as far as temptation went. But this wasn't just simple temptation; this was basic survival.

After the second cigarette, Walker was inclined to rephrase that. It wasn't survival; it was sudden death. His lungs burned, and he had a head rush that brought him as close to passing out as he ever wanted to get. And if he didn't pass out, he was probably going to be sick. Stubbing out the butt, he exhaled his last drag, then took a long swallow from a bottle of beer. Resting his head against the back of the sofa, he wedged the bottle between his thighs and contemplated his bare feet propped on the coffee table.

He wondered how many times he would relive these few weeks with Riley. How many times he would dredge up memories of her. Of her sitting outside the barn with him, smoking cigars. Of her teaching him how to rope. Of her dragging him into a western-wear store and getting him outfitted in jeans and boots. Of her sitting between his up-raised knees in the circle of his arms, her back flush against his chest as they watched the spectacular flourish of a set-ting sun. Of her lying beside him.

As if sensing his companion's mood, Max came over and laid his head in Walker's lap, an anxious look in his eyes. Walker gave the dog a wry grin as he ran his fingers through his thick ruff. "It's pathetic, isn't it, Maxwell, watching a grown man wallow in his misery like this?"

Max perked up his ears and gave a small woof. Walker smiled and tugged his ears. "How would you like to come to New York with me, boy? I'll find you some hot females and an endless supply of fire hydrants. You'd love it." Finding his chest suddenly too full to handle, he patted his leg, and Max put his paws in Walker's lap, whining softly. Ridiculously affected by the dog's response, Walker caught the dog's face as though he were human, his own voice raw and hurting as he whispered gruffly, "Look after her for me, boy. I don't want her to be unhappy. And I don't want her to miss me for too long." His eyes smarting, Walker downed the remainder of the beer, not sure how he was going to get through the goodbyes without breaking down like a damned baby.

Friday morning was tough. And the day didn't get any better. Walker got through it by drawing on resources he didn't even know he had. But beneath it all, he felt as though he was trying to cram the rest of his life into the next few hours. John McCormick made it somewhat easier by asking him not to tell Molly until after supper that he was leaving. The older man knew his wife would be upset, and he wanted to put off telling her for as long as he could. Walker didn't argue. If Molly McCormick made even one of her warm, maternal gestures, he'd fall apart like wet cardboard. Because the family was in on the conspiracy, it made it easier to play out.

Once Dana and Brent got home from school, Walker kept his attention, and everyone else's, focused on shooting a family portrait. It was the first time he had spent much time around Riley's older brother, his wife and their two kids, but by the time the whole McCormick clan had squabbled and reorganized their way through three or four poses, Walker realized Wayne was a force to be reckoned with. He had the devil in his eyes, pure charm in his grin, and Walker knew damned well he and Riley together were the unholy terrors their mother claimed them to be.

By the time Walker had shot two rolls of film, the formal sitting had fallen apart at the seams. He shot another half dozen rolls before and after the picnic supper, pictures of a family simply being a family. He probably would have made it an even dozen if Brent, aided by Dana and the damned dog, hadn't wrestled him down and confiscated the camera, then turned the tables on him.

The hardest to deal with was Riley. For the most part, she kept up her end of the charade. He knew it was getting to her when she left the picnic table suddenly, under the guise of getting more lemonade. When she came back out, he knew damned well she'd been crying, and that just about finished him. If it hadn't been for John McCormick's steadying hand on his shoulder, Walker wouldn't have made any bets on how he would have handled that.

It wasn't until later that night, after Wayne and his family had gone, that the mood changed—and then it got even worse. The rest of the family was gathered around the kitchen table having a late night snack when John Mc-Cormick finally told Molly.

Walker knew what was coming the minute Riley's father started fumbling with his paper napkin, then cleared his throat.

His jaws locked together, Walker gripped his mug, unable to look at anyone, dreading what was coming.

John raised his head and looked at his wife, his voice a little rough around the edges when he said, "Walker will be leaving tomorrow."

Molly looked from her husband to Walker, a tight catch in her tone as she asked, "What do you mean—leaving?"

Walker felt as though there was a rock caught in his throat as he tried to speak. "I'll be heading back to New York tomorrow, Molly. I've got what we need here, and they want me back."

There was a taut silence, with no one looking at anyone, then Molly shot her husband a distressed look, obviously shaken by the news. There was another heavy pause, then she glanced back at Walker and spoke, her voice uneven. "Oh." She folded her hands in her lap, then took a steadying breath, lines of strain around her mouth. "I didn't realize you'd be going so soon." She tried to force a smile. "We're all going to miss you, Walker."

He had to clear his throat before he could get the words out. "I'm going to miss you, too." He scanned the suddenly solemn faces around the table, then stared at his clenched hands and spoke, a gruff catch in his voice. "You've all been great."

There was a long lapse; then Molly spoke again, a forced brightness in her tone. "What time does your plane leave in the morning? We'll have to see you off."

The muscles in his throat worked as he remained silent for a moment. He stared at his hands, unable to look at Riley. He had deliberately not told her his plans, plans he had deliberately made to avoid the emotional risks of one last night together. He didn't trust himself, and if he stayed the night and she came to him, he knew damned well he wouldn't be able to say no. As it was, he didn't know how he was going to manage this final bit of time together. Evading Riley's gaze, he finally looked at Molly, his voice like sandpaper. "I'll be leaving tonight, Molly. I have a seven a.m. flight, so I'll spend the night in the city."

The stunned silence was so brittle it had an edge to it, and Walker lowered his gaze, waiting, his body wired with a nerve-grating tension.

There was the rough sound of a chair being shoved back from the table, and Walker looked up. Without a word, Riley rose, her chin up, her body stiff, as she left the table. There was no mistaking the look on her white face. The muscles in Walker's jaw jerked as he lowered his head, wishing like hell he could have told her some other way. But he'd had no choice; he'd needed the buffer of other people around him. He simply didn't trust himself enough to tell her on her own. He was so torn up inside that if she so much as touched him, he would lose it. As sure as hell, he would not be able to stop himself.

Dana's voice was thick with tears when she offered, "We'll come help you pack, Walker."

Inhaling heavily, he raised his head and met the teenager's gaze, his voice impassive when he said, "Everything's already loaded."

There was a stricken look in her eyes. "Then you're leaving right away?"

He toyed with the mug of cold coffee in front of him, wishing that disconnecting from these people wasn't so damned hard. "Yeah. I'm leaving right away."

Feeling too exposed to meet anyone's gaze, he shoved his chair back and stood up. His voice rough, he said, "I'll say goodbye to Riley, then I'll be back."

The screen door slammed loudly behind him as he stepped out onto the back step, the thickness inside his chest nearly crippling him. He wasn't even gone, and he missed them already. The door slammed again, and a fatherly hand clapped him on the shoulder. "Let's walk a piece," John McCormick said gruffly.

With the older man's hand still on his shoulder, they went down the steps and started across the yard. When they reached the rail fence beside the garage, Riley's father stopped and leaned against the shoulder-high post. He didn't say anything for a moment, then he spoke, his voice quiet. "Do you love her, son?"

Walker shoved his hands in his pockets and stared into the twilight, the soul-deep ache leaving his voice uneven when he answered. "Yes, sir, I do."

John McCormick rested one foot on the bottom rail and gazed out across his land. "We had a long talk last night, Riley and I. She said she feels the same way about you."

The painful weight in his chest expanded, and Walker rammed his hands deeper into his pockets. "Yes, I know."

"But you aren't going to do anything about it."

"No, sir, I'm not."

Riley's father didn't say anything for a moment; then he shifted his position and rested his forearms on the top rail, his hands laced together as he squinted into the distance. "I'd like to know why, if you don't mind."

Walker clenched his jaw, a tight-lipped expression on his face as he peeled a piece of dried bark off the rail. He crumbled it between his fingers, then abruptly tossed the mulch onto the ground and stuffed his hands back in his pockets. His tone was clipped when he finally answered. "I've got a side to me she's never seen, and I know I'd end up hurting her. She'd be unhappy, and I don't want to do that to her."

"She seems to think the opposite, son. She doesn't think she'd be unhappy at all. She seems to think you're a good man." His arms still resting on the top rail, his foot hooked on the bottom, John McCormick stared at his hands, his profile solemn. "I've always thought my daughter had pretty good judgment when it came to people. And I have no reason to think otherwise now." He raised his head and stared out across the land he loved, then he straightened and clapped Walker on the back. "You'll find her on the rise west of the barn,'' he said quietly. ''She goes out there when she has something on her mind.''

Walker listened to Riley's father walk away, feeling so hollow, so torn apart inside, that it was almost more than he could handle. He clenched his jaw harder, the knot in his throat convulsing, wondering what it would have been like to have a father like John McCormick. The hollowness intensified, and he closed his eyes, experiencing a new definition of pain.

He found Riley where her father had said he would. She was sitting huddled against a slab of granite, her knees upraised, and even in the fading light, he could see the starkness in her expression and the trails of dampness down her face.

Jamming his hands in his pockets, he looked across the valley, his mind locked on one thought. This was it; this would be the last time he'd ever be alone with her. There were a thousand things he wanted to say, but only one that really mattered. In a few short weeks, she'd become his still center, his light in the darkness. He wanted to hang on and never let go, but he couldn't tell her that. He could never tell her how very much she meant to him.

The muscles in his jaw knotted, and his hands closed into fists, the rawness inside him making it hard to speak. ''Along with my many other shortcomings, I take the easy road whenever possible, Mac. I knew if I told you ahead of time what my plans were for tonight, we would have ended up in a wreck. And I didn't want that to happen.'' He turned to face her, his voice even gruffer than before. ''I don't trust myself around you, McCormick. I never have.''

She wiped her face with the heel of her hand, then looked up at him, anger and hurt overshadowing the pain in her eyes. ''Don't you ever get tired of carrying that big heavy conscience around?'' she challenged, her voice shaking. ''I'd like to take that damned nobleness of yours and stuff it somewhere dark and painful.'' She angrily dashed away a new overflow of tears as she got to her feet and came toward him, temper sizzling from her. "Just where do you get off making my decisions for me? And what in hell gives you the right to think you aren't worthy of being loved? We're all imperfect, Walker. You're just a little more imperfect than most."

He hadn't been sure what to expect from her, but this wasn't it. He knew he had hurt her badly, and he had expected the tears, but he sure in hell had never expected her to come out fighting. He would have smiled if the ache in his chest hadn't been so big. God, but he was going to miss her. Feeling as though some huge hand was clenching around his heart, he brushed her hair back behind her ear, trying to memorize this image of her. "Ah, McCormick," he whispered unevenly. "Don't ever let that incredible fire of yours go out."

Her chest heaving and fire in her eyes, Riley stared at him; then she made a low, grating sound and slipped into his arms. A sob was wrenched loose as she turned her wet face against his neck, her voice catching. "Damn you. I hate you for doing this." She drew a deep, jagged breath, then demanded brokenly, "Just don't say goodbye."

Unable to see, Walker hugged her hard and buried his face in her hair, his own voice ragged as he whispered, "No goodbyes, McCormick. I never say goodbye."

His hand tangled in her windblown hair as he tucked her face against the warmth of his neck, his face pressed against her head. He didn't know how in hell he was ever going to let her go. But he knew the longer he put it off, the harder it was going to be.

Dragging the heel of his hand across his face, he loosened his hold. Feeling as if he had a baseball wedged in his throat, he brushed back a tendril of hair, putting some space between them. "I gotta go, sunshine," he whispered unevenly. "Walk me back to the Jeep."

She dragged the back of her hand across her face, then withdrew from his embrace, leaving one arm around his waist as he turned with her. His arm around her shoulder,

Walker hugged her against him as they started up the path, the ache in his throat so big, so tight, he couldn't even swallow. He didn't have a clue how he was ever going to get through the next twenty minutes. Just the thought of letting go of her for the final time, of knowing this was the last time he'd ever feel her warmth against him, was enough to bring him to his knees. How he was going to get through the last goodbye, he didn't know.

Walker separated the strands of the barbed wire fence and held it as she climbed through, then twisted through himself. As he stood up, Riley whispered his name, then turned into his arms and buried her face against his chest. He held her head against him as he pressed his cheek against her hair, his voice so gruff he could barely get the words out. "I'm going to clear out of here as quick as I can," he whispered raggedly. "I'm going to kiss you once, then I want you to go to the house. I'm going to bring the Jeep up, and I'm going to say goodbye to your folks. I can't drag it out, Mac. It's going to kill us both if I do."

She nodded once; then another sob escaped as she slipped her arms around his waist. Fighting back the awful ache that was tearing him to pieces, Walker swallowed hard, then caught her face and tipped it up, drawing a painful breath as he lowered his head. Her mouth was warm and moist, her lips tasting of tears, and he closed his eyes, the ache deepening in his chest. So sweet. Lord, she was so sweet. The air was instantly trapped in his lungs, and his heart slammed into triple time as she offered him everything. He tightened his hold on her face, desperately deepening the kiss as he tried to absorb enough of her to last him a lifetime. His face twisted by raw emotions, he dragged his mouth away and hugged her hard, his jaws locked against the internal agony of having to let her go. Kissing her once more on the temple, he made himself release her, his tone rough as he whispered vehemently, "Go. For God's sake, go."

She placed her palm against his face, her eyes shimmering with tears as she gazed up at him. Touching his mouth one last time, she turned, leaving him standing at the fork of the path, her form diminishing in the fading light. Walker watched her, his vision blurring, knowing he had just let go of the rest of his life.

Chapter 8

Walker stood at the window of his hotel room overlooking the airport terminal, watching the first thin streaks of dawn creep over the eastern horizon. Hell, he hadn't known he was capable of feeling such emptiness. Nothing he'd ever experienced had come close to equaling this. Nothing. And he knew it was something he was going to have to learn to live with. The hole wasn't going to go away; he'd left part of him behind when he pulled out of the McCormick yard. Saying goodbye to the McCormick family had been tough enough, but Riley's final tear-dampened kiss through the open window of the Jeep had nearly killed him.

But what had done him in, what had finally brought him down, was the damned dog following the Jeep down the lane and onto the main road. As if sensing the finality, Max hadn't stopped at the gate as he usually did, but continued the chase, and Walker had finally had to stop and order him home. By the time he got back in the vehicle, he couldn't see a damned thing. He'd never know how in hell he had made it back to the city without totaling the car.

That recollection nailed him right in the solar plexus, and Walker dragged his hand down his haggard, unshaven face, trying to make the muscles in his throat work. The damned dog—God, it was almost laughable.

Letting the drape fall back across the window, Walker rubbed his eyes and exhaled heavily, then glanced at his watch. There wasn't much point in trying to grab any sleep now. He might as well shave and shower, then head over to the terminal to check in. Four hours to Toronto, a two-hour layover, the hassle of clearing customs, then the final leg— maybe, if he was lucky, he'd be so damned exhausted, he'd sleep through most of it. An image of Riley pushed into his mind, and Walker tightened his jaw. And then again, maybe he wouldn't.

The sun had cleared the horizon by the time he stepped out of the lobby onto the crosswalk leading to the main terminal. The brightness hit him square in the face, and his eyeballs felt as if they were about to incinerate. Shifting his camera case to his other hand, he slung the straps of his leather garment bag and carry-on over one shoulder, then rammed his sunglasses on, self-castigating humor flickering through him. He'd felt better after a five-day drunk.

A current of air grabbed at his hair as the electronic door opened before him, and he squinted, his bloodshot eyes refusing to adjust to the loss of brilliance. The flicker of humor resurrected itself. One look at him, and an airline would have a whole new definition of a red-eye flight.

Through a film of exhaustion, he spotted the big red maple leaf emblem for Air Canada, and hiking the straps higher on his shoulder, he started across the concourse. A fragrance of sunshine insinuated itself into his consciousness, and the awful ache rose up again. He clenched his jaw against it, the knot in his throat contracting as he tried to contain the wrench of emotions. God, he didn't know how he was going to make it through the next hour, let alone a whole day—or a lifetime. But he would—somehow. He'd made it from the hotel to the terminal without thinking about her—a space of thirty seconds. Next time he'd make it to forty.

Knowing he was playing stupid head games with himself, he got in line at the first-class check-in counter, the muscles in his face fixed. If he could make it as far as the plane without making a fool of himself. If he could just make it to the damned plane.

The fragrance caught him again, and he abruptly looked away, his vision blurring. Lord. He was going to lose it.

"Walker."

That one word, the sound of that voice, put his whole body in free-fall. His heart stalled, driving his stomach to his shoes. Surfacing from shock, he jerked around, his heart slamming into overdrive as his gaze connected with that of one Riley McCormick—one very pale, somber, but determined-looking Riley McCormick. The second shock wave hit when he realized that John McCormick was standing just on the edge of his field of view.

Walker's gaze slid from her father back to her, the frenzy in his chest compressing his lungs. Finally breaking the visual connection, he stalled for time as he set down his camera case, then rammed his hand in his back pocket. Keeping his expression impassive, he focused on the two of them again, thankful his eyes were obscured by sunglasses. "John. Riley. I didn't expect to see you here this morning."

Riley glanced at her father, and the older man touched the brim of his Stetson in a familiar gesture. "Mornin', Walker." He shot his daughter another look. "I'll wait for you upstairs in the coffee shop," he said quietly. He swept the two of them with another glance, then turned and walked away.

Walker shifted his weight to one hip, gripping the luggage straps across his shoulder as he turned back to Riley. It was then that he saw the two pieces of luggage sitting on the floor beside her, and his stomach hit rock bottom again. His hand clenched on his hip, he looked up at the concrete rafters, swamped by so damned many feelings he didn't know whether he was going to sink or swim. Exhaling heavily, he looked back at her, his expression fixed as he tipped his chin toward the luggage. "Do you mind telling me what in hell that's all about?"

She stared at him for a moment, her face etched with strain, her gaze solemn and steady; then she looked away. "I want to strike a deal with you, Walker," she said unevenly.

His heart started to do funny things in his chest as he studied her profile. Feeling as though he was about to go down for the third time, he reached out and caught her by the back of the neck, urging her to look at him.

His voice was gruff when he asked, "What kind of deal?"

She swallowed hard, trying to blink away the first glimmer of tears. "It's a compromise. You spent four weeks with me on my turf. I think it's only fair I spend four weeks on yours."

She might as well have grabbed him by the heart. So many emotions tore through him that he couldn't tell one from the other, but the strongest, the one that filled up his chest and made his own eyes burn, was a kind of hope that was almost crippling. And a nearly savage kind of wanting. God, such wanting. Wanting to drop everything and haul her into his arms, wanting to pull her inside him, wanting to hang on to her and never let go. Unable to hold her gaze, he trailed his knuckles along the curve of her jaw, his hand shaking, raw emotion jammed up in his throat. Trying to come to grips with his feelings, with what she was offering him, he stroked her bottom lip with his thumb and spoke, his voice catching on every word. "That's not a good idea, McCormick."

Taking his hand between both of hers, she turned his palm against her mouth, tears leaving tracks of dampness. Walker gripped her fingers as she brushed her mouth across the taut ridges of his knuckles, then laced her fingers through his, palm against palm. Walker was going down fast, and he tightened his hold, her touch a lifeline.

Riley wiped her face with the back of her free hand, then placed it against their joined hands, her voice shaky as she looked up at him and whispered, "That's too bad, Manley, because I don't care if it's a good idea or not. I can't let you walk out of my life without a fight." Sensing that he was weakening fast, she pushed the final button. She reached up and brushed her hand against his jaw, the look in her eyes hitting all his nerve ends. Her voice was low and husky, and so, so gentle. "Don't you know I'm so damned much in love with you that I can't think straight?"

That did it. Walker gripped her hand and looked away, fighting to hang on to the swell of emotion that was threatening to break loose, trying to will away the sudden smarting in his eyes. He couldn't handle this now. What he was feeling was too big, too intense, too deep, too private, for public display, and he knew if he touched her, he'd come apart, seam by seam. All he could do was hang on to her hand and lock his jaw against the awful ache that clenched like a fist around his throat. With that one statement, she had filled up all the dark and empty spaces in his soul; he hadn't known it was possible to feel so full.

On a tremulous breath, Riley laid her hand flat against his taut face, silently urging him to look at her. Swallowing hard, Walker met her gaze, his chest so crowded with feelings that there was no possible way he could utter a single word.

Her long thick eyelashes spiked with tears, she tried to smile, her voice breaking as she whispered, "Don't say no, Walker."

Stripped naked by the look in her eyes, Walker shrugged free of the straps on his shoulder, and, struggling against the thickness in his chest, he pulled her into his arms, his resistance in shreds, not giving a damn if the whole world was watching. Right or wrong, he wouldn't walk away from her again. She was his light at the end of the tunnel.

He absorbed the warmth and strength of her for a moment, trying to collect all those feelings that had trampled his good intentions; then, without looking at her, he smoothed back her hair with unsteady fingers. "Let's book your ticket. Then I want to go talk to your father."

Chapter 9

Riley McCormick took off the headphones, the drone of the 747's jet engines infiltrating the first-class cabin. The aircraft rocked through a pocket of turbulence as it lumbered through heavy weather. She shifted her head on the headrest, her expression softening as she gazed at Walker. He was slouched down in his seat, sound asleep, his face turned toward her. He looked like a gunslinger, his rumpled hair and day's growth of beard giving him that dark, dangerous, desperado look. All he needed was a cigarillo clenched between his teeth. Her amusement faded, her expression sobering as she stroked the back of his hand with her thumb. Even in sleep, he hadn't let go of her hand.

Experiencing a rush of emotion, she swallowed hard and continued to stroke his hand, wishing she could control the throat-aching tenderness he aroused in her. He was so complex, so intense, so inward. A man of many contradictions. He could take her from the protected to the protector in a heartbeat; he could take her from anger to intimacy with a look, and he had the power to hurt her like no other person could. But he wouldn't. Not deliberately.

Riley tried to ease the tightness in her throat. Needing to fuss over him, she drew his jacket up and tucked it around his shoulder, not even trying to disengage her other hand. If he needed to keep her close, then he could keep her close. She didn't care. She would become his Siamese twin if that would erase the look of desolation that was nearly always present in his eyes. She swallowed hard, angry at herself for feeling so emotional, angry at whomever or whatever it was who had taught him to be so hard on himself. Four weeks. She had four weeks to take that look out of his eyes, to convince him that he had a right to be loved. And she did love him.

The pitch of the engines changed, breaking her train of thought. There was an announcement over the intercom that they were on the final approach, and she glanced up to find the seat belt sign already on. She released her seat and adjusted it to the upright position, then shifted toward Walker, a smile appearing in her eyes. There was something very sweet and appealing about him in an unconscious state. He had his arms crossed under the cover of his jacket, one hand fixed around hers, his breathing deep and even. Her smile deepened. He really did look like an outlaw. He needed a haircut, his jaw was dark with a stubble of beard, and there was something about the jut of his chin that carried a hint of danger, of steely determination, of pure male challenge. Her amusement became even more acute. She must be out of her mind. Any woman with half a brain could see this was a dangerous kind of man.

She watched him for a moment longer, then reached over and smoothed the back of her hand against his dark jaw, wishing she didn't have to disturb him. There were lines around his eyes from too many sleepless nights. "We're on the final approach, Walker," she said quietly. "It's time to rise and shine."

Barely conscious, he stirred and straightened in his seat, then blinked to clear his vision. He pushed down the jacket she had covered him with, then dragged his hand down his face before turning to look at her. The intense blue of his eyes were dulled by sheer grogginess, and he forced his eyes open wide as he shifted his legs, trying to fight off the last dregs of sleep.

It took him a moment to come fully awake; then he gave her a sleepy smile that came right out of the bedroom. Shifting his hold on her hand, he caressed her palm, the slow erotic touch turning her whole arm to sponge. "So, McCormick, have you changed your mind?" His voice was gruff and had the texture of gravel.

She closed her hand to still his disturbing little caresses, her voice only slightly uneven as she teased, "If I'd known what a lousy traveling companion you were, I would have picked up someone else at the airport."

He gave her a husky laugh, then brought her hand to his mouth and kissed her knuckles. "I asked you if you'd changed your mind. I didn't ask for a travel commentary."

"Changed it to what?"

"Keep it up, McCormick," he murmured gruffly, "and you'll be on the next Greyhound bus back home."

Her mood sobering, Riley glanced down at their joined hands, wishing she was wiser, wondering what was going through his mind, wondering if she'd pushed too hard. She rubbed the back of his thumb with her own, trying to ease the sudden knot of apprehension in her chest. She glanced up at him, her gaze steady. "Are you sorry I'm here, Walker?"

A startled expression flitted across his face, and he straightened, his touch not entirely gentle as he captured her face in his free hand. His voice was just loud enough for her to hear. "Don't ever misconstrue the reasons I did what I did, Riley," he said, his tone low and vehement. "I want you, believe me. I want you here. I want you in my bed. I want you across the breakfast table from me, but that doesn't mean it's right. And the only, the absolute only, reason I'll ever be sorry is if you end up getting hurt.'' His expression altered, his eyes darkening as he smoothed his knuckles along her jaw, the caress so sensual it made her heart flutter. His voice dropped a notch as he dragged his middle finger across her bottom lip and said, ''And the minute I get you home, I'm going to show you just exactly how much I want you.''

Riley's insides dropped with a roller coaster rush, and she closed her eyes, her lungs malfunctioning from a nearly paralyzing attack of anticipation. After driving herself crazy night after night, imagining what it would be like to be completely and totally loved by Walker Manley, she was fast approaching the time when she would find out. And she wasn't sure if she could keep from disintegrating into tiny little pieces in the meantime.

He smoothed his hand along her jaw one more time, his voice husky and very soft and underscored with just a touch of amusement when he said, ''You'd better start breathing again, McCormick. We could get into a real wreck here if I have to administer mouth-to-mouth resuscitation in front of all these nice people.''

Riley's heart ricocheted off her ribs, and she forced herself to take a deep shaky breath, her pulse still erratic. Her gaze locked with his, and the breathlessness hit her a second time when she saw the look in his eyes. She finally managed to make her mouth work. ''How long is it going to take us to get there?''

He let go of her hand, snapping his seat into an upright position, then gave her a grim smile. ''Too damned long.''

Riley felt as though she were caught in some weird state of suspension from that point on. It was as if she were moving through a dream sequence—landing at La Guardia, deplaning, moving through the terminal, waiting for their luggage—nothing on the periphery registered. The only reality was that the waiting was almost over, and she felt as if she had a whole flock of birds loose in her chest.

Somehow Walker steered her through the unrealness, through the crosscurrents of a milling crowd, his unrelenting grip anchoring her. He looked dark and formidable, his mouth compressed into a hard line, his body language a warning to anyone who considered infringing. But in spite of the very clear message he was sending to anyone who crossed his path, Riley was getting a different one altogether. She'd never felt more protected in her whole life. He used his own body as a buffer against the jam of people around the luggage carousel, letting go of her only when he absolutely had to. It was as if he knew that every sensation she was experiencing was so extreme that she could shatter with a single touch. And the only touch he wanted her to experience was his.

When they stepped outside to flag a cab, the heavily overcast weather seemed to disconnect her even more, with the sky settling on the ground in a damp gray drizzle. The only things that registered were the smell and taste of the rain, and the warmth of his hand against the back of her neck as he ducked her head to help her into the cab. Shoving his customized camera case on the floor on the far side of her, he squashed in beside her and slammed the door, then dragged her into the curve of his arm as he gave the driver directions.

It was the smell of him, the weight of his arm around her shoulders, the way he caught her by the back of her head and forced her face against his neck—it was all that and a crazy flurry of anticipation in her chest that made her pulse hammer, made her want to curl into him and never let go. She closed her eyes, suffocating from the fever of expectation that was climbing higher and higher. The pressure had built to an unbearable level, and desire nearly suffocated her. Her body had been primed for him for weeks, and tonight there would be no barriers. Not physically, not emotionally. The thought of him inside her, deep and desperate and driving, made her heart labor even harder. Tonight the waiting would finally end. But she didn't know if she could keep from disintegrating until then.

Huddling in his embrace, she pressed her face even deeper against the curve of his neck, her fingers clutching his jacket. If she could have climbed inside him, she would have.

As if tuned in to her every thought, Walker dragged her closer into his embrace, his fingers tangling roughly in her hair. He brushed his mouth against her forehead, his voice very strained as he whispered gruffly, "Hang on, McCormick. If this cabbie gets his butt in gear, it shouldn't take us much more than thirty minutes."

Riley closed her eyes and tried to quell the frantic pulse in her throat, to quell the anticipation and agony of waiting, the delirium of wanting. Thirty minutes. She locked her jaws together and slid her arm behind him, clutching the back of his jacket, need like a flood inside her. Walker swore and held her head tighter against him, his heartbeat wild beneath her head. "Hang on, Mac," he muttered, his voice rough with tension. "Just a few more minutes."

Walker's hold on her didn't slacken throughout the entire drive. He held her tight and secure, as if realizing she was balanced on a very fine edge. By the time they reached his building, she was nearly in a state of shock—dazed, weak and shaking so badly she could barely function. She closed her eyes and leaned against the wall of the aging freight elevator as Walker threw their luggage in beside her, then slammed the metal gate across the opening. Punching the button for the top floor, he reached for her, whispering gruff assurances as he caught her by the back of the neck and pulled her toward him. Riley turned in to his embrace and slipped her arms around his waist, needing his strength, needing his warmth, needing *him*.

The elevator stopped, and with his arm still around her, Walker opened the door and shoved their luggage into the shadowed cavernous space of his studio. He hugged her against him, then led her into the dusky interior toward an alcove tucked behind a permanent backdrop.

The living quarters were also heavily shadowed, the rattle of rain against the wall of windows the only sound penetrating the gray dusk. Walker shouldered the door shut and wrapped his arms around her, a shudder running through him as he buried his face against her neck. He hauled in a jagged breath and tightened his hold. "We're in big trouble, McCormick," he whispered unevenly, his voice muffled with strain. "I wasn't expecting this, and I'm not prepared. I don't think I have anything here."

Feeling too shaky to stand, Riley clung to him, her own voice breaking with unbearable tension when she whispered, "I am. I took care of that two weeks ago." With need breaking over her, she turned her head, desperate for him. "Don't stall, Walker," she whispered, her voice compressed by the unbearable pressure swelling inside her. "I don't think I can stand it if you do."

He muttered something, then took what she offered, hot, hungry and searching, as if he was starved for the taste of her mouth. Riley sagged against him, overpowered by him, by the hot, thick, heaviness that was slowly, surely dragging her down.

Every nerve stimulated to nearly unbearable sensitivity, she drew his tongue into her mouth, wanting to draw him deeper and deeper insider her until there was no way out. Clutching her face between his hands, Walker emitted a ragged groan, then fumbled with her rain-dampened coat, stripping it from her with frantic roughness. Riley shrugged it free as he dragged it down her arms, then clutched him close as she feasted on the moistness inside his mouth. Walker inhaled sharply, and hungrily moved his mouth against hers as he dragged her hips hard against him. Widening his stance, he fitted her against the cradle of his thighs, the hard, thick ridge behind the placket of his slacks making her sob as their two bodies meshed.

Thrown into a delirium of desire, Riley made a wild sound, her head falling back as he thrust against her, driving her into a blind fever. Forcing her hands between them, she choked out his name as she fumbled with the clasp on his slacks. She needed him. Now, inside her, hard and thrusting. She would go out of her mind if he prolonged things any further.

The instant her fingers breached his waistband, Walker wrenched his mouth away, his breathing tortured as he caught her hand. "No," he rasped out against her ear, gripping her wrist and immobilizing her hand against him. "Not here . . . not like this." He hauled in a labored breath, then buried his face in the curve of her neck, his whole body rigid with control.

Riley closed her eyes and forced air into her laboring lungs, a kind of panic spiraling through her. She couldn't endure the throbbing emptiness that swelled inside her, the heaviness that kept getting thicker and thicker. He had to end it. And he had to end it before she shattered into a million pieces. She touched the thick, hard bulge beneath the fabric. Her voice breaking with desperation, she said, "Please, Walker. Don't stop. Please. I want you inside me . . . now." She twisted her face, finding his mouth, hers hot, desperate and devouring as the frenzy possessed her. Walker remained stock-still for an instant, for a heartbeat; then, on rough exhalation of air, he jammed her hips against him, rubbing against her, unable to restrain the storm any longer.

Feeling as if she was falling, feeling as if she was hurtling through space, Riley hung on to him, nearly incoherent with need. The sound of Walker's voice penetrated her delirium, but she was past comprehending. The only thing that she was aware of through the consuming fog of desire was the strength of his arms around her as he half carried her across the room, as he lowered her onto something slick and soft.

Through her fevered haze, Riley knew he was trying to slow the frantic pace, to defuse the explosion, but she was past defusing. Every time he touched her, every time he whispered to her in a voice that was thick and ragged, Riley slipped farther into the vortex that was pulling her down deeper and deeper.

Their bodies desperately molded together, they fought to surface from the too-long-denied desire that kept dragging them down. Sure she would shatter if Walker let go of her, Riley sobbed and caught his hips, locking him against her in a futile attempt to maintain the pressure. A shudder coursed through Walker, and his tortured groan was muffled against her mouth as he came apart, no longer in control, claimed by need, possessed by the hard, thrusting rhythm. Fighting against the obstruction of clothing, frustrated to a frenzy by that one remaining barrier, Walker stripped away her clothes, his breathing harsh and jagged in the darkened room, then fumbled with the zipper on his pants.

With a hoarse sound, he pressed his hand hard between her thighs and went still, his breathing harsh, his face twisted into a grimace of agony as he tried one last time to temper his rampaging need. But Riley was beyond temperance, and she reached up and caught the back of his head, drawing him down as she moved against the hard comfort of his hand.

Another tremor shuddered through him, and he choked out her name as he pressed her back and shifted on top of her, the sensations of flesh against flesh, of the hard thickness of him unrestrained between her thighs, putting Riley over the edge. She forced her hand between them, and finally, with the agony of waiting finally over, opened herself to him and guided him home. He ground out a single word of encouragement as he locked her hips hard against him, as he let the storm find its own focus, let it seek its own tempo. She wrapped her legs around him, cast adrift as he roughly thrust into her, carrying them higher and higher as the swell built and built until the heat and pressure pulled together into one final detonation. They clung to each other, hung on for dear life as one last thrust catapulated them over the edge into one final mind-shattering swell, and the crest claimed them. Riley sobbed out his name as Walker ground his hips against her, and a ragged, tortured groan was torn from him as her body convulsed around him in violent spasms, drawing his release in an eruption of heat. And they were lost—lost in each other, lost in the grip of a pleasure so raw it wrung their souls as together they soared into a starburst of pure, pulsating color.

When Riley finally came back down from the wild climb Walker had taken her on, she was hanging on to him with every ounce of strength she had, so profoundly moved, so overwhelmed by the emotional explosion, from the raw, wild passion he had discharged, that she was weeping in his arms.

Walker lay heavy and spent upon her, his face pressed into the damp skin of her neck, his body trembling from the aftermath of what they had shared. On a shaky intake of air, she tightened her hold on the back of his neck, then smoothed her other hand up his back beneath his unbuttoned shirt. She had known that a physical union with him would be earthshaking—but she'd had no idea that any man could carry her to the outer limits of reality. Never had she expected that.

Slowly Walker collected his strength, and, bracing his weight on his elbows, he took her face between his hands and kissed her with comfort, with tenderness, with unspoken love. Riley gave him full access, wanting to hang on to him and never let him go. He filled her body, her mind, her spirit—and she loved him.

He brushed his mouth against hers in a sweet, gentle caress; then, on an unsteady sigh, he reluctantly raised his head and gazed down at her. The dusk in the room softened his features, but the solemn, intense look in his eyes, the gentle way he brushed back the damp tendrils of hair, made it hurt to breathe. And he didn't have to say a word for her to know just how much she meant to him. Her throat ached from trying to hold back the tears.

With infinite care, he wiped away the traces of moisture along her temple; then he tipped up her chin and kissed her once more, his hold on her face possessive and oh, so sweet.

When he raised his head again, the trembling in his hands had abated a little. He wiped the dampness from her bottom lip with his thumb, then met her gaze again, his eyes so dilated they were almost black. He took a deep, steadying breath, then gave her a half smile, his voice rough and uneven when he said, "You pack one hell of a wallop, McCormick."

Riley's expression remained solemn as she caressed his jaw, no trace of a smile in her eyes. "I love you, Walker," she said quietly.

Walker stared down at her for a moment, his expression unreadable; then he shifted his gaze and began combing his fingers through her hair. She heard him try to swallow; then he made an indistinct sound and rested his forehead against hers, his forearms bracketing her shoulders. When he finally raised his head, there was moisture caught in his bottom lashes. His voice was roughened by emotion. "I know you do," he whispered gruffly. "I know you do."

Moved by his admission, Riley caught his face between her hands and pulled his head down, kissing him with all the tenderness he aroused in her. She didn't care if he refused to say the words; she knew he felt them, and that was all that mattered. On a shaky sigh, she raised his head and looked up at him, a touch of humor in her eyes. "I might have had to fight dirty to get into your bed, Manley," she whispered, "but Lord, it was certainly worth it."

He stared at her a moment, as if surprised at her switch; then he gave her an engaging, lopsided smile. His voice still a little gruff, he murmured, "I hate to rain on your parade, sunshine, but you still aren't in my bed."

She grinned up at him as she looped her arms around his neck. "Thank God. It feels like a gym mat."

The laugh lines around his mouth creased as he gazed down at her, the look in his eyes making her breath catch. He watched her with that glimmer of amusement for several seconds, then finally relinquished a response. "It feels like a gym mat because it is, smart mouth."

Riley could tell he was waiting for her to ask him about it. She decided that she wasn't going to give him the satisfaction. "I see."

Shifting his thighs between hers, he propped his head on one hand, a gleam in his eyes. "Don't you want to know why I have a gym mat in my living room?"

"No."

He laughed then, his eyes so full of life and love it made her heart contract. Still grinning down at her, he gave her nose a flip. "God, you're a snot. I should have left you at the airport." He continued to watch her as he idly stroked her bottom lip with his thumb, the amusement leaving his eyes, his expression sobering. "I'm sorry our first time turned out this way," he said quietly. "I didn't intend for things to get so out of control."

She reached up and touched his face, her own voice husky. "I don't recall trying to fight you off, Walker."

His smile didn't quite reach his eyes, and she caught a glint of self-recrimination.

She cupped her hand against his face, stroking his cheekbone with her thumb. "Don't, love," she whispered. "I've been waiting so long for this, I wouldn't have cared if we were in the elevator."

His expression lightened, and amusement returned. "Four weeks hardly qualifies as a long time, McCormick."

She traced his brow, her voice suddenly uneven. "I had nights that seemed four weeks long, Walker," she whispered. "I'd lie awake, wanting you, wanting this."

He dropped his head and gave her a soft, lingering kiss, his breathing unsteady as he whispered against her mouth, "I was trying to do what was best, Mac."

She held his head down, her fingers caught in his hair as she caressed his bottom lip with her tongue. "But you were wrong. This is best."

He drew in a deep, ragged breath and raised his head, humor in his eyes. "It sure in hell is." He kissed her again and whispered against her ear, "You're sure I shouldn't have used something?"

"No, Walker," she said with exaggerated patience. "*I've* been using something for two weeks."

"Well, damn," he muttered.

The way he said it made her laugh, and she hugged him, loving the feel of him still inside her, of his weight on top of her. Sliding his arms around her, he trailed a string of kisses down her neck; then, bracing his weight on his forearms, he looked down at her. "Are you ever going to tell me what your parents had to say about this?"

She met his gaze directly. "They would have preferred an alternative, but they don't crowd my decisions, Walker. They trust me to make the best ones for me."

"What about your mother? How do you feel about leaving her?"

Riley didn't try to dodge how she felt about that. She swallowed hard and looked away, sobered by that stark reality. "I'm scared to death for her, but she wanted me to come. Dana and Brent are finished with school for the summer, so they'll be there for her. And Dad promised me he'd call if there was even a hint she was doing too much." She swallowed again and met his gaze. "She deals with things, Walker. She refuses to cross bridges, and she lives every day the best way she knows how. I guess if I've learned anything from what's happened to her, it's that you don't leave any regrets behind—it might mean taking a few risks, but you make every day count." She managed a smile, but her voice was unsteady as she went on. "And she said she'd gamble four weeks on you."

Walker held her gaze for a moment, then very carefully tucked one curl behind her ear. His voice wasn't quite steady, either. "Your mother is one hell of a lady."

"Yes, she is." There was a brief silence; then, needing very much to lighten the mood, Riley lifted her head and kissed the underside of his chin, the dark stubble of his beard rough against her mouth. "So, Manley," she warned huskily, "you'd better make this junket worth my while."

He tucked in his chin to block her tormenting advance, laughter in his eyes. "Not only are you a snot, you're a nuisance, too."

She bit him lightly on the neck, then lifted her hips a little to ease her skin away from the sticky mat. It was hardly anything, just a slight tilting of her pelvis, but the effect was staggering. Walker sucked in his breath and closed his eyes, his jaw taut as he went stock-still. And Riley experienced a wild fluttery sensation in her belly as she felt him thicken inside her. Her heartbeat went wild, and she slid her arms around him and hung on, the flutter of anticipation intensifying as she rocked once more beneath him. He exhaled sharply through gritted teeth, his body rigid as he turned his face into the curve of her neck.

Riley closed her eyes and tried to draw air past the flutter, every nerve sensitized to how hard he was. Before she could move again, he grasped her hips and immobilized her, his breathing harsh against her ear, his grip like iron. He held her like that for several moments, as if collecting his strength; then he started to ease away from her. But she tightened her legs around him, holding him fast, unable to endure a physical separation. Walker swore softly and rested his head against hers; then, with a tensing of the muscles across his shoulders, he braced his weight on his forearms and raised his head. His gaze was dark, intent, sensually absorbing, and Riley felt suffocated by a rush of heat. She let her eyes drift shut, her pulse going crazy as he cradled her head in his hands and brushed her mouth with a whisper of a kiss, then moistened her lips with his tongue.

She opened her eyes and looked at him, then rocked her pelvis against him again, tightening her muscles around him. His face contorted, and he clenched his jaw, and when he finally looked at her, his eyes were glazed with need. The muscles in his neck were corded with tension, his voice raspy and strained. "Riley. Baby." His rib cage expanded on a shuddering breath; then he looked at her, the heat of desire darkening his eyes, their intensity transfixing her. "This isn't how it should be for you," he said, his voice gruff. "In the middle of the floor on a gym mat, with a hothead who couldn't even wait long enough to get his jeans off."

Her voice went all soft and husky. "I don't need the right setting or the romantic frills, Walker," she whispered. "I just need you."

He stared down at her, then closed his eyes in a tortured grimace and slid his arms under her, his hold fierce, desperate, needy—as if he couldn't let her go. Sensation after sensation pulsed through her, and Riley moved again, but this time Walker met her with a slow countering move that staggered her senses. And she closed her eyes and hung on, knowing now how fast, how hard, how high, he was going to take her.

A damp grayness infiltrated her mind, and Riley stirred and turned. Strong arms pulled her back into the curve of a hard, male body, and his warm breath feathered across her naked shoulder. She opened her eyes, half-asleep and slightly disoriented. She smiled drowsily and snuggled back against the warmth. She might be slightly disoriented, but not so out of focus that she didn't know where she was and whose hand was cupped around her breast. She stared off across the room, taking in the character of the loft. She smiled sleepily. It was all very Walker.

It had been two in the morning when he had finally pulled her up, kissed her very thoroughly, then carted her up the wrought iron stairs to bed. She had been so sated, so drugged on sex and satisfaction, that she was practically incoherent from it, but he hadn't been satisfied with that. He'd made love to her again, but this time he kept her hanging on the edge until she completely unraveled, until she couldn't even remember coming down.

Sleep pulled at her, and she let her eyes drift shut. Smoothing her hand across the back of his, she cradled his palm securely against her. Until now, she'd had no idea this degree of contentment even existed.

She was just on the edge of sleep, in that disconnecting zone of unconsciousness, when a loud thumping reverberated on the door downstairs. Jarred sharply awake and startled by the sound, she bolted upright and clutched the sheet in front of her, trying to get her bearings. Everything focused with unpleasant clarity when she heard the door slam open and a male voice call out, "It's time to rise and shine, so haul your butt down here, you lazy sluggard. I brought breakfast."

"Oh my God," Riley breathed, raking her hair back off her face.

Walker rose up on his elbows, his eyes so glazed and bleary it looked as if someone had poleaxed him. If he'd looked like a gunslinger before, he *really* looked like one now, unshaven, rumpled and sexy as hell. He sat up and scrubbed his face with his hand, trying to focus.

The voice rang out again. "If you don't get your lazy butt down here, Manley, I'm going to come up there with a bucket of ice."

Walker shut his eyes in an exasperated, disgusted grimace, using language John McCormick would have washed his mouth out for.

"Walker! Last call, damn it!"

Still calling Michael names that would have scorched metal, Walker launched himself out of bed and yanked open a starkly modern wardrobe. He snatched up a pair of slacks and started pulling them on, swearing the whole time.

Riley looked from him to the staircase, then back to him, still trying to get her bearings. Walker shot her a disgusted look and hissed between his teeth, "It's Michael. And I'm going to kill him."

The only thing that came together in her head was something so dumb it was pathetic. She clutched the sheet tighter and whispered back, "He has a key?"

Walker snatched up a shirt and started for the stairs. "Yes, he has a damned key. And to cop one of your homilies, I'm going to stick it somewhere dark and painful."

For some reason she couldn't resist. "Up his nose?"

Walker shot her a partly amused, partly exasperated look as he started down the stairs. "Right idea but wrong hemisphere." Then he disappeared. Riley was left to stare after him, wondering what in hell she was supposed to do. A sudden flash cut through the fog in her mind, and she dropped her forehead on her upraised knees, wincing from acute embarrassment. Great. Walker's clothes, her clothes—*all* her clothes—were strewn from one end of the living area to the other. She closed her eyes and groaned. It was evidence a blind man couldn't miss. A new thought gave her something else to wince over. The clothes she'd had on were downstairs and so were her suitcases—along with two men, one of whom was going to want to know, with the devil in his eyes, exactly what was going on. Michael Bonner didn't get that sparkle from being a nice guy, that was for certain.

Accepting the fact that she was going to have to face the music sooner or later, Riley slid off the bed and wrapped the sheet around her as she went over to the wardrobe. Selecting a sweat suit, she went to the bathroom—a profoundly hedonistic, decadent bathroom—found a new toothbrush in a drawer, brushed her teeth, washed her face and got dressed, then, with a sigh of resignation, headed for the stairs. It was time to dance.

A few steps from the bottom, she wanted to turn tail and go back upstairs and never come down. Michael was leaning against the large island that separated the kitchen area from the living area, a broad grin on his face, her slacks and shirt lying on the floor not three feet in front of him. It was enough to make a stripper cringe.

As she saw it, she had two choices: she could either stick her head in the rain barrel and end it all, or she could brazen it out. The choices were narrowed by the fact that this was New York and there wasn't a rain barrel in sight. Heaving a sigh, she decided to brazen it out. She hauled up her nerve and spoke, her voice still rusty from sleep. "Good morning, Michael."

She had to admit it—when Michael realized who the clothes belonged to, the look on his face was almost worth the price of admission. His jaw dropped, his eyes glassed over, and he looked as if someone had just clobbered him on the back of the head with a fence post. While he was still in a state of shock, she began picking up the trail of clothes. The mat was part of a mini gym set up in the corner adjacent to the door, and she snatched up her bra, which was draped over a set of barbells. Clutching all the evidence, she went back and dumped it in a chair, determined to play this charade out to the bitter end, and equally determined not to let Michael see that her scalp was parboiled by embarrassment. She tried her best to disarm him with a smile. "Did I hear you say something about breakfast?"

The unexpectedness of her being there had obviously stripped the gears in his brain, and he remained stalled in park. Feeling she had at least salvaged something, she glanced at Walker. He had been lounging against the fridge when she first came down, his arms folded across his chest, his stance outwardly relaxed but his body language all dominant, challenging male. But now he was watching her with a grin, the former hardness in his face relaxing into unmitigated approval. "Nice move, Mac. Yank the rug out from under him, then kick him while he's down."

The sound of Walker's voice seemed to release Michael from his trance, and he shook his head. Awe underscored his tone. "Well, hell," he said with an element of unbelief.

With an indolent thrust of his shoulder, Walker pushed himself away from the fridge and moved toward her with a predatory saunter. Fixing her with a private, very intimate gaze, he hooked his arm around her neck and hugged her against him. His tone animated with amusement and approval, he said, "You're slick, McCormick. Real slick. Getting rid of the evidence while he's still in a coma."

Riley turned her face into his shoulder, trying to focus on the humor in the situation, still in the midst of I-wish-I-was-dead embarrassment.

Michael finally collected his wits. Leaning his full weight against the island, he crossed his ankles, his thumbs hooked in his pockets as he stared at the two of them. He had a wicked, wicked gleam in his eyes, and his mouth kicked up in a wicked, wicked smile. "I not only brought breakfast, Manley, I also brought *you* a check for ten thousand dollars."

Walker froze, and Riley glanced up at him. She caught the tail end of a strange expression as Walker looked at the ceiling and swore, his jaw set in disgust.

The twinkle in Michael's eyes became downright gleeful. "You forgot about that, didn't you?" He slapped his thigh and chortled when he saw the look on Walker's face. "My God, I don't believe it. You *did* forget!"

Shooting him a rude look, Walker refused to give him the satisfaction of a response. Michael looked like he was ready to split open, so thoroughly was he enjoying himself at Walker's expense. He finally expelled the last of his laughter on a sigh, then shook his head. "Talk about poetic justice." He looked at Riley, shook his head again and grinned in unqualified admiration. "Welcome to New York, Riley. I thank you for bringing the half-wit home."

Walker emitted a snort of disgust and turned away, jamming his shirttail into his slacks.

Riley's intuition was working overtime, and she gave Michael an absent smile, then glanced at Walker. The set of his shoulders radiated annoyance, but she was picking up on something else altogether. Why did she have the feeling that lover boy had just been caught red-handed? Riley mulled that over for a moment, then glanced back at Michael.

Her head tipped to one side in a speculative gesture, she narrowed her eyes. If Walker Manley was that annoyed, it must be over something really embarrassing. She kept her tone deliberately placid. "Tell me, Michael, does this ten thousand dollars have anything to do with me?"

Walker swiveled around, but Michael, who was grinning like a Cheshire cat, never gave him a chance to speak. "It sure does, honey."

"Keep your mouth shut, Bonner," Walker snapped. "And don't call her 'honey.'"

Michael lifted his hands in a would-you-get-a-load-of-him gesture, and Riley nearly laughed. Walker Manley was definitely rattled. It was clear by the cold look he shot Michael that he was itching to strangle his agent, but when he looked at her, she could see a hint of red creeping up his neck. "Look, Riley. It was just a stupid bet we made when we were both falling-down drunk. It's not a big deal," he said.

Knowing she might never get another chance like this to make him squirm, she planted one hand on her hip and made her demand in a tone she used on small children. "What bet, Walker?"

He raked his hand through his hair, cast another helpless glance at Michael, who was thoroughly enjoying this, then gave her a frantic look. "Riley—hell, it wasn't anything."

Ignoring him, Riley swiveled her attention to Michael. In the exact same tone of voice, she said, "Michael?"

Tipping his head to one side, Michael folded his arms across his chest and grinned at her, mischief in every laugh line. "Now, Riley. I think Walker should be the one to make the explanations. After all, it was his drunken arrogance that got him into this in the first place."

Riley turned back to Walker, not allowing even a glimmer of amusement to show. "He's not doing a very good job of bailing you out, Walker. Are you sure you want him to dig you in any deeper?''

Walker shot Michael another disgusted look, then went over to the row of windows and stood staring out. ''Michael can tell you whatever he damned well pleases,'' he snapped. Then he went on to suggest in very innovative, graphic and specific terms, what Michael could do with his check.

Riley managed not to laugh. This was classic Walker at his irritated, sarcastic best. She looked at Michael, raising her eyebrows in the same expression her mother used when she wanted an answer.

Michael's grin broadened. ''That's what I've always liked about Manley—he has the disposition of a pit bull.''

Riley wasn't about to be sidetracked. ''The bet, Michael?''

Michael watched her, the deviltry in his eyes almost masking the thorough assessment he made of her. As if satisfied by what he saw, he met her gaze, the glint in his eyes intensifying. ''Well, it was like this, ma'am. About five weeks ago, my client and I had a meeting with George Nicholson concerning the new advertising campaign for Priscella Cosmetics. As a point of interest, this meeting took place in the Silverado Saloon.'' He paused, watching Riley assimilate this bit of information, then continued. ''Now, in defense of my client, I must explain that he'd just completed six weeks in hell and he was dog-tired—which isn't a great combination for our boy Walker. Anyhow, George wanted to hire a well-known model for the Priscella campaign. Our Walker was deep enough in his suds that he took loud and vocal exception to George's choice and started shooting off his mouth.''

Michael fixed a twinkly look on her, the laugh lines around his mouth creasing even more. ''And since I was pretty deep in the suds myself, I was equally obnoxious. Walker said that he could haul anybody in off the street, and, with his genius behind a camera, he could turn this no-name into the next Carole Armitage." His grin deepened as he cast Walker a quick look, then focused his attention back on Riley. "Since I always found his kind of conceit hard to stomach, I said he couldn't. Then our George got mixed up in it, and somehow or another, a bet landed on the table. The deal was that George got to pick the model and location, and Walker got four weeks to produce a portfolio. If he defaulted, he paid me. If he pulled it off, I paid him." Michael flipped the check back and forth, eyes dancing, then dropped it on the counter. "George let me know yesterday that Priscella is definitely buying. So this, ma'am, is my end of the bargain."

Riley stared at him, her eyes narrowing dangerously. Her voice was very, very calm. "And I was the no-name, right?"

Michael rested his full weight against the island, barely able to contain his enjoyment. "You were."

Her temperature climbing, Riley went over to the island and picked up the check. She'd been singled out because of a stupid scheme cooked up in a damned bar. Her indignation rising like mercury, she turned to face Walker, prepared to tell him what she thought about being classed as a no-name.

But the words dried up when she saw the look on his face. He was watching her, his expression closed and sober, as if her anger was inevitable. His expression didn't give her much. Just a glimpse, but in that instant, she saw inside the man. And what she saw were the remnants of a childhood that had shaped him—a child who had learned from painful experience not to expect approval or acceptance. In that flash of perception, she suddenly understood why he was such a solitary man. And her indignation died as quickly as it had flared.

Shaken by her insight, she scrambled for a way of dealing with the damned check. Easing a shallow breath past the knot of empathy, she somehow managed to control her expression. Giving him a level look, she started to tear the check, but caught a glimpse of Michael's broad grin out of the corner of her eye. Deciding he was just as responsible as Walker for this bit of insanity, she stopped.

Calculating an alternate plan, she glanced from Walker to Michael, then back to Walker. She loved him to bits, but he wasn't getting off scot-free, either. Selecting a pen from the bunch jammed in a huge mug, she sauntered across the room, a smile of pure malice lightening her eyes. Her voice was soft, silky, her don't-argue tone pure Molly Mc-Cormick. "You're going to endorse this check to me, Walker."

Walker stared at her, his expression unsmiling and shuttered; then he silently took the check and pen from her hand. He went back to the island and signed it, and Riley had to really fight to ease the cramp in her throat. He was still expecting the worst, and it broke her heart. It might take her a lifetime, but damn it, she was going to erase those shadows from his eyes.

Without meeting her gaze, he handed her the check, then rammed the pen back into the coffee mug. Riley played out the charade. She gave the check a cursory glance, then looked at him. "Aren't you going to ask me what I'm going to do with it?"

He still wouldn't meet her gaze, and his tone was a little too quiet. "Whatever you want."

Ah, Walker, she thought, don't you know you can trust me? Aloud, she said, "That's nice. Because this is what I'm going to do. Both of you need to be taught a lesson, but tearing up the check doesn't quite do it. Now, ask me what I'm going to do."

Finally Walker looked up, and Riley caught a flash of surprise in his eyes. He held her gaze for a moment, and a rush of relief made her giddy when she saw the first glint of amusement appear. He slung his weight onto one hip, his tone rife with exaggerated patience. "Okay, McCormick. What are you going to do?"

She gave the two of them a TV-hostess smile. "I'm going to donate it to the charity of your choice. Then you won't have to wrestle with your conscience."

Michael let out a loud groan, but Walker said nothing, the intensity of his gaze as he scrutinized her making her insides go all quivery. He reached out and tucked a strand of hair behind her ear, his touch oddly intimate, his whiskey-rough voice just loud enough for her to hear. "If I had a choice, I would rather wrestle."

It was as if she could see right into his mind—naked, hot, damp bodies rolling around on the gym mat—and a crazy, warm weakness broke loose in her chest. She had to clench her hands to keep from touching him. Lord, he was going to drive her crazy.

Chapter 10

She knew he was gone before she even opened her eyes.

Her heart pounding frantically, fear heavy in her chest, she stared blindly into the darkness, trying to separate reality from the distortions of her subconscious. It was Sunday night, her second night in Walker's bed, and it was the early hours of morning. And something had brought her sharply awake.

Riley rolled onto her back, the leftovers from an unknown fear skittering through her. She knew, without reaching out, that the space beside her was empty. Her heartbeat heavy in her chest, she stared at the skylights, trying to will away the fizzle of dread.

The particular hush of night permeated the darkened loft, and she forced herself to steady her breathing as she focused on the rectangles of eerily diffused light above her. Her pulse rate finally settled, and she exhaled slowly and sat up, dragging her hair back from her face. Her alarm, she was finally able to recognize, came from the fact that Walker was gone. She gave herself a moment to adjust; then she picked up a shirt of his and slipped it on, not liking the agitation in her stomach. Something besides sleeplessness had driven him from their bed, and the dread she had awakened to renewed itself. There had been perceptible changes in him since he'd returned home. He was pulling into himself; she could sense it.

Slipping soundlessly down the spiral staircase, she found him standing before the bank of windows, dressed only in a pair of slacks, his profile backlit by the night aureole of the city. His arm braced against the frame, he stood staring out, his preoccupation total. And she knew that whatever ghosts had put the bleak expression in his eyes were stalking him tonight.

Hugging herself against a sudden chill, she moved from darkness toward an arc of half-light, wanting very badly to erase that look in his eyes. Her voice was soft, textured by gentleness, when she whispered, "What's the matter, Walker?"

He straightened and turned, nothing showing on his face except solemn disquiet in his eyes. "Hi. I didn't hear you come down."

Rubbing her forearms to ward off the unsettling chill, she moved out of the shadows, wishing she knew how to hold his phantoms at bay. Whatever the dark and destructive ghosts were that pulled at him, they followed him relentlessly. And she didn't know how to fight something she couldn't see.

She stopped in front of him, trying to read his expression in the faint light. With his back to the window, the angles of his face were obscured by shadows, but she felt his gaze on her when she smoothed her hand up his naked arm. "What's the matter, Walker?" she asked again.

He gave his head a shake and covered her hand with his, lifting it to press a rough kiss against her palm. She sensed such bleakness in him. Unable to stand it, she slipped her arms around him, his hair silky around her fingers as she pulled his head down against her shoulder. "I missed you in bed," she whispered, wishing she could see inside his mind.

Walker released his breath on a jagged sigh, enfolding her tightly against him as he pulled back her hair and kissed the curve of her neck. He didn't say anything for a moment, but when he spoke, his voice was gruff. "Nothing's the matter. I just couldn't sleep."

For some reason a recollection from childhood surfaced, a recollection of her mother coming into her room in the dead of night to comfort her after a bad dream. And she wondered if anyone had ever comforted him in the dead of the night, when his demons haunted him. Easing a breath past the tightness in her throat, she pressed a kiss against his temple. She wanted to force him to talk to her, to provoke him into a fight where he would let it all out, but this was Walker. And he hadn't given anyone access to his soul for a very long time.

Swallowing again, she slowly combed her fingers through his hair, her voice uneven as she tried for lightness. "What's the matter? Not enough action tonight?"

He gave a soft laugh and tightened his arm around her hips, drawing her firmly against him. "Fishing for compliments, McCormick?"

She smiled, giving him a reprimanding pinch. "That's not what I meant."

He raised his head and moved his mouth across her ear, his voice still rich with amusement when he said, "I think you're fishing, Mac. But if you want the unembellished truth, my internal clock is still ticking away on Mountain Standard time."

"You know what you can do with your internal clock, Manley."

An undercurrent of humor was still in his eyes as he took her face between his hands and kissed her hard. "Lord," he said against her mouth, "no wonder your mother shoved you out the door. You were likely driving her crazy."

Responding to the feel of his hands against her face, Riley tried to ignore the accelerating breathlessness in her chest. "Leave my mother out of it. This is between you and me."

"Yes," he whispered huskily as he slowly and thoroughly moistened her bottom lip. "It certainly is."

Her eyes drifting shut, Riley gave herself up to the pure sensual pleasure he was arousing in her. She followed his lead, wanting to bring him back to her, to block out whatever it was that colored his life with such sorrow. She wanted the only shadows in his eyes to be shadows of desire. Those she could handle. Those brought him to her; they didn't separate her from him as the other, darker ones did.

Walker didn't leave their bed again that night. But Riley remained awake after he'd gone to sleep, only slightly comforted by having him in her arms. He lay with his face nuzzled against her neck and his arm tucked around her waist, as though, even in sleep, he needed to keep her close. Struggling against the prolonged ache in her chest, Riley continued to stroke his head.

She didn't know how to deal with this man. She didn't understand him, yet she understood him perfectly. The one thing she was sure of was that, for whatever reason, he carried a heavy burden of self-blame, and because of that guilt, he kept punishing himself. Whatever this *thing* was that haunted him, it had the power to destroy. And that frightened her. She couldn't fight something she couldn't even see.

It was eleven when she awoke the next morning. The bed was empty again, but a scrawled note was propped up on the nightstand.

7:00 a.m. I wish I could have been here to wish you good morning, but George had a meeting set up with his people, and I had to be there. Phone your mother and make sure everything is okay. The number for Priscella C.'s is in the Rolodex file in my workroom if you need me, and I've left keys on the island—the downstairs door locks automatically, so don't get locked out. And *don't* get lost. I'm going to try my damnedest to get home by two. You have no idea how hard it was to leave you alone in my bed—especially with only a sheet between me and temptation. I'll likely spend the rest of the day hyperventilating. Be home as soon as I can. W.

Riley's throat filled up, and her chest hurt from the wealth of emotions that one little note aroused—it revealed far more than he realized, and it touched her right down to her very soul. *If you need me*—she wondered if he had any idea just how much she did.

The effect of the note stayed with her as she tidied up around the apartment. There was some minor clutter, but beneath the surface everything was in perfect order—his closets, the linen shelves, the kitchen cabinets. And although the scattering of CD cases on a shelf indicated his elaborate and very pricey entertainment center was frequently used, his extensive record, cassette and CD collections were meticulously catalogued. She'd seen evidence of this part of his personality before—in his frustration with any uncontrolled disorder on the shoot, in his demanding, perfectionist's approach to his work, in how neatly he kept his quarters at the ranch. Normally such a trait wouldn't have upset her, but this was Walker, a man who had sorrow in his soul.

That awareness was compounded when she went back upstairs to shower and change, then went to his wardrobe to snitch a rugby jersey. There, too, was evidence of that ingrained preciseness. She slowly ran her hand down a stack of perfectly folded sweaters, fighting a growing lump in her throat as she envisioned a very small boy, struggling to find approval. And she experienced the same hollow feeling she'd had when confronting him over the check. She had no proof, but she knew she was right.

Determined to shake the mood she was in, she walked three blocks to the open-air food stalls she and Walker had passed on Sunday, on their way home from getting groceries. It was going on two when she returned to the loft, and with one ear turned to the elevator, she washed the vegetables and put them away, then arranged a bowl of fruit for the counter. When she caught herself watching the clock, she decided she was going to have to find something to do while Walker was at work or she would drive herself crazy.

The phone rang, and she reached across the counter to answer it, intuition telling her it was one Walker Manley on the other end.

"Manley residence."

There was a brief pause, then a curt retort. "The Manley residence belongs to my parents, Riley. You *can* just say hello."

She read the testy tone immediately. "What's the matter, Walker? Did someone steal your parking spot?"

She heard him exhale sharply, and she could almost visualize him standing there, his hand rammed on his hip, his gaze raised to the ceiling, trying to collect some patience. She leaned back against the cabinet, amusement tugging at her mouth. Walker was definitely short on patience.

She heard him take a deep breath, then he spoke, his voice unbelievably flat. "Something's come up. I wanted to let you know I'm going to be late."

The flicker of amusement evaporated, and Riley was instantly focused, hearing a hard, bitter edge to his voice that she'd never heard before. Her stomach did a nosedive. "What's wrong, Walker?" she asked quietly.

There was another brittle silence; then his voice faded, as though he shifted the phone. "Nothing that a damned good swift kick wouldn't fix." She heard him take a deep, composing breath, and his voice was a little less harsh when he continued. "I'm sorry. I'll be home as soon as I can."

Disturbed more by what he hadn't said than by what he had, Riley made some ....d of conciliatory comment, then hung up, an uneasy feeling settling heavily inside her. There were a number of em.. ons she'd seen in Walker during the past weeks, everything from frustration to a barely controlled annoyance to a kind of emotional withdrawal, but this was the first time she'd seen any evidence of real rage. And it *was* rage she'd heard, cold and deep.

Folding her arms tightly against a sudden chill, she leaned against the window frame and watched the river in the distance, feeling stranded and very much alone. She had crowded into Walker's life, so sure that coming here would give them the time they needed to build bridges. She had never really considered the possibility that maybe the gulf was simply too wide.

As the day wore on, the knots in her stomach got tighter and tighter, and Walker was always on the periphery of her thoughts. In an effort to keep from thinking, she walked back down to the market and picked up some additional items, then came back and started baking. She had to do something to keep busy or she would be climbing the walls before he got home.

It was nearly eight o'clock when Riley heard the freight elevator lumber up the shaft. She dumped a tray of muffins on the counter to cool, trying to ignore the butterflies in her stomach. She heard the door open, and she braced herself and turned, the butterflies multiplying.

Riley wasn't prepared for the sweep of relief that hit her when he came through the door. She took a measured breath to quell the flurry inside her, then dredged up a smile. "Hi. I figured fresh muffins would bring you home."

Walker tossed a manila envelope on a sleek, black lacquered credenza in the entryway, his profile unreadable in the angled light. His apology was abrupt, almost rudely brief. "Sorry. I didn't think I'd be this late."

Her stomach hit rock bottom. She'd seen that closed-down expression on his face before. It had been in the Silverado, when the three of them had come out to talk to her about the campaign, and she remembered how his eyes had gone flat, how he'd pulled away and physically distanced himself from her. Suddenly she felt as though she had landed on a tightrope. She tried to keep her tone light. "Would you like me to fix you something to eat?"

He looked at her, his eyes chilling. There was an unyielding set to his jaw that made her insides shrink, and she again sensed the rage simmering inside him. He stripped off his tie and tossed it on the island. "You're not here to wait on me."

Riley turned back to the counter, stung by his tone, but not wanting him to see that she was. She began piling the muffins on a tray, her hands not quite steady as she tried to rationalize the hollow feeling his response had inflicted. She heard him go upstairs; a short time later he came back down, and she heard the clank of weights from where the gym equipment was set up. She turned, the hollow sensation expanding.

He was flat on his back on the bench press, dressed in a pair of old sweat pants, his body working like a machine as he went through the routine, his muscles bulging and straining with every lift. It wasn't the fact that he was obviously pushing himself to the very limit with weight and speed that nailed her squarely in the heart; it was the look on his face that nearly killed her. Anyone who didn't know him would see only the hardness, the almost cruel set of his jaw, but what she saw beneath that was a raw, lacerating pain. This wasn't exercise. This was physical punishment. This was savage self-abuse. This was the physical pouring out of some deep, destructive force. And she couldn't stand there for a second longer and watch him do that to himself.

She went upstairs, badly shaken by what had happened, and lay on the bed, grateful for the darkness. Fear moved in, fear not for herself, but for them. Whatever it was that was driving him to that kind of physical mistreatment was fixed firmly between them tonight. And she didn't know how to get around it.

The minutes stretched out like hours as she lay there, her whole body wired to every sound coming from downstairs. She tried to block them out, but she waited, poised on the edge of the worst kind of suspense, hoping that each sound would be the last. But then a new sound broke loose, the rattling, staccato sound of fists on a speed bag, the sound of Walker trying to hammer out his rage.

The purge lasted for nearly two hours; then, finally, finally, silence took over. Feeling as though she'd been put through an emotional wringer, Riley slowly got up from the bed, her legs trembling, her insides in a mess. She went to the bathroom and splashed cold water on her face, then with shaky hands, stripped off her clothes and put on a nightshirt.

Still trembling, she shut off the bathroom light and went back into the bedroom, tension still pulling at her. Unable to make herself crawl between the covers, she sat on the top stair, listening for some sign of him. The only sound she recognized was that of the shower from the downstairs bathroom, and she huddled in the dark, waiting. After fifteen minutes she couldn't stand it any longer, and crept down the stairs. Her heart in her throat, she pushed open the bathroom door.

As the door swung open, a tightness constricted her heart. Through the Plexiglas of the shower stall, Walker's form was shrouded by the cloud of steam, but it didn't hide the aftereffects of two hours of physical abuse. Spent and haggard, he was leaning against the tiled wall, his eyes closed, the spray from the shower nozzle beating against him. It only took one look for her to know the man had nothing left.

Fighting back a knot of emotion, Riley yanked opened the shower door and reached in to shut off the water. Determination, a fierce kind of caring and an irrational anger surged up in her. Damn it, damn it, for once she was going to take care of him. She didn't care what kind of a fight he put up. Dragging the towel from where it was draped over the door, she stepped into the enclosure and started drying him off, trying to put aside how upset she was. She loved him, damn it, and she couldn't watch him do this to himself.

Walker made a weak effort to still her hands. "Riley, don't."

She shoved his hand away, refusing to look at him. "Don't tell me 'don't,' Walker," she interjected, anger warring with a nearly suffocating need to look after him. "Enough is enough."

She would have dragged him out of the shower if she had to, but, surprisingly, he didn't put up a fight. Still refusing to look at him, she fixed the towel around his hips, then pushed him toward the door. "You're going to bed, and you're going to bed right now. And, damn it, for once don't give me an argument."

She didn't look at him. She knew that if she did, she would lose the spurt of anger that was keeping her going. And she was not going to cry. She wasn't. She ignored the fact that he had pushed himself to the point of pure blind exhaustion. And she ignored the fact that she wanted to hold him so badly she could barely stand it. Right now, her main objective was to get him into bed. Then she could take care of him.

Once in the sleeping loft, she turned on the goosenecked lamp by the bed, pulled back the comforter and swept the pillows onto the floor. "Get in. On your stomach."

Filled with so much feeling for this man that she could barely contain it, she stomped into the bathroom. She closed her eyes, making herself take several deep breaths, trying to discipline herself, trying to ease the emotions that kept filling up her chest. She shoved back her hair with both hands, trying to dam up her feelings; then she snatched up a bottle of lotion and went back into the bedroom.

All her self-lecturing nearly bought it when she saw him stretched out on the bed, the muscles across his back twitching from overuse. And she realized how many other times he must have pushed himself to the limit to have the muscle development he did. It made her mad and protective and emotional all over again.

She climbed on the bed and straddled his hips, then took the top off the bottle of lotion.

He stirred, his voice muffled in the crook of his arms when he spoke. "Riley, you don't have to—"

And this time she didn't scold him. "Shh," she whispered softly, soothingly, then smoothed her lubricated hands up his back.

Walker emitted a low groan as she kneaded the engorged, stressed muscles across his shoulders, and Riley leaned down and kissed the still-damp crease of flesh between his shoulder blades. Then, without speaking, she slowly and thoroughly began working the soreness, the tightness, the last of the tension, from him. Placing the heels of her hands in the small of his back, she worked up and out, stretching out the knots with strong rotating strokes, trying to relieve, trying to soothe. As she slowly worked up his spine, she could feel him relax until he lay completely pliant beneath her.

She reached his shoulders again and kneaded across their breadth, then used her thumbs to massage his neck. Walker exhaled on a low groan, his hands going limp. "Ahhh...Mac, that feels good."

Riley's mouth lifted in a smile, her expression still tinged with somberness. "I know," she murmured, wanting to maintain the hypnotic calm. She massaged his scalp, her smile touched with real amusement as she felt him turn to mush beneath her. Knowing how much he was reveling in the pure physical pleasure she was giving him, she worked down his arms, paying special attention to the erogenous zones in his shoulders, his elbows, his wrists.

A fluttery kind of weakness pumped through her as she felt him lose himself in the sensations she was provoking. Loving him with her hands, needing the feel of him like she needed her next breath, she let her touch become more caressing, more sensual as she slowly massaged one palm. His rib cage expanded raggedly between her thighs as Walker pressed his face into the bed, and Riley closed her eyes, her own pulse escalating, setting off a crazy frenzy in her chest. She wanted this touching, this weakness, to go on and on forever. She wanted to absorb his heat and his pleasure through her hands.

She wanted him to experience only the sense of touch. Nothing else. She wanted his other senses overwhelmed by that alone.

Feeling almost drugged by the feel of him, she reached out and shut off the light, closing off the distraction of sight. Rising up on her knees, she touched his shoulder, and Walker responded to the pressure and rolled over beneath her, the towel twisting free.

The intimate connection of his hard arousal made her weak, and she tried to draw breath around the surge of heat and weakness that made her legs tremble. She gripped his arms, her head dropping back as he smoothed his hands up the insides of her thighs, his touch sensitizing her skin to an excruciating level.

His voice was husky, as intimate as his lover's touch. "What do you want?" he whispered hoarsely. "Tell me what you want."

She rolled her head, her lips parting as sensation upon sensation piled in on her, the sensory stimulation coming from her hands, from her thighs, from the slow stroking of his hands along her skin. Barely coherent, she somehow managed to answer him. "I want this." She rocked her hips against his in a long, tormenting stroke, bringing a pleasure so perfect it made her clutch his arms. And with a rush of wet heat, her hunger changed, and suddenly touching wasn't enough. She wanted it all. A fevered languor claimed her as she slowly rode the hard ridge of flesh trapped between them, her grip on his arms her only anchor, his slow, countering thrust her only reality.

Disengaging her grip, Walker fumbled for the switch for the lamp, then caught her hands, a guttural sound torn loose as he met another stroke with a roll of his hips. His voice low and ragged, he pleaded, "Look at me, Riley. Open your eyes."

Rotating her head in a delirium of pleasure, Riley struggled with the weight of passion and did as he asked, her eyes dilated and unfocused with desire.

His face distorted with the agony of hard, hungry arousal, Walker met every one of her slow, tormenting strokes with one of his own, his gaze riveted on her. Riley watched his eyes glaze over as the tension built, the sensations centering where their bodies fused together. The heat and hunger collected into an unbearable need, and Riley cried out, her control disintegrating as her whole body clenched, tightening toward the final release.

His face twisted with restraint, Walker moved with her, his voice raw and ragged as he whispered, "Let it happen. Let me see it happen."

On a low sob, she rose up and took him inside her. He thrust against her, driving her up and up until the tension exploded in a cataclysmic eruption, her body's convulsions milking his hot release. And on a hoarse incoherent sound, he crushed her against him, the delirium claiming them both.

Shattered and trembling, Riley hung on to him, tears slipping out from beneath her lashes. Walker raked her hair back from her face, his fingers tangling in the silky strands as he roughly cradled her head against his shoulder, his hold on her fiercely enveloping. He pressed his mouth against her forehead and asked, his voice raw with emotion, "God, Mac, how am I ever going to let you go?"

Chapter 11

God, Mac. How am I ever going to let you go?

Riley watched the rain drizzle down the windows, part of her brain assimilating the statistics on the radio stating that this was the wettest, coldest summer New York had had in years. But the other part of her mind kept playing Walker's words over and over, the sobering reality of what those words meant settling inside her like a rock. She could have interpreted the comment as something immediate, something said in the heat of passion, but deep down, she knew it was more than that.

Heaving a deep sigh, she turned and stuck her hands in the pockets of her slacks as she studied the apartment. Most of the furniture was black. Black lacquered wall unit and entertainment center, black-trimmed tables, black leather sofas. All very modern, all very expensive, but black nonetheless. The walls, the counters, the woodwork, with the exception of the pegged oak flooring, was all done in flat white. Black and white—with no varying shades in between. Very much like Walker himself.

The effect should have been stark, almost sterile, but it wasn't. There was too much of Walker here. Most of the artwork was enlargements of black-and-white photographs he had taken, but his choice had nothing to do with conceit. Every shot revealed something that had touched him, had moved him in some way, from a haunting shot of three old women sitting on a park bench to shots of the city to one of a single white birch tree, stark and barren against a winter landscape. These were parts of Walker's soul, and what troubled her most was that there was no joy in any of them.

The wall that separated the living area from his workroom held another grouping of black-and-white photographs, all showcased on black matting, each one a gripping study of human frailty. They were so moving, so poignant, they made her throat cramp every time she looked at them. And they, too, were Walker.

She turned away and wandered around the living area. When he was gone, she had nothing to keep her occupied except her disturbing thoughts. She trailed her fingers along the clean lines of a modernistic sculpture, two pieces of metal twisted together to create a subtle but powerful emulation of an intimate embrace. He saw the passion and poignancy in everything. She repositioned the piece and wandered over to the corner nook of bookshelves, then turned back to the window and considered the rain. What she needed was a long walk.

A loud knocking startled her, and she hesitated, then went to the door. Besides themselves, there were only two people who had access to the studio: Michael and David, Walker's assistant. It could only be one of three people, and it wouldn't be Walker.

Who it was was one Michael Bonner, carrying a wet squall jacket, wearing a lopsided grin and a purple-indigo-and-emerald-green sweater she would have killed for. Her hand braced on the open door, she eyed the sweater, then him, deciding he looked far too complacent. She decided to give that complacency a little nudge. "I'll let you in if you give me that sweater."

His grin broadened into pure deviltry as he started pulling one arm free of the sleeve. "Sounds fair to me."

She knew darned well he didn't expect her to take him up on it. But after his unexpected and somewhat embarrassing arrival that first morning, she figured he owed her one. She grinned and opened the door for him to enter. "Sounds fair to me, too."

Michael stopped, a startled expression flitting across his face. He stared at her a moment, then narrowed his eyes, a reluctant grin kicking up one corner of his mouth. Riley allowed herself a little smile, suspecting that not too many people one-upped this man. He shot her another look, then pulled the garment off over his head, his indigo cotton shirt riding up his midriff. His tone made it very apparent that this had cost him. "This is my favorite sweater, you know."

She tipped her head to one side, doing her best to hold down a grin. "It'll be mine, too." She took the sweater, then waved him in. "There's fresh iced tea in the fridge. Want a glass?"

He tried to sound affronted. "I'd better get *something* out of this."

Michael was fiddling with Walker's very impressive stereo system when she brought him the iced tea. He hit a control, and pure sweet blues and the soft wail of a tenor sax poured out, the haunting sound a continuation of the rainy day. Michael adjusted the tone, then took the glass she extended to him.

Riley settled herself in the corner of one sofa, watching him as she took a sip. "Walker won't be home for a while. He had a meeting at Priscella."

Michael settled deep into the sofa opposite her, propping his feet on the coffee table. "I know. I just came from there. He's done a hell of job on this one. It's the best commercial stuff he's ever done."

Riley knew from bits and pieces of conversations that Michael and Walker went back a long time. Keeping her tone casual, she plotted a course. "How long have you known him?"

"Since we were kids. We went to school together."

"Then you know his family."

Michael's gaze swung back to her, his expression suddenly shuttered. He stared at her a moment, then answered, his voice flat. "Yeah, I know his family."

Riley's insides instantly knotted, and she was grateful for the rainy-day dusk that had filled the room. Her fingers felt nerveless as she clutched the cold glass. "Walker never talks about them."

Michael swirled the ice in the glass, then took a drink, something deliberate and distancing in his lack of response.

She had lived with an active and accurate intuition for too long to ignore it. When he didn't meet her gaze, the nerves in her stomach tightened. She didn't give him a chance to waltz. "But you already know that."

His gaze locked on her; then he glanced down and carefully rotated his glass on the arm of the sofa. His tone was devoid of expression when he answered. "Are you digging, Riley?"

She watched him, trying to assess his expression. "Yes."

Michael stared back at her, then dropped his gaze, absently wiping the condensation from the side of the glass with his thumb. When he finally looked back at her, Riley recognized the directness in his gaze, and she knew he wouldn't do her the disservice of misinterpreting her response. His voice was quiet when he finally spoke. "Walker doesn't play head games. If he wants you to know something he'll tell you."

Trying not to acknowledge how much his response unsettled her, Riley glanced down at her own drink, wishing she wasn't so outside it all. She knew this "something" sat squarely between her and Walker, and that made her very uneasy.

Michael set his glass down on the coffee table and rested his arm across the back of the sofa, deliberately sidestepping the issue. "Walker's going to be tied up most of the day. I thought you might like to go sightseeing."

Riley watched him, considering a number of things, but mostly how far she could push this conversation without infringing on Walker's privacy. She didn't say anything for a moment, then spoke, her voice quiet. "Are you the designated baby-sitter, Michael?"

Michael held her gaze for a moment, then slouched down, tucking his hands under his armpits as he studied his boots. "I'm just doing a favor for a friend," he said, his tone also quiet. He hesitated for a moment, then glanced up. There was an unblinking steadiness in his eyes as he considered her. Finally he spoke. "I'm going to give you some advice, Riley. If you want something permanent from Walker, you're going to have to push him. You're the best thing that's happened to him in a long time, maybe ever. But no matter how he feels about you, he's not going to pursue anything permanent. The bottom line is that he doesn't believe he deserves anything good in his life."

A hollow feeling unfolded in her, and Riley looked away. She didn't know why Michael's comments bothered her; he had only confirmed what she already knew. She'd seen that denial in Walker's eyes too many times not to recognize it. She tried to keep her voice even. "I know that. But I don't know why."

"Then you're going to have to ask him. He's been hit from behind by too many people already. I'm not going to do anything that could even be remotely construed as telling tales out of school. I wouldn't do that to him." He set his glass down on the coffee table, then laced his hands together. He considered what he was going to say for a moment, then glanced at her, his expression unsmiling. "I'm going to say it one more time. You gotta force his hand on this. He'll just let the clock run out if you don't.'' Slapping his thighs, he stood up, his tone putting closure on Walker as he said, ''Come on. I think you need to go for a walk in the rain.''

Over the next few days, Riley thought a lot about what Michael had said, about her forcing the issue with Walker. But ever since the night he'd nearly killed himself lifting weights, she'd sensed a realignment in him. It was as if the more connected they were, the more internal he became, as if her being there had made him more vulnerable. It didn't take Freud to figure out that he carried a heavy burden on his conscience, but every time she saw that bleakness in his eyes, she felt as if she'd failed somehow, and she tried to compensate by loving him the best way she knew how. But the bleak look recurred with increasing frequency. She knew she was losing him, little by little, and it frightened her.

When he came home late Friday night and locked himself in his darkroom after barely speaking to her, she knew something had happened. She also knew he wasn't going to tell her what it was. She finally went to bed by herself, her insides in knots, waiting for him to come up. But he didn't, and she finally fell asleep, feeling very isolated and alone.

When she awoke the next morning, she was still alone. Nor had Walker's side of the bed been slept in. Experiencing a shot of alarm, she scrambled into a pair of sweats and flew down the stairs.

She found him in his workroom. And he was a mess. His hair was rumpled, his eyes were bloodshot, he desperately needed a shave, and the pants he had on looked like they had come out of a war zone. But his face—God, his face—there was such exhilaration in his eyes, it made her hurt to look at him.

He gave her a peculiar, intent look, then glanced out the windows, a startled expression flitting across his face. He closed his eyes in self-disgust. He heaved a sigh and looked at her, his gaze dark with apology. ''Ah, hell, Riley—I'm sorry. The time just got away on me.'' Catching her hand, he pulled her over to the huge drafting table. "Come here. You gotta see this."

Riley glanced down, then looked again, something sweet and miraculous unfolding in her. "Oh," she breathed. "Oh, Walker." On the table was the sum total of her life. Dozens and dozens of pictures of the ranch, of her parents, of her family, of the ranching community where she'd grown up, of Max smiling at the camera. And they were wonderful. But what was most wonderful was what the photographer had seen through the lens of his camera. The joy, the love, the tranquility, the hard work, the commitment—he saw the roots, the continuation. More moved than she could say, Riley picked up a picture of her mother sitting in silhouette against a sunlit window, her hands folded on the table in front of her. A profile shot, it was a study of reflection, beauty and quiet contentment. She had to blink hard to keep the tears back.

"I really like that one," Walker said softly, taking the picture from her.

She put her arms around him and hugged him hard. "Thank you, Walker. They're wonderful."

He looped his arms around her hips and hugged her back. "I thought I'd make up a big album for your parents for Christmas, and maybe more personal albums for the others. What do you think?"

Riley smiled at how pleased he was with himself, and at how slick he was about dodging her praise. She also smiled because he was talking about Christmas. In a strictly diversionary tactic, she dug her fingers into his ribs. "I think you're too cute for words."

He instantly collapsed around her, letting his breath go on a protest. He pulled away from her, his eyes gleaming with a get-even look. "You snot. You're going to pay for that."

She grinned back at him and made a sassy face. "Give it a rest, Manley. You're so damned tired, one good shove will put you out for the count."

He narrowed his eyes at her and began moving to the right. Still smiling that predatory smile, he spoke again, his tone smooth and certain. "You're going down, McCormick."

Amusement made her voice break, and she moved away, shaking her head. "Don't be a ditz. You'll hurt yourself."

"Not very likely." His eyes were bright with anticipation, and his grin was getting cockier by the minute. "Down, McCormick." His arm flashed out, and he swept her legs with a lightning fast move. "You're going down now." Somehow she managed to catch him behind his weight-bearing knee as she hit the floor, and before he had time to get a hold on her, she rolled away and scrambled to her feet, moving out of range to the more open space in the living area. Darned if she was going to make this easy for him.

He nailed her again with another lightning fast move, and it finally dawned on her that the speed came from years of discipline and practice. Watching him like a hawk, she maneuvered into a new position. "Martial arts, huh?"

He grinned. "You bet."

She grinned back at his smugness. "Think you can take out a woman, Manley?" she taunted, waiting until he moved in front of a huge leather ottoman. He was enjoying this; she could tell. She slid to the right, and the minute his weight wasn't centered, she nailed him with a good old-fashioned tackle, bringing him down on top of the ottoman, then using her weight to dump him onto the floor.

Riley should have known not to mess with a man's ego. And the fact that she couldn't stop laughing didn't help much, either. She had to resort to fighting dirty, but that didn't stop Walker. He finally caught her around the waist from behind and started dragging her toward the bathroom, threatening her with a cold shower. Riley grabbed the corner of the island and the support post, using them as anchors.

His chest heaving, Walker tried to disengage her fingers. "Let go, darlin'. Take your licks like a man."

Out of breath and laughing, Riley fought him off. "Not in this lifetime." She tried to twist away, but he caught her wrist, slowly breaking her hold. The phone rang, and Riley tried to use it to her advantage. "Let me get that. It's probably my parents."

Holding her tight against him, Walker gave a breathless laugh and pried her fingers loose. "Nice try, McCormick. But you're out for the count." Freeing her hold, he locked both arms around her and tried to drag her back. "The answering machine's turned on. You can call them back after we've settled this."

Frantically trying to thwart his superior strength, Riley grabbed for the phone. Walker caught her arm and locked it against her waist, his breathing more ragged. "Shower first, sunshine. Nice and cold."

By the third ring, Walker had manhandled her out of the kitchen area and was doing his damnedest to haul her toward the bathroom. Riley had other plans and was doing *her* damnedest to stop him.

The phone rang again, and the answering machine cut in with Walker's message, followed by the sound of the tone; then a man's voice came over the recorder. A sharp, autocratic voice.

And Walker went dead still.

"It's time we had a talk, Walker. If you insist on causing this kind of stir, at least have the decency to talk to me about it. We'll expect you at two tomorrow. I suggest you try to be on time for a change."

The sound of the disconnection echoed in the suddenly brittle stillness. Walker didn't move, not a single muscle. Then, as if collecting his power, he withdrew his arms from around Riley's torso and slowly straightened.

Her heart faltered at his abrupt shift in mood, and she turned to face him. "Who was that?"

His voice had a hard, bitter edge to it. "My father."

It was as though that single admission was the fuse that released his fury. He swore, slamming his fist against wall.

The unexpectedness and violence of his reaction stunned her, and Riley stood rooted to the spot, alarm speeding through her. When he cocked his arm back, she saw the fresh scrape across his knuckles, and something let go inside her.

"No!" Grabbing his wrist, she stepped in front of him before he could lash out again. "Don't! Don't do that to yourself."

Walker tried to jerk his arm away, but she wouldn't let go. Her heart racing like a trip hammer, she slid her arms around him and hung on. Badly shaken by what had just happened, she closed her eyes and weakly rested her forehead against his shoulder, an overdose of adrenaline pumping through her system. She didn't know what had set him off, or why. But one thing she did know: there was much more to this than just plain fury.

For a moment she thought he would try to jerk away from her, but he stood there, his body locked stiff, every muscle clenched and trembling. And Riley thought of a young, unbroken stallion she'd seen once. Challenged and cornered, the horse had exploded, savagely lashing out with his front hooves. But once the handler had him under control, the stud had stood with all four legs braced, the muscles in his hindquarters trembling, his sleek black hide wet with nervous lather. And even as young as she was, she'd known it would have taken only one wrong move to unleash the fury again.

She'd known that then. And she knew it now.

Her heart still laboring from the surge of adrenaline, she flattened her hands against his back and pressed her face tighter against his shoulder, aware that she, too, was trembling. She didn't know what to say, so she said nothing, slowly increasing the pressure of her embrace, willing him to relinquish his rage.

It took a while, but little by little she felt the tension in his back ease, and finally he let go of it all, as if expelling it through his lungs. Drawing a deep, cleansing breath, he folded her into a tight embrace, a final tremor coursing through him.

Riley closed her eyes in shaky relief, not quite sure where to go from here. There were too many questions she didn't have answers for. But almost immediately she sensed a change in him, as if he was deliberately closing himself off. As before, she could almost feel him centering himself; then he slackened his hold and pulled away.

Uncertainty eating at her, she watched him, knowing he would simply withdraw into silence if she let him. Taking a shaky breath, she took the plunge. "Talk to me, Walker," she whispered unevenly. "Tell me what's going on."

Turning his back to her, he put his hands on his hips and tipped his head back, as though trying to draw up some inner calm.

"Walker?"

His voice was flat when he finally answered her. "It's a family matter. It doesn't involve you."

Still shaky inside, Riley folded her arms tightly across her chest, moving so she could see his face. Her pulse suddenly thick with trepidation, she watched him, knowing how tenuous her situation was, remembering what Michael had said. When she spoke, her voice wasn't quite steady. "If it affects what happens between us, it does involve me, Walker."

He turned, not a trace of emotion on his face as he stared at her. "This has nothing to do with us."

The intractable tone of his voice hit her wrong, and a flicker of anger shot through her. He was doing it again, damn it, only this time she wasn't going to let him get away with it. She moved closer, deliberately invading his space. "Really?"

"Yes, really. It's none of your business."

None of her business? Her temper started to climb, and she let her arms drop, moving another step closer. She kept her voice very, very quiet, but there was no mistaking the tone. "Well, I beg to differ. When you start smashing your hands against walls, when you lock yourself in your dark-room and don't come out for twelve hours, when you damned near kill yourself lifting weights, it sure in hell is my business."

Walker didn't back off. "Look," he said with deliberate patience, "I told you what I was like. But did you listen? No."

"No, Manley. You *didn't* tell me what you were like. You gave me all the excuses you use to build walls. If you don't want to deal with something, you just haul up a bad mood."

"That's a crock, and you know it. You don't know a damned thing about me."

For some reason, his retort hit a nerve, a very painful nerve, and Riley was horrified to discover that she was on the verge of tears. She folded her arms across her chest again, swearing she wasn't going to let him make her cry. "How can I? You keep holding pieces of yourself back. Do you think I'm so shallow that I can't accept the fact that you're not perfect? Is that what you think, Walker? Do you think that at the first sign of trouble, I'm going to change my mind about how I feel about you?"

Something flickered in his eyes, and he looked away. And Riley knew that she'd hit a nerve, as well. She'd wanted to make him mad, damn it. She hadn't wanted to hurt him. She tried to ease a breath past the awful tightness around her lungs. "Why can't you just talk to me?"

His hands on his hips, his jaw rigid with control, Walker stared back at her, his expression fixed. "My family isn't like yours. I don't want you dragged into this mess."

"Is that it, or do you just want me out of your life?"

Walker watched her a moment longer, the hardness in his face replaced by a disquieted expression. Finally he turned away and went over to the windows and stood staring out. When he finally spoke, his voice was very gruff. "No, that's not what I want. The problem is with me, Riley. It's never been with you."

The rawness in his voice completely finished off her brief flare of anger, and Riley closed her eyes and leaned back against the island, trying to will away the shaky feeling in her legs. She wanted to go to him in the worst way, but she felt as though she'd hit a brick wall. And she didn't have the resources to take the confrontation any farther. Heaving a sigh, she opened her eyes and looked at him. "Are you going to keep the two o'clock appointment with your parents?"

There was a brief silence, then he answered. "Yes."

"Will you take me with you?"

Another silence, only this one was longer. "No."

Riley stared at him a moment, then dropped her hands. "Well, I guess that's that." There was nothing more she could say.

She stayed out of his way for the rest of the morning. By lunchtime, she had developed a blinding headache. Walker ate the lunch she prepared, his eyes bloodshot from lack of sleep, then withdrew to his workroom. Unable to handle the tension or the headache any longer, she went upstairs and lay down, then indulged herself in a good cry.

Covering her eyes with her arm, she ignored the tears that slipped down her temples into her hair, wishing she didn't feel so damned displaced. But silence separated them, and she felt as if everything was slipping through her fingers like a handful of smoke.

She was so deep in her unhappiness that she wasn't aware he'd come up the stairs until she felt the mattress dip. He tried to move her arm so he could see her face, but she wouldn't let him. He moved it anyway, and more tears slipped into her hair. She heard him try to swallow as he smoothed his thumb down her temple, wiping away the moisture.

His voice was like gravel when he finally spoke. "These past few weeks with you have meant everything to me, McCormick. I want you to know that. I've spent a lot of years trying to work through some heavy-duty crap, and I haven't done a very good job of it. I don't know if I'll ever be able to put it all together. But you've never been part of the problem, sunshine. You have to know that.''

Her throat aching so badly she couldn't possibly speak, Riley slipped her arms around him, silently urging him down beside her. Exhaling raggedly, he shifted, stretching out beside her as he gathered her in a tight embrace.

Slowly stroking her back, he held her for a long time, trying to soothe away the rawness. And when she finally grew quiet, he made love to her with such profound tenderness, with such exquisite care, that she came apart in his hands. And afterward, exhaustion claimed him and he fell asleep, still holding her.

She lay safe and warm in his arms, watching dusk creep into the room, bringing uncertainty with it. Doubts piled in on her, and feeling as though they would smother her if she stayed there, she slipped out of Walker's arms and went downstairs. It was the early hours of the morning before she went back.

Like the previous morning, Walker was already up when she awoke, the gray drizzle of another rainy day settling heavily inside her. She found him standing in front of the windows with a towel draped around his naked shoulders, his hair still damp from a shower. Her heart contracted, and she rubbed her upper arms against a sudden chill. Feeling as if there was no warmth left in her, she finally spoke. ''I want to go with you today.''

He turned and stared at her a moment, then turned back to the window. His voice quiet, he said, ''You don't have any idea what you'd be getting into.''

''No, I don't.''

''This won't be a nice family get-together, Riley. I told you, my family isn't like yours.''

''I never expected them to be.''

He made a contemptuous sound and braced his arm against the frame. She hesitated, afraid, uncertain, knowing she was playing with the rest of her life. When she finally spoke, her voice was uneven. "What happens now is up to you, Walker. I'm not going to fight you on this, but we can't go on like this, either."

"Is that an ultimatum?"

"I don't give ultimatums. You should know me better than that."

He turned to face her, nothing showing in his expression. But there was a hint of anger in his voice. "It sure as hell sounds like one."

Riley held his gaze, not even trying to disguise how raw she was feeling. Her voice broke a little when she finally spoke. "You either trust me, or you don't." She had to pause before she could go on, and she looked up at the ceiling, trying to will away the ache that kept getting worse and worse. She did not want to come apart in front of him. God, she didn't. On that thought, the tightness eased a little, and she took a shaky breath. Feeling as though she was putting her very life on the line, she met his gaze again. "You're either in, or you're out, Walker. It's time to either fish or cut bait. It's up to you."

He stared at her for a very long time; then, finally, when she was sure he wasn't going to respond at all, he turned back to the window. And she knew he'd made a decision. His voice was clipped. "Then I guess we fish, sunshine."

She closed her eyes, nearly sick with relief. She looked at him again and, her voice still shaky, asked, "Then I can go with you?"

There was another long pause. "Yes."

Turning, Riley went upstairs. Cold and shaking, she crawled onto the bed and sat with her arms locked around her knees, her head weakly resting on her wrists as the aftershocks of fear hit her. She had been so damned afraid he would say no—and she didn't know what she would have done if he had.

They barely spoke after that, every hour an endurance test. As much as Riley dreaded the approaching confrontation, the waiting was even worse. She was relieved when it was time to get ready to go, and she dressed with more care than she could ever remember taking. Walker had bought her a sage-green raw silk outfit that a fashion house had selected for one of his shoots. When he'd brought it home, all elegantly gift wrapped, he'd told her he'd had to buy it because it was the exact same color as her eyes. It was a gorgeous outfit, and it looked great on, but that wasn't the reason she wore it; she wore it because he had given it to her with love in his eyes.

When she came downstairs, he was at the sink rinsing out a glass. He stopped and stared at her; then, as if he couldn't stop himself, he reached out and caressed one of the chunky earrings she had on. That one light touch nearly undid her, and she had to clench her jaw against the sudden thickness in her chest.

He let his knuckles slide down her neck; then the muscles in his face hardened, and he turned away. "We'd better get going."

The black Porsche parked in the ground-floor bay shouldn't have come as a surprise, but it did. Whenever they'd gone out before, they'd either walked or taken a cab, and she knew he had a vehicle outfitted for location shoots. But the Porsche was an unknown—like the situation facing her.

The only thing Walker told her was that his parents lived in Connecticut, and that it was about an hour-and-a-half drive. But if the Porsche had come as a surprise, her stomach dropped to her shoes when he turned onto a paved drive nearly buried in the trees, passing through elaborate, electronically controlled wrought iron gates mounted on massive stone pillars. The driveway was long and secluded, but the deeper they went into the canopy of trees, the bigger the butterflies in her stomach grew. She sat beside him, a horrible feeling of alarm sliding through her. When the house and grounds came into view, she could do nothing but stare, dumbfounded by what lay before her. The house was incredible—a sprawling stone structure with a drive-through portico at the front that was supported by huge white pillars. She counted eight chimneys before she closed her eyes, her mind swamped. She had seen wealth before, but nothing like this.

Walker parked under the portico, and without looking at her, got out and walked around the front of the car. He opened her door, his expression hard and mocking, his tone deprecating when he said, "Welcome to the old homestead."

Still reeling from the shock, she slowly climbed out of the low-slung car, every speck of color draining from her face. She should have known. She should have seen the indicators. But she had missed them all. And it had nothing to do with wealth. It had to do with all the things that perpetuated wealth—the innate drive to succeed, the discipline and single-mindedness, the vision, the talent—that had been bred into him. But that wasn't what got to her. It was the expectations that went with that kind of money, the kind that might have been passed on to a son.

Walker's grip on her chin jolted her back, and she looked up at him, trying to will away the burning sensation in her eyes. There was a cold glitter in his gaze. "This isn't mine, Riley. This has nothing to do with who I am."

She wanted to tell him it had everything to do with who he was, but she knew he wouldn't understand.

Walker dropped his hand and turned away, slamming the car door. He started up the steps, and Riley pressed her hands together, the butterflies going crazy. He stopped and turned. He stared at her a moment, then came back down, the lines around his mouth softening. He stuffed his hands in his pockets and looked away, the muscles in his jaw flexing. There was a taut silence, then he released his breath on a heavy sigh and glanced back at her. He studied her briefly, his eyes dark and unreadable; then he very carefully untangled a strand of hair caught in her earring. "I'm sorry,

Mac,'' he said huskily. ''I need my butt kicked. If you don't want to go in, believe me, I understand.''

The regret in his voice touched something very deep inside her, and Riley tried to relax the knot in her throat, her butterflies gone. There was no way she was going to let him go in there alone. Not sure how steady her voice would be, she caught his hand and laced her fingers through his, acknowledging his apology with a reassuring squeeze. When she could finally manage a shaky smile, she looked up at him, her gaze steady. ''Let's get one thing straight, Walker,'' she whispered unevenly. ''You aren't dragging me anywhere. The only place I want to be is where I am.''

Walker studied her, his gaze unreadable. ''Don't be so sure.''

Chapter 12

A light breeze swept through the portico as they climbed the stairs, and Riley shivered slightly, feeling as if every nerve was exposed to it. But the chill was incidental; what she was most aware of was how hard her heart was hammering and how tightly Walker was holding her hand.

He didn't look at her, his profile cast in unyielding lines as he reached out and pressed the ornate door chime. A new wave of apprehension slithered through her, and she locked her fingers around his, frantically wishing she knew what was facing them beyond the heavily carved oak doors. Her survival instincts were sending out all kinds of warnings, but something deep inside assured her that she was exactly where she ought to be. She prayed to God her intuition was right.

The door was opened by an elderly black woman. She was white-haired, plump, with the posture of a drum major, her gray apparel and white apron clearly a uniform. But it was her face that riveted Riley. Lined with age, it had seen trials and tribulations, but it was also a face that revealed a wealth of comfort. Brown snapping eyes crinkled at the corners as her face lighted up with a smile that had enough voltage to illuminate all of Maine. "My, oh my, Mr. Walker. Aren't you a sight for these old eyes."

The hard lines around Walker's mouth relaxed into a lopsided grin, the warmth in his expression making Riley's throat contract.

"Hello, Maddy," he said gruffly. "I thought you hung up your duster a long time ago."

The older woman took his face in her wrinkled hands and gave his head an admonishing little shake, the reprimand in her tone negated by the tears in her eyes. "Don't get sassy with me, Mr. Walker, or I'll dust your britches."

Walker let go of Riley's hand to receive the woman's welcoming hug, and the lump in Riley's throat expanded when she saw him squeeze his eyes shut before he tightened his arms around the older woman and tucked his face into her shoulder. Riley stood there, swallowing hard, moved by the reunion, comforted by the fact that there was someone here who obviously cared about this man.

Maddy blotted her face on Walker's shirt, then caught his head. She gave him a resounding kiss on either cheek, then leaned back and looked up at him. Her eyes twinkled with another smile as she caught his cheek in a maternal pinch. "You been keeping your nose clean and your skivvies washed, or you been up to no good again?"

Walker's expression held a glint of amusement. "Clean on both counts, and I don't spit in punch bowls anymore, either."

Maddy chuckled and patted his cheek, then turned to Riley, a sharp, assessing look in her eyes. Walker put his arm around Riley's shoulder and drew her against him. "I'd like you to meet Riley McCormick, Maddy. She's visiting from Canada."

Maddy studied Riley for a moment, then swung her attention back to Walker, her eyes narrowed in contemplation. "Well," she said decisively, "it's about time."

She took the hand Riley offered in both of hers, a sly gleam appearing. "This boy's had his hand in my cookie jar since he was two years old, Miss Riley, and he's put more gray hair on this old head than Old Man Time."

Riley grinned. Her tone laced with a touch of conspiracy and a whole lot of understanding, she said, "Thirty years is a long time to put up with Walker."

Walker shot Riley a look, his eyes narrowed in a warning; then he looked back at the older woman, a wry expression lurking around his mouth. "She gives me nothing but a hard time as it is, Maddy. She doesn't need any help from you."

Maddy's eyes were still twinkling as she gave Walker a head-to-toe once-over. "I can see you're suffering, Mr. Walker. I can tell by that devil shine in your eye." She looked back at Riley and gave her head a rueful shake. "This boy could charm the skin off a snake, Miss Riley. Got hisself outta more trouble with that smile of his..."

Riley glanced at Walker, laughter in her eyes. "It takes more than a smile to get him out of trouble these days, Maddy."

Maddy gave Riley a broad, approving grin. "You'll do, child. You'll do." Turning her attention back to Walker, she sighed heavily, her expression sobering. "We best go in. They're waiting for you in the library."

A new wave of apprehension hit Riley as they entered the house, and she tried to ignore the sudden palpitations that settled in her chest. She glanced at Walker, the unaccountable feeling of dread intensifying when she saw the hard, inflexible look on his face. She wished she didn't feel so unfortified.

Passing in front of the wide, sweeping staircase, they followed Maddy across the oak-paneled foyer to a set of ornately paneled doors, their footsteps sharp and staccato on the inlaid Italian marble surface. Maddy knocked, then opened the door, her voice carefully modulated as she announced, "Mr. Walker's here, ma'am."

Maddy opened the door wider and stood back, her hand on the brass handle, silently ushering them into the room. Just before they stepped through the door, she touched Walker's arm. Her voice so low only they could hear her, she said, "You come back to the kitchen after, you hear? I got a big chocolate cake waiting for you."

Without looking at the older woman, Walker caught her hand, silently acknowledging her with one final squeeze. Then, with a militant set to his jaw, he touched Riley in the small of the back, then followed her into the room.

Riley's first impression was of quiet warmth. Elegant, richly appointed, with dark oak bookshelves, vaulted ceiling and casement windows, the room featured a huge field-stone fireplace that was flanked by French doors opening onto the terrace. Leather and wood and priceless antique furniture infused the room with a mellow graciousness. It was a room that had ripened with history, a room that offered elegant sanctuary. She looked up at him, not sure how to proceed.

But he didn't acknowledge her glance. His profile was rigid, his jaw set in challenge as he stared at the man who was rising to his feet behind a massive cherrywood desk.

The physical resemblance between the two men was startling. Mr. Manley's hair was salt-and-pepper, his face weathered; Walker was taller, leaner, his build more streamlined. The eyes were different, but the older man's revealed the same edge of steel, and his jaw was set in the same intractable expression. *Like father, like son.* And Riley knew that if there was a battle of wills between them, it would be bloody.

"You're late, as usual."

Walker stared back at him, a cynical half smile making his eyes go a cold, icy blue. "It's nice to see you, too." Walker shifted his gaze, and his voice took on an impassive tone. "Hello, Mother."

Her attention fractured by a dozen impressions, Riley shifted her head, noticing for the first time the woman standing behind a Queen Anne wing armchair. Walker's mother stood watching him, her hand resting on the brocaded back, the lines around her eyes shadowed with acute distress.

Riley could see the pulse in the woman's neck clear across the room, and the tautness in her body was clearly evident. Perfectly groomed, her silver hair swept up in an elegant French roll, Mrs. Manley made Riley think of a piece of very fragile porcelain. Poise and breeding radiated from her, and Riley suspected that poise and breeding were, right now, all that was holding her together.

When the older woman finally spoke, her voice was very unsteady. "Hello, Walker." Mrs Manley drew on her poise as she stepped out from behind the chair and moved toward them. She managed a nervous smile as she looked at Riley.

Walker made the required introduction with an abruptness that bordered on rude. "My parents, Jackson and Vivian Manley. Riley McCormick."

Jackson Manley cast Riley a scant glance, then leveled an icy glare at his son. The anger in his voice was barely restrained. "With all due respect to Ms. McCormick, I did not intend this to be a social call."

Shoving his hands in his pockets, Walker watched his father with an insolent stare, silently challenging him with his loose-hipped stance. His mouth lifted in a cold, cynical smile, his tone contemptuous, he spoke. "We could always count on you to screw the niceties, couldn't we, Dad?"

The older man approached him, the veins on his neck distended with anger. "Niceties? Is that what you call what you've been up to? You didn't even have the decency to face us with this bit of ridiculousness. Do you have any idea how badly you upset your mother with this?"

Anger glinted in Walker's eyes, the only other indication of his feelings a twitch in his jaw. He held on to his temper, but his tone was deadly. "I think we'd better talk this over in the study, don't you?"

"What I have to say can be said right here. I want this idiotic legal manipulation stopped. And I want it stopped now."

Walker's eyes narrowed, and his lips went white. But it was his voice—cold, cutting and furious—that made Riley shiver. "Manipulation? *You* want to talk about manipulation? You waited until I was out of the country, and you— *you*—made the decision to ship him off to some institution without saying a damned word to anyone. Without any consideration for whether it would be best for him. Screw everyone else, as long as it suits you."

"Just one damned minute!"

"After what you tried to do, I wouldn't give you the time of day, let alone a minute. I'll fight you every step of the way if I have to, but you're not going to bulldoze your way through this one."

Jackson Manley's rage broke loose, and he pointed his finger at Walker. His tone vicious with condemnation, he retaliated, "You're such a big man, aren't you? Taking care of things. Well, you'd better think back, boy. Let's lay blame where blame is due. If you'd taken better care of things fourteen years ago, we wouldn't be in this mess. And he wouldn't be where he is now, would he?"

A terrible silence filled the room, and Walker stared at his father, not a muscle moving in his face except a tic in his cheek. Then Walker turned on his heel and strode out of the room, leaving a stillness that reverberated with the echoes of a festering and unforgiving anger. Riley stood rooted to the spot, stunned, unbelieving, suspended in horror.

A sound broke through her dazed state, and she swiveled her gaze to where Vivian Manley was leaning heavily against the chair, her hand covering her face, terrible violent sounds coming from her. And those sounds shattered the unreality of it all and released Riley from the paralysis of shock. Whirling, she went after Walker, a sick shaky feeling washing through her and wedging her heart high in her throat. Something had just happened that had never happened before. She was sure of it. She knew it from the awful silence that had echoed and reechoed with the bitter accusations, from the utter stillness that had transfixed both men, from the dread that was chewing up her stomach. But, most of all, she knew it from the glimpse she'd had of Walker's face as he turned to leave. It was the look of a man who'd taken a crippling blow square in the gut.

As shaken as she was by the ugly scene, a few things were brutally clear. Some sort of tragedy had fractured the family, and a long-festering blame had finally been voiced. But what horrified her most was that it was Walker's father who held the smoking gun.

She'd had some idea of the depth of self-punishment Walker had lived with. She'd seen the evidence in the stark expression in his eyes, in his dark moods, in his bleak conviction that he deserved nothing good in his life. But this new insight scared her to death, and the first tentacles of panic uncurled inside her. The accusation his father had leveled had given confirmation to how he felt about himself, and that confirmation would drive him farther into himself—and farther away from her. Her panic grew.

As she rounded the wide staircase, she slammed into Maddy, who was coming around the other side, the whites of her eyes stark against her dark face. She grasped Riley's arms, her voice thick with alarm. "He's headed to the creek, Miss Riley. You gotta get him. You gotta stop that boy before he does something rash." Her expression crumpled, and she covered her face with work-worn hands. "His daddy may as well have cut off both his arms, saying something like that. Hearing that is goin' to nigh well kill him."

Her own alarm escalating, Riley interrupted. "Where's the creek, Maddy? Which way do I go?"

Staunchly swiping at her face, Maddy straightened her shoulders and pointed through the open door. "There's a trail that cuts through those trees there. Just follow it and it'll take you past the stables to where he is."

Something weird happened to her lungs. "Stables?"

"Yeah. Past the trees." Maddy wiped her face with her apron, her tone calmer as she focused on where her responsibilities lay. "I got to go, Miss Riley. This is going to tear Mrs. Manley up something awful. You go find that boy. He's going to be hurting plenty after this ruckus."

It was crazy, but it was the sight of the unused stables that sent panic sluicing through her, and Riley took off down the path, a senseless litany revolving in her head. *Please, Walker. Please, please, please.*

Twigs snagged in her hair, and she couldn't seem to draw enough breath as she dodged around the dead branches protruding along the nearly overgrown path. Her heart hammering against her ribs, she broke through into a small grassy clearing—and into the remnants of childhood.

Riley felt as if she'd hit an invisible wall. A weathered tree house, crumbling with age, was nearly obscured in the heavy foliage of a huge old tree; a tire swing, twisting in the breeze, the rope frayed and gray with age, hung suspended from a thick branch that angled out over a sharp bend in the fast running stream. And upstream, across the water, the bluff was scarred with countless tracks that looked like they had been cut by dirt bikes. A knot of emotion tightened around her hammering heart, and Riley pressed her fist against her chest, trying to hold back the sudden ache of tears that climbed up her throat. Childhood. After what had happened in the library, after his own father had turned on him, after he'd been charged and found guilty, he had come here, had returned to this sanctuary of his youth.

Desperate to find him, she started along a trail that followed the creek; then, following some sudden gut feeling, she turned and headed upstream, her heart laboring more from a clenching fear than from her flight through the trees. She had to find him. The thought of his being alone was more than she could handle.

She fought her way through another copse of overgrown trees, the churning in her stomach escalating when she broke into another long open area and saw no trace of him. Frantic, she scanned the area, a terrible feeling making her insides twist. She had to find him. But she didn't have a clue where to look. As she turned to go back, she caught a movement along the shallow bank of the stream, and her heart lurched when she saw a sliver of color beside a huge boulder embedded in the bank.

She closed her eyes in a nearly disabling wave of relief; then, hauling in a deep, steadying breath, she started toward him.

He was sitting with his back against the rock, his elbows braced on his upraised knees, his bowed head resting against his interlaced hands, and even from a distance she could see his legs trembling. Compassion wrenched her very soul as she neared him and saw the ravages that had been wrought. His face, contorted with pain, was drained of all color, and the knuckles on both hands were white. But what tore at her more than anything was how tightly he had his eyes closed, and the traces of moisture that spiked his dark lashes. At that precise moment, the magnitude of the guilt he carried became a real, tangible thing for her. And she wanted to strangle Jackson Manley for what he had done to his son.

Feeling as if her heart was going to come through the wall of her chest, she drew a deep steadying breath, praying she had the wisdom to say the right words. She knelt beside him, wanting so badly to put her arms around him, her instincts warning her not to. Fortifying herself against a possible rebuff, she smoothed her hand up his arm and spoke, her tone soft and comforting. "I'm sorry, Walker. So very sorry."

Inhaling raggedly, he dug his thumbs into his eyes, then raised his head and turned away, his mouth obscured by his laced hands. When he spoke, his voice was so gruff it was barely audible. "It's not your problem, sunshine. I'm sorry you got mixed up in this."

Her hand still resting on his arm, she sat down facing him, her hip flush against his, wishing he would look at her. She continued to stroke his arm, wanting to infuse him with warmth, with her unspoken assurance. There was nothing she could say that could alter what had happened; her only hope was that she could influence the outcome. "I'm here of my own volition, Walker," she said quietly. "So don't assume responsibility for me." She glanced down, absently fingering the rolled-back cuff of his shirt, trying to find a way of approaching sensitive ground. The question framed, she glanced up, her gaze sober as she studied his profile. "You weren't expecting this today, were you?"

Walker dropped his hands, his gaze shifting as he picked up some pebbles from the ground between his knees. His tone was derisive and edged with bitterness. "My father adheres to very rigid principles of behavior, McCormick. Outbursts of temper are not acceptable, and a Manley does not air dirty laundry in public." He flipped his wrist, tossing the pebbles along the rocky creek bed. Resting his forearms on his knees, he laced his fingers together and stared at his hands. "What I expected was a cold reception, a lecture in the privacy of his study, and maybe an uncomfortable luncheon served in the conservatory. But a nice loud, ugly shouting match—no, I never expected him to be that human."

Her mouth suddenly dry, Riley locked her arms around her knees, trying to quell the nervous flutter that was suddenly loose in her chest. Right or wrong, she had to know. Dredging up every bit of courage she had, she looked at him. Her voice uneven, she said, "That's not what I meant."

He picked up another handful of pebbles, shaking them together in his hand as he stared across the water. The only thing that came back was silence. Riley's stomach twisted into a sickening knot, and she gripped her hands tighter. "I need to know, Walker."

He flung the rocks and got to his feet. He walked away a few paces, then stood staring across the creek. "Want to check out the dirty laundry, is that it, Mac?"

Riley hunched her shoulders against a sudden chill. "I don't give a damn about dirty laundry, Walker. I just want to know what this is all about. You told me once you had a brother, and I want to know why no one ever mentions him. I want to know why your father is filled with such rage, and I want to know why your mother is so damned fragile." Her throat started closing up on her, and she had to swallow twice before she could get the rest out, her voice still breaking. "And I want to know why you don't trust me, Walker. Why you think I'm going to turn my back on you."

He turned, his face drawn with emotion, an emotion that he allowed to surface as white-hot anger. "You want to know? You want to know?" He strode over to her and grabbed her arm, yanked her to her feet and headed toward the trail. His tone was savage. "Well, damn it, if that's what Missy McCormick wants, that's sure in hell what she's going to get."

Stunned by how violently his veneer had finally cracked, Riley tried to pull free, trying to reason with him. "Walker, for God's sake—"

"Just shut up. You want the answers. Well, lady, you're sure as hell going to get them."

By the time they reached the car, Riley felt as if she'd been mauled. Her shoulder ached, and her wrist felt as if it had been rubbed raw by his brutal grip. But Walker didn't give her a chance to recover. He opened the door and practically shoved her inside, then slammed it so hard the whole car rocked. Riley's mind was still reeling, her body still numb with shock, when he yanked open his door and climbed in. Her surface reaction was to let him have it for hauling her around like some damned rag doll, but one look at his face and any anger she had evaporated.

Fixing her gaze straight ahead, she tried to will away the awful sensation in her middle, feeling his agony as clearly as if it were her own.

He started the car and shoved it into gear. His voice flat, he ordered, "Do up your seat belt."

Fumbling with the harness, she wordlessly complied, blinking against the threat of tears. He was hurting and alone in whatever hell tormented him, and she didn't know how to reach out to him. She didn't know how to stop the pain.

The drive was a nightmare of silence—stiff, alienating, fraught with unbearable tension. And as the miles sped by, Riley's apprehension doubled and redoubled, until she felt almost sick from it. She had no idea what she was facing, and the look on Walker's face really shook her. She hadn't known that degree of cold, unforgiving self-contempt was even possible.

The plaque on the gate said Stonehaven; the formal gardens and immaculate landscaping indicated money. As the trees and shrubs slipped past, the building came into view, and for all the careful architectural innovation, the sprawling bungalow was clearly an institution of some sort. From the scattering of people on the terrace and in the gardens, Riley guessed it was some kind of extended-care facility. She glanced at Walker, but his expression was even more grim, white lines etched deeply around his mouth.

She fixed her gaze ahead, her apprehension turning into acute dread. In Walker's mind, he had launched himself on a course of self-destruction. He was determined to reveal the very worst about himself. He was going to show her, prove to her, why he was so unworthy as a human being. And it scared her to death.

Ignoring the parking lot tucked in a grove of trees, they drove up the sweeping circular drive, parking across from the main door. Without looking at her, Walker got out of the car and went around the front, his mouth fixed in a hard thin line. Trying to ignore the trembling in her hands, Riley opened the door and climbed out. She barely had time to close it before Walker had her by the arm and was marching her toward the sliding doors. Scrambling to keep up, Riley tried to collect herself, tried to draw up some semblance of composure through the absolute confusion inside her. She knew he was using anger as a shield. But knowing that didn't ease the knots in her gut or the frenetic pounding in her chest. She prayed to God she could handle whatever was in store for her.

She had a scattering of impressions as they entered the lobby. An unobtrusive information desk, huge baskets of freshly cut flowers, comfortable sofas in intimate arrangements, subdued, soothing colors. But that was all she had time to see. Walker hauled her down one of the wide corridors fanning off the lobby. They had nearly reached the end when he stopped and whirled her to face him, his eyes blazing, his hard, cold expression almost a sneer. "You want to know about my brother? You want to know why my father is filled with such rage and why my mother's a basket case? You want to know, McCormick, so here it is. Fourteen years ago, I was driving my brother's car, and I missed a curve doing eighty miles an hour. Tyson was a passenger—my passenger." He gave her a smile that chilled her to the bone. "So let's go meet Tyson, Ms. McCormick, and you'll understand what this afternoon was all about." With that, he caught her by the upper arm and shoved her through the last door on the right.

The drapes in the room were drawn, the dimmed light coming from a valence covering the indirect lighting over the hospital bed. The figure in the bed was lying in a fetal position, his back to them, apparently asleep. But it wasn't the man in the bed who made Riley's heart falter. It was the metamorphosis in Walker. The moment he rounded the foot of the bed, his expression altered. And there was no way Riley could hold back the raw emotion that climbed up her throat and made her chest hurt. Never in her whole life had she seen such an agony of gentleness, of regret, of remorse, in someone's eyes.

Walker seemed to forget she was even in the room. With practiced ease, he lowered the guardrail, then hitched his hip on the edge of the bed, placing his hand on the other man's shoulder. "Ty. Are you asleep, buddy?"

His brother stirred, and with stiff, spastic movements, slowly shifted. His voice was thick and slurred. "Walker?"

Walker's lopsided smile didn't reach his eyes. "Yeah, it's me. I brought a friend with me this time. Someone I want you to meet."

"A friend?"

"Yeah. Would you like to sit up?"

There was a jerk of the head, and Walker reached for the controls, slipping his arm beneath his brother's shoulders as he elevated the head of the bed. Again with practiced ease, he shifted Tyson's position, then arranged the pillows to support his head. And as Walker withdrew his arm, Riley got her first unobstructed look at Tyson Manley.

The shock of comprehension hit, and everything swam out of focus as the missing pieces fell into place. She closed her eyes, the chill of realization settling like a rock in her stomach. She understood it all: the starkness in Walker's eyes, the pain, the self-punishment. And she wondered how he had survived.

Her first coherent thought was that she would handle this or die trying. Her second thought was that she could not let Walker see how badly shaken she was. Closing her eyes, she took a composing, fortifying breath. She *could* handle this. Granny Davidson had suffered a stroke when Riley was seventeen. And from what she could see, this was not so different.

Her insides in a mess, her expression devoid of any emotional reaction, she moved over to the bed, allowing only the most basic part of her mind to function. But it was hard to maintain the facade, for Tyson Manley was clearly a shell of his former self.

Old scars showed clearly on his temple, but those scars were only on the surface. It was his twisted, disabled body, the slackness in one side of his face, his inability to hold his head erect, the shrunken arm and the clawlike hand, that told the story. She'd spent enough time at the hospital with Granny to know what the signs meant. They meant a permanent, disabling and irreversible brain injury. An injury that had tragically altered Tyson Manley's young life and left a burden on his brother's conscience that would haunt him until the day he died. It was hard, cold, unalterable reality, and nothing—not anger, not penitence, not any amount of self-reproach—was ever going to change that.

Sticking her hands in the pockets of her slacks, she went to stand beside Walker, experiencing an unexpected, nearly overwhelming surge of affection for the man in the bed. He was so like Walker. But what eased the ache around her heart was the sharp glint of awareness in his vividly blue eyes as he focused on her. Damaged he might be, but Tyson Manley was no man's dummy.

Meeting his gaze directly, she smiled down at him, liking that glint. "Hi, Tyson. I'm Riley." Recalling how Granny D. had needed time to assimilate impressions, she gave him a moment. Riley also recalled how Granny D. had hated being treated like an invalid, how she'd hated people always shouting at her because they thought she couldn't hear. Riley had learned a lot from Granny D.—like the fact that pity and concerned looks didn't cut it. Fighting against the thickness unfolding in her chest, she forced a lightness she didn't feel and grinned down at him. "Now I know why Walker's been so slow about introducing us. You're much better looking than he is—probably much nicer too."

There was an instant of silence, then Tyson's face contorted and a great braying laugh came right from his diaphragm. Walker shot her a startled, dumbfounded look, which she totally ignored. Taking Tyson's twisted hand between both of hers, she leaned over and kissed him on the cheek, stubbornly suppressing the urge to cry. Fixing her smile in place, she straightened and met Walker's brother's gaze, giving his hand a gentle squeeze. "I'm pleased to meet you, Tyson," she said, her voice only slightly uneven.

Tyson clutched at her hand, his gaze riveted on her. "Riley."

Riley didn't dare think about the anguish centered around this man. Nor did she dare think about Walker. She would grieve for them both later. Much later. Still holding Tyson's hand, she sat beside him, then quietly began to talk. She told him about how she'd met Walker, about her trip to New York, about what the weather was like. Anything she could think of. And the whole time, Tyson never took his eyes off her face, and he never let go of her hand. Every once in a while he interjected with a word and she tried to grasp what he wanted, and the whole time she felt as if the ache in her chest was going to suffocate her. And the whole time she was painfully aware that Walker was as far away as he could get. He had opened the drapes on the windows and stood staring out, one arm braced against the frame, the other on his hip. If it wasn't for his unregistering stare, for the harsh set of his profile, she might have felt a little more secure about his reasons for bringing her here. But she knew by the look on his face that there was more to this than Tyson's condition.

Distracted by those unsettling thoughts, Riley didn't immediately pick up on the telltale signs that Tyson was tiring. But when she realized he was struggling to absorb each word, she knew he'd hit his limit. She stroked the back of his hand and asked, her voice quiet, "Are you getting tired, Tyson?"

He closed his eyes and jerked his head. "Tired."

"Would you like me to lower your bed a bit?"

He moved his head again, and Riley reached for the controls. She watched his face as she lowered the head of his bed, and when he opened his eyes and focused on her, she stopped. "Like that?"

"Yes." With spastic movements, he shifted one arm and turned his head toward the window. "Walker?"

Walker straightened and came over to the bed, his face impassive. But when he got to where Tyson could see him, he dragged up a smile.

Riley let go of Tyson's hand and carefully laid it on his chest, then stood back, locking her arms across her chest. His gaze fixed on Walker, Tyson made a weak gesture toward him. Placing his hand under his brother's jaw to help support his head, Walker leaned over him. "What, buddy?"

"Sunday?"

The corner of Walker's mouth lifted in a more genuine smile. "Yes, it's Sunday."

There was a glimmer in the other man's eyes; then his taut muscles relaxed, and he let his head rest against Walker's hand. He closed his eyes for a moment, then looked back up at his brother. "You said—you—were coming—Monday."

"I'll be back. You can count on it."

Reassured, Tyson closed his eyes again. Walker watched him for a moment, then made sure the pillows were securely arranged to support his head. Pulling up the covers, he gave his brother's shoulder a light squeeze. Straightening, he went to the windows and closed the drapes. His voice flat, he said quietly, "He'll be out for a couple of hours. We may as well go."

She followed him to the door, stifling the urge to go back and check Tyson one more time before they left. But the grim look around Walker's mouth told her that he'd had about all he could take for one day.

The drive back to the city was a repeat of the one to Stonehaven, except this time the silence had a different tone. The level of tension wasn't there. In spite of how utterly drained Riley felt, her mind wouldn't let go. Over and over again, she processed the scene at the Manley estate, the different comments Walker had made, her own assessment of things. And although he had made damned sure she got the whole picture, she felt disturbingly more isolated. It was as if he'd let her in, then he'd walked out.

Darkness had settled by the time they reached the city, and it started to rain just as they pulled into the alley behind Walker's building. Hitting the control mounted under his dash, Walker wheeled the Porsche onto the low ramp that led into the bay where he stored the vehicle. He waited as the metal door slowly rose, and as soon as it was high enough, he eased the car into the darkened loading dock, hitting another control that turned on the overhead lights. He switched off the engine, set the parking brake, then took the keys out of the ignition.

The slam of the car doors echoed heavily in the empty space, the sound triggering a strained tension. Riley preceded Walker up the few steps to the fire door that led to the freight elevator, her insides churning.

Semidarkness infused the loft, and Riley fumbled for the switch that turned on the track lighting over the island in the kitchen. She dropped her handbag on the corner, then went over to the windows and stared out at the halos around the streetlights across the street. Clasping her arms in front of her, she absently rubbed her upper arms, feeling chilled to the bone. She wished she had her mother's wisdom right now. She wished she had anything other than this feeling of trepidation that kept overlapping everything else.

Hearing a cupboard door open, she turned. Walker was at the counter, a bottle of Crown Royal in his hand, and she watched him pour himself a stiff drink. She realized it was the first time she'd seen him with anything stronger than a beer. That realization triggered another association, and she remembered the case of beer he'd brought to the ranch when he'd come to apologize. And her chest clogged up from the memory.

Clasping her arms tighter, she swallowed hard, hoping her voice would hold. "Would you like me to make you something to eat?"

Without looking at her, he put the cap on the bottle, then downed nearly half of the whiskey he'd poured. Leaning back against the cupboard, he swirled what was left in his glass. His tone was flat. "No, I don't want you to fix me something to eat."

Shifting her gaze, Riley rubbed her thumb against a seam in her sleeve, dreading what was ahead of her. She steeled herself and looked at him. "What was that all about with your father?"

His jaw locked as he stared down at his drink. After a moment, he turned back to the counter and poured himself another shot. "You don't want to know."

"Yes," she said very quietly. "I do."

He lifted his head and looked at her, his gaze unreadable; then he shifted his head. She could tell by the way he rocked his glass back and forth that he was considering whether to answer her or not. Straightening, he went to stand in front of the windows several feet away from her. He took another drink, then finally spoke. "Stonehaven's undergone some administrative changes, and we've been advised that as of the first of October, there will be a new policy. All the patients must be ambulatory. Which means Ty has to be moved. The medical director has always felt it would be in Tyson's best interests if he was in a center where he could get more specialized care. I think he's right, but my mother wanted him at Stonehaven because it was only a twenty-minute drive from home. Now that Tyson has to be relocated, my old man got it in his head that it would be better for my mother if he wasn't so close, if he was far enough away that she couldn't go over there every day. In that respect, he's probably right. But my father takes things to the extreme. While I was away, he made arrangements to move him to a rest home in California. I found out about it right after we came back."

Right after—the night he nearly killed himself with the weights. Feeling slightly sick, Riley closed eyes and massaged the bridge of her nose with her thumb and forefinger, so drained she could barely think. California. It wasn't a move. It was banishment from everything familiar. Exhaling heavily, she raised her head and looked at Walker, her heart contracting as he took another drink. He looked so damned battered and alone.

He drained the glass and set it on the window ledge, then stuffed his hands in the pockets of his slacks. Resting his shoulder against the frame, he went on, his tone emotionless. "I don't intend to let that happen. Tyson needs to be around the people he knows." He reached out and picked a blob of paint off the window sill, then stuck his hand back in his pocket. There was a gruff catch in his voice. "He wouldn't understand why no one came to visit him—it would be the worst thing they could possibly do to him." Picking up the empty glass, he turned from the window, his face chiseled with strain. He rolled the last bit of liquid around the bottom, his tone barren when he continued. "As I said, I can't let that happen, so I've started legal proceedings to get full guardianship." He looked up at her, one corner of his mouth lifting in a humorless smile. "So that's the story, sunshine."

Feeling as if everything was slowly slipping out of focus, Riley held his gaze, trying to sustain a sense of reality. She had to force herself to speak. "Does this mean you'll have to go to court?"

"Possibly."

"Won't they listen to reason?"

He made a derisive sound. "You were there. You heard him. Do you think he's going to listen to reason?"

Caught in his own sobering thoughts, Walker absently smoothed his thumb down the curved lines of the metal sculpture, his expression heavily reflective. Giving the piece of art one final caress, he set his glass down on the table, then stuck his hands in his pockets and turned back to the window.

Riley watched him, her insides twisting, trying to scrape up the courage to ask the next question. Taking a deep breath, she faced her uncertainty square on. "But it's not just about guardianship, is it?"

It took him a long time to answer, and when he did, his voice was very quiet. "No."

Feeling suddenly shaky, she went to the sofa and curled up in the corner, trying to draw up some warmth from deep inside herself. Her voice held the same element of quiet his had. "Tell me about the stables I saw at your parents' house, Walker."

He shot her a startled look then turned back to the window. There was a trace of humor in his voice when he answered. "So you noticed."

"Yeah," she said softly. "I noticed."

He continued to stare out the window. "We used to have a string of polo ponies. Tyson and I used to play quite a bit."

Riley leaned her shoulder against the back of the sofa, a hint of a smile surfacing. "And here I thought you didn't know one end of a horse from another. You play dumb like a pro, Manley."

She could only see his profile but she saw the corner of his mouth lift. "It's what I do best."

Riley watched him a moment, then began toying with a loose thread on the hem of her jacket. "What happened to the horses, Walker?"

He went very still, then slowly turned his head to stare at her, the oddest expression in his eyes. Finally he turned back to the window and rested his shoulder against the frame, the stark lines of his face reflected in the glass. His tone was quiet, without inflection, when he started to speak. "We were at a polo match the day it happened. It had been one of those long, hot summers made for raising hell, and we were so young and stupid and cocky—nothing could stop us. Ty had just turned twenty-one, and he'd spent more time in the clubhouse than he should have. He wasn't fit to walk, let alone drive, so I loaded him in his car and headed home."

Not moving a single muscle, Riley watched him, afraid he wasn't going to continue—equally afraid that he was. He stuck his hand back in his pocket, the lines around his mouth more deeply etched. His voice was thick and unsteady when he finally continued. "We were just a couple of miles from home when he decided he was going to be sick. I was watching him instead of the road, and I hooked the edge of the pavement and shot off a curve. The police report said we were doing about eighty—which was very likely. Anyway, we clipped an approach, and Ty went through the windshield. The impact smashed his skull. He was in a coma for three months, and in the hospital for another eight. The day my father was told the damage was permanent, he came home and sold every horse on the place."

And sold you out, as well. Riley looked up at the ceiling, trying to draw up some calm to stifle her anger. Anger wouldn't do either one of them any good. She had seen the blame, the bitterness, the unforgiving fury, on Jackson Manley's face. She experienced a flash of the same unforgiving fury toward him, but she smothered it. That was a road she refused to travel. She waited for the moment to pass, then drew a measured breath. When she finally spoke, the words wanted to stick in her throat. "The accident— were you hurt?"

There was a stillness, not a sound, then Walker turned to look at her, a confused expression appearing. "What?"

Riley also went still, a disquieting thought slowly taking form. "Were you injured in the accident?" she asked again.

He held her gaze for a split second, then picked up the glass and walked over to the kitchen area. "Not much."

"What does that mean?" Rising from the sofa, she followed him, bracing her weight against the island in an attempt to still her sudden shaking. "What does 'not much' mean?"

His voice had a hard edge to it. "It means zip, Riley. This has nothing to do with you."

The anger that had been simmering beneath all the other emotions rose to the surface, and Riley was unable to keep herself from reacting. "Nothing to do with me? I watch you beat yourself to death with regret, I watch you struggle with this awful guilt you carry, I watch you put limitations on our relationship because of this terrible tragedy. I love you, Walker. Whether you like it or not, I'm a player in this game. And, damn it, I don't quit just because the road isn't covered with roses." Pain and fearfulness, and the feeling that she was hanging by her fingertips, got mixed in with the anger, and she lost it. Truly lost it. "Damn it, I'm not like your parents, Walker. I am *not* going to hold you accountable for the rest of your life for what happened to Tyson. I'm not going to hold your conscience for ransom because of a fourteen-year-old mistake. Can't you see that?"

Slamming the glass down on the counter, he turned, his face white with raw emotion. "I *am* accountable, Riley. Every damned day I wake up, I am accountable. If I could trade places with him, I would. If I could sell my soul to undo what I did, I'd do it gladly. But I can't. I can't change a damned thing, and I have to live with that for rest of my life."

It was at that precise instant that Riley realized why Walker had taken her to Stonehaven. It wasn't a show of trust—he was providing himself with a reason to send her away. And fear mixed with the anger. "I know that. But it doesn't have to affect us. I know you love me, Walker. You don't have to say the words for me to know it. That's separate from Tyson. That's not part of the guilt."

Before she even had time to brace herself, he was across the space that separated them, his eyes blazing as he spanned her chin and snapped her head back. "It isn't separate, damn it! And it sure in hell *is* part of the guilt. What do you think kept me from touching you for so damned long? How do you think I feel every time I'm so deep inside you the whole universe spins? That'll never happen for Tyson, sunshine. Never again. Every time I wake up at night and you're there beside me, I think of him alone in that hospital bed, knowing all those things have been taken away from him because of my carelessness." He jerked his hand away and turned. His tone harsh, he went cruelly on. "Loving you doesn't make it any easier, Riley. It only makes it worse."

Everything went so still. The room, the raw emotion, her heart. Everything. For an instant every single sense went dead; then her pulse caught, and Riley closed her eyes as a sickening chill spread through her. Five words—and she knew she'd lost it all.

She picked up her handbag, determined to play things out to the bitter end, repeating the words she'd said the night before. "Well, I guess that's that, isn't it?"

Not a sound broke the silence.

Chapter 13

She found the first-class airline ticket lying on the table when she got up the next morning. Beneath it was a note.

I'm sorry, Riley. I never meant to hurt you.

W.

She stared at the note, a numbing paralysis starting in her head and spreading down through her whole body. Like a blind person, she fumbled for the chair and sat down, her knees suddenly too weak to hold her. Propping her elbows on the glass surface, she buried her face in her hands, her mind unable to process the reality. He was gone. Just like that. Nine words scrawled on a piece of paper, an airline ticket, and it was over.

Letting her hands drop to the table, Riley slowly raised her head, numbly staring at the papers spread on the smoked-glass surface. Documents of an emotional bankruptcy. Foreclosure on the rest of her life. Her mind refusing to digest anything beyond the shock, she picked up the airline folder, an empty ache working its way through the numbness. But it was numbness that made her fingers cold as she opened the folder and slipped out the ticket, the red lettering blurring against the white. Swallowing hard, she ran her thumbnail down the perforated edge, not wanting to acknowledge what it really meant.

One bit of data swam into focus, and Riley stared at the stub, a jolt of awareness fracturing the numbness. It was the second half of an open-return ticket. She dropped it on the table and bolted from her chair. A return ticket. He had bought her a return ticket when they'd left Calgary. Even then he had been so certain. She hadn't known anything could hurt, could emotionally devastate, the way that one airline ticket did. She stood there, helplessness mixing with the cold, sickening realization that there was no recourse. There was absolutely nothing she could do.

Something snapped, and her temper fired. Sweeping up the wooden bowl in the middle of the table, she slung it across the room—hurt, frustration and anger mixing together into one grand fury. Damn him! Damn him for doubting her. Allowing her anger to override everything else, she strode over to the counter, yanked open the drawer where the telephone book was kept and slammed it on the island. She found the number for the airline and, snatching up the phone, punched in the numbers, her hands shaking so badly she had to redial three times.

By the time she got an agent, she was so mad she couldn't see. She dashed away the tears, hating herself for that show of female predictability. A man would have put his fist through the wall and had it over and done with. Now there was predictability. The flicker of amusement surprised her, and she managed to book a flight for that afternoon with a degree of calm. But when she couldn't get the telephone book back in the drawer, she pitched it across the room as well, and the tears started all over again.

She managed to hang on to her rage for four hours, while she packed, when she took the door keys off her key chain, when she laid them on the table by the abandoned airline ticket and the note. She would buy her own damned ticket home.

She even managed to dredge up another fortifying spurt when she slammed the grate of the freight elevator for the last time. But after the outside door closed and automatically locked behind her, when she crossed the sidewalk to where her cab was double-parked in the rain, a wrenching sense of loss hit her, and it was all she could do to get in the vehicle. It was truly finished. But she would survive. She only felt as if she wouldn't.

She refused a porter's help at the airport, needing the physical struggle of fighting through the crush of people with her own suitcases. She was standing in line to buy her ticket when a recollection flashed into her mind with such clarity that it was almost as if it were happening all over again. She remembered Walker crossing the concourse at the airport in Calgary, his unshaven face lined with fatigue, his eyes bloodshot and hollow—and she remembered the unguarded look on his face when he turned and saw her standing there. She saw the love and she saw the pain—and she knew, really *knew,* what his leaving her had cost him.

"Lady, are you buying a ticket or just taking up space?"

Overwhelmed by the feelings the memory had evoked, Riley turned to stare at the man behind her, who was watching her with open annoyance. And she knew she couldn't leave like this, not even if Walker Manley had left a whole damned airline lying on the table.

"Hey, lady. Will you get a life? I ain't got all day here."

"Sorry." Fumbling with the shoulder straps on her bags, she moved from the lineup. A case of the shakes hit her, and she leaned back against a long row of luggage carts, covering her face with one hand. God, what was she doing? She was at the airport, she had locked herself out of Walker's apartment, and she didn't have a clue how to find him. And she was so damned unglued, she couldn't come up with a rational plan if her life depended on it. She had to think, damn it, and she had to stop crying. Now. She had to stop crying *right now*.

After wiping her face with the heel of her hand, she shoved her hands in her jacket pockets, staring across the departure concourse, trying to come up with some options. Her gaze lighted on the row of telephones, and she thought of Michael Bonner and his key.

Hefting up her luggage, she made her way through the current of people, not even thinking about what she would do if she couldn't track Michael down. She found the listing for his agency, and with her heart wedged squarely in her throat, she dropped the change into the slot and punched out the number.

A low, sexy female voice answered. "Bonner Agency."

Riley had to clear away the enormous constriction before she could get the words out. "Could I speak to Michael, please?"

"I'm sorry. Mr. Bonner isn't available at the moment. Could I take a message and have him call you back?"

Riley jammed her hand back into her pocket, the first vestiges of panic climbing up the walls of her stomach. Tears threatened again, and her voice broke badly when she scrambled desperately for a message. Something rational. "It's Riley McCormick calling. Would you tell Michael—" She had to pause, the clog of tears making it impossible to speak. "Tell him that I'm at the airport—tell him I have to talk to him. I'll call back in—"

Miss Sexy Voice's tone changed, becoming more crisp. "Would you hold for a moment, please?"

Turning her back to the concourse, Riley fished a Kleenex tissue out of her pocket and blew her nose, deciding that the first thing she was going to do when she got off the phone was go to the ladies' room and have a good bawl, then shape up. She had to stop this stupid, senseless crying.

"Riley? What's wrong?"

The sound of Michael's voice completely unhinged her, and she closed her eyes, resting her forehead against the framework separating one phone from another.

"For God's sake, talk to me, Riley."

Struggling to present at least a shred of coherence, Riley managed to get out an explanation, aware that the woman at the next phone was watching her with undisguised interest.

Turning her back on the eavesdropper, she finished telling Walker's agent what had happened, determined, *absolutely* determined, to get a grip on herself.

"Where are you?"

She hauled in a tremulous breath, wondering where his brain had been. "At the airport."

"I know you're at the airport," he answered with the kind of patience used on small children and old people. "Where at the airport?"

At any other time, his tone would have amused her. Drawing another deep, steadying breath, she told him.

"I'll be there in half an hour. Forty minutes max."

"I can take a cab—"

"You stay right where you are. I'm coming for you, so don't give me a hard time." Riley could hear him moving, and his voice faded, as though he'd shifted the phone from one ear to the other. "Hang in there, sugar. I'm on my way."

It was the gruffness in his voice that did her in. She was blinded by tears again, and hated herself for it. She wasn't going to make it to the ladies' room, that was for certain. She shoved her suitcases four feet to the side and sat down on top of them, not giving a damn about the funny looks she was getting. It wasn't every day that her life came apart at the seams.

True to his word, Michael made it in just under forty minutes. When he saw her, he stopped and gave his head an unbelieving shake, then dodged his way through the pedestrian traffic. Still shaking his head, he crouched down in front of her, a glimmer of humor in his eyes. "Well, if it isn't Orphan Annie."

Certain she was all cried out, Riley managed a wobbly smile. "You're such a comfort. Everyone else thinks I'm nuts."

He gave a chuckle, then his face softened with concern. "How are you doing, kid?"

She leaned her head against the wall, a catch in her voice. "Just wonderful. I've cried my way through a box of Kleenex tissues, and my head feels like it's stuffed with cotton balls, but other than that I'm fine."

Michael studied her for a moment, an empathetic smile hovering around one corner of his mouth; then he stood and hauled her to her feet. "I think it's time you and I had a long talk."

Her part of the talk took place on the drive back into the city. His part of the talk took place back in Walker's apartment. Michael poured her a drink that stripped the remaining skin off her throat, then sat down on the coffee table in front of her. Resting his forearms on his thighs, he laced his hands together and stared down at them. "I think it's time you knew some of the background, Riley," he said quietly.

She didn't say anything, and he raised his head and looked at her, his expression solemn. "I've known Walker since we were kids. I always envied his relationship with Tyson—they were always so tight. Walker and his father never got along. Jackson Manley had very fixed views on what he expected from his family, and there was never any room for error. Walker didn't fit the mold his old man kept trying to shove him into, and they fought about everything—his friends, what he was going to do with his life, how he behaved in public, how he did in school. When he was a kid, Walker used to make an effort, but his dad wouldn't give an inch. Finally Walker quit trying. Tyson was different—different disposition, different temperament, less intense—didn't have that stubborn streak Walker does. As far as Jackson was concerned, Tyson could do no wrong. The really crazy thing was that that favoritism never affected the relationship between Tyson and Walker. Tyson used to run interference all the time. He'd cover up for him, take the blame for some of Walker's escapades, do things to keep the lid on. I think in some ways Tyson admired Walker's rebellious streak.''

Riley ran her thumb along the edge of her glass, sobered by the fact that none of this came as a surprise. She should have seen it—after what had happened yesterday, she should have been able to put those pieces together on her own. She wiped the bottom of the glass on her slacks, then looked back at Michael. ''And then there was the accident.''

He exhaled heavily and stared at his clasped hands. His voice took on a weightier edge. ''Yeah. Then there was the accident.''

''I need to know the whole story, Michael,'' she said softly.

He looked up at her, his eyes shadowed. ''Walker gave you the basic facts. What he didn't tell you was that the only reason Tyson played polo was to keep his old man off Walker's back, because Walker loved to play. His maternal grandfather got him started at it, which was bad news to begin with, because Jackson and his father-in-law didn't exactly see eye-to-eye. Walker was one hell of an athlete and an even better horseman. He loved it. His Grandfather Jefferson died when he was about fourteen—just when things were really turning sour with his father. Polo became his old man's prime target. Jackson never let up about it. When Tyson took it up, it was a different story.'' Michael held her gaze for a moment, then looked down at his hands again and went on, his tone quiet. ''And what he also left out was how the accident happened.''

Her own voice was calm, but a flutter of dread started in her belly. ''And how *did* it happen?''

Michael abruptly got to his feet, but Riley caught a glimpse of his expression as he rose, and she realized he, too, was haunted by memories. His hands jammed in his back pockets, he went to stand before the grouping of photographs, his stance almost defensive. Finally he reached out and straightened one. His voice was rough when he spoke. "Tyson was really wasted that day. It took two of us to get him in the car. Walker did up his brother's seat belt—I saw him, but after they got going, Tyson thought he was going to be sick so he undid it. But instead of opening the window, he took it in his head he was going to be sick out the door. Walker tried to grab him, but Tyson put up a fight, and that's when it happened."

The following silence was heavy, weighted with the grim reality of what had happened. It was Riley who finally broke it. "Had Walker been drinking?"

Michael turned and looked at her, a strained expression on his face. "No. It sounds warped as hell, but I think it might have been easier for Jackson Manley to deal with if he had. Other than the speed, Walker had been playing by the books that day. He was stone-cold sober, he'd tried to talk Tyson into going home two hours before they actually left, he'd put Tyson's seat belt on, and skid marks on the road were a clear indication he'd tried to stop before he lost control. But it was Jackson's golden-haired boy who'd been falling-down drunk, who had chucked his dinner in the lobby of the club, and that nearly killed the old man. So he took it out on Walker."

"Like selling off all the polo ponies?"

"That was part of it. Especially when most of the horses were legally Walker's—his Grandfather Jefferson had left them to him when he died. Jackson never came right out and *said* it was Walker's fault—at least, he didn't until yesterday. But he let him know where he placed the blame. Walker finally had enough and pulled the pin. He hadn't been back for even a visit in at least five years."

"What about his mother?"

Michael shrugged. "She pretty much fell apart after the accident. In all honesty, she was so torn up about Tyson, I don't think she even saw what it did to Walker—at least, not then. I don't know about now." He paused, his expression heavily introspective, then he let his breath go on a deep sigh. "Walker avoids her, too. When he's in town, he goes out to Stonehaven three or four times a week. But he always goes in the afternoon or evening so he won't run into her."

"What happens when Walker's away—like this summer?"

Michael reached out and touched the shade on one of the floor lamps, then shoved his hand in his pocket and came back to where she was sitting. "He checks in with the nursing staff every day. The staff tells Tyson that he's called, and that's usually enough to keep him happy. But there were a couple of times this spring, when Walker first started the magazine shoot, that Tyson got really agitated. His doctor thought it was because he was overanxious about Walker, so I took out a video—it was a profile on Walker one of the networks had done. Tyson must have had them play that thing a thousand times. So I had some video footage shot when I went up to talk to Walker about this Priscella deal, and that's their ace in the hole. He'd watch those tapes twenty-four hours a day if they'd let him." He sighed heavily and sat back down on the coffee table, his shoulders hunched as he rested his forearms on his thighs. "That's why this whole thing with California is so damned nuts. It's as if Jackson resents Tyson's dependency on Walker. It's crazy."

Riley was so emotionally wrung out, she was practically numb. And at this point, numb was a safe state to be in. She took a sip of her drink, then sighed and rested her head against the back of the sofa. "Does Walker stand a chance of getting guardianship?"

Michael looked up at her, his gaze direct. "I think so. Davis Jefferson was no pauper, let me tell you. When he died, he left sizable trust funds for Tyson and Walker—each of them got limited access when they turned eighteen. Walker's been paying all of Tyson's medical bills since day one. And it's been a bundle over fourteen years. So, yes, legally, I'd say he stands a damned good chance. And I suspect Jackson Manley knows that."

Eighteen, and his brother's keeper. There should be an Eleventh Commandment. Thou shalt not abandon thy children. Worry lines etched in her face, Riley absently rubbed at an old scar on one knuckle as she mulled over what Michael had told her. There was a brief lapse, then she spoke again, her voice very husky. "The accident—was Walker hurt?"

Michael studied her, his gaze oddly intent, a hint of a smile in his eyes. "You never forget whose corner you're in, do you?"

Discomfited by his observation, she swirled her drink. "I did today."

"You're here now," he pointed out quietly.

She managed a weak shrug, then redirected him. "Was he?"

Michael's expression was grave. "Yeah, he was," he said gruffly. "Multiple rib fractures, one broken leg, the other knee torn to hell, some internal injuries. He was in the hospital for four weeks. The first day they let him up in a wheelchair, he disappeared, and they found him in intensive care—with Tyson." Michael leaned over and picked a piece of lint off the floor, then rolled it between his fingers, his expression reflective. Letting his hands go lax, he looked up at her. "He's never going to stop blaming himself for what happened to Tyson, Riley. You've gotta know that before you take this any further."

Emotion welled up inside her, and she looked away, concentrating on forcing it back. When she finally spoke, her voice had a catch in it. "I know that, Michael. But he doesn't have to keep punishing himself, too."

Michael studied her, his gaze somber. "Is that what you think he's doing now—punishing himself?"

"Partly."

He reached out and lifted her chin so she was looking at him, his tone gentle. "Don't put a twist on this, kid. Don't think he's bailed out because he has doubts about you. He's been beating himself up for so long, he doesn't know how to stop.''

Riley tried to ease the ache in her throat, her eyes brimming with tears. ''I can't just walk away, Michael. Not unless I'm dead sure that's what he really wants.''

He gave her a reassuring half smile. ''That's not what he wants, Riley. It's what he thinks he deserves.''

Looking away, she quickly dried her face, absolutely determined she was *not* going to cry anymore.

Michael's pager went off, and he pulled it out of his jacket pocket, checking the tiny screen. He heaved an exasperated sigh and got up. ''Hang on to that thought, and give me a minute to check this call. I didn't tell my secretary where I was going, and she's probably broken a fingernail.''

Riley leaned her head back against the sofa and closed her eyes, the strain of the past two days finally catching up with her. She wanted *not* to cry anymore, she wanted her head to stop aching, but most of all, she wanted Walker to come home. She opened her eyes and stared at the grouping of photographs on the wall. So much aloneness. In a sudden flashback, she saw him the night he'd come to the barn, standing there in the dim light, the night sky behind him—and such torment in his eyes. And even then, at some unconscious level, she realized he needed someone to forgive him. Knowing that kind of thinking was going to get her into major trouble, she forced her attention back to Michael.

He was standing with his hip braced against the island, absently rearranging the pencils and pens in the mug as he waited for his call to go through. He shifted the receiver closer to his mouth. ''Yeah, Joyce. What's cooking?''

He straightened, shooting Riley a startled look. ''When? Was that all he said?''

She caught a flicker of something in his eyes before he turned slightly and stared across the room, grimly intent on the lengthy explanation. A very unpleasant feeling unfolded in her, and every muscle in her body was tensed by the time he hung up. If she'd have any doubts before, she had none when she saw the expression on his face.

Bracing herself, she met his gaze squarely. Her voice controlled, she asked, "What's happened to him?"

He stared at her a second, obviously considering his response, then he exhaled heavily. "He's done a disappearing act. He called and left a message that his assistant is taking over his next assignment. I'm also supposed to let George know he's off the Priscella campaign."

Riley needed to do something. Anything. She abruptly set down her glass and stood up, trying to ignore the panic that suddenly assailed her. She stuffed her hands in the pockets of her jacket in an attempt to hide her agitation. "I've got to find him, Michael. I can't just sit here and do nothing."

A hint of a smile showed around Michael's eyes. "So you can give him hell, right?"

Riley managed a wry smile back. "Right."

His expression softened, and there was a tone of quiet assurance in his voice when he spoke. "Don't worry, kid. We'll find him."

But they didn't. Michael made a dozen calls that day, but the only thing he was able to find out was that Walker had stopped by the nursing home. Riley discovered that all his cameras were still in the studio, but the duffel bag of extra clothes he always took on shoots was gone.

By Tuesday night she was nearly frantic. She had an awful feeling in the pit of her stomach, and no matter how many lectures she gave herself, it just wouldn't go away. She nearly drove herself crazy listening for the elevator, and she practically wore a path to the windows. She finally broke down and phoned her parents at midnight New York time. She didn't call to talk to them about what had happened; she called because she needed to hear the sound of their voices. And because she'd never felt quite so alone in her whole life.

Wednesday was no better, but she hung on to the hope that Walker would at least check with Michael. But he didn't, and she spent another restless night, listening for him to come home. It was about noon on Thursday when the real crusher came. Michael received a brief note from Walker in the morning mail, saying he'd decided he needed some time to himself, that he had lined up another photographer for his upcoming assignments, and he would be back in a few weeks. It was later that same day that Michael found out Walker's boat was missing from the marina. When Riley found out that the *Sea Hawke* was a thirty-foot cabin cruiser and fully equipped for a voyage, she had to face the fact that Walker was not going to walk through the door.

She awoke the next morning to another day of rain, and after a sleepless night, the heaviness of the weather dragged her spirits even lower. Michael showed up midmorning with a list of marinas along the coast, and for a couple of hours she experienced a brief flurry of hope. But by the time they got to the second to last one on the list, hope had taken a severe beating, and she was back to feeling helpless.

And for her, there was nothing worse. The lack of sleep had prompted a persistent headache, and she was so tired she could barely think. She went over to the coffee table where Michael had spread out a map of the coast, the list of marinas and Walker's appointment calendar. Sitting on the floor beside the table, she folded her arms on the clutter of paper and rested her head on them, watching Michael pace back and forth, the phone in his hand, the extension cord trailing behind him. It would make one hell of a photograph, she though with a small flicker of humor. *Man Tethered to Technology.*

Shifting her head, she rested her chin on her wrists and stared at Walker's black leather day diary lying in front of her. She trailed her fingers across the cover, then heaving a sigh, she straightened and drew it closer. Michael had already checked out the appointments in it, but that had turned up nothing. She started idly turning pages. The number of entries she found concerning Tyson—dental appointments, doctor's appointments, the purchase of a new motorized wheelchair, reminders for things he needed—seemed endless. She thought of the man alone in the hospital bed, the man with the same intense blue eyes as Walker, the man who had looked so much like his brother that it made her heart ache. She thought about how Walker shouldered the full responsibility for his care—and how he had also shouldered the responsibility for his brother's aloneness. And that made her heart ache even more.

Fighting the thickness in her chest, she looked over at Walker's agent, making a decision based on impulse alone. "Hang up the phone, Michael," she commanded unevenly.

Shifting the receiver, he frowned at her. "Just a minute. They're checking their log."

"He's not going to be in a marina, Michael. You know that, and I know that. We've just been playing games with ourselves, and all we're going to have to show for it is a huge phone bill." She carefully closed the daybook, trying to will away the ache in her throat. Then she looked back at Michael and spoke, her voice quiet. "But there is something I'd like you to do for me."

He stared at her, the receiver still to his ear; then, as if reluctant to admit she was right, he pressed the disconnect button with his thumb. "So what's this thing you want me to do?"

"I'd like you to take me out to see Tyson."

Michael looked at her, considering what she'd said; then he hung up the receiver and went over to the island and set the phone down. He stared down at the instrument for a moment, then turned to face her. "I'm not sure that's a good idea, Riley."

She trailed her fingers across the lettering on the cover of the daybook, trying to find the words to explain. "I don't want to involve him in this, Michael. It's just that he's a major part of Walker's life—and I'd like to know that part a little better." *And I can't stand the thought of both of them being alone.*

Michael stared at her a moment, then grinned. "It's a deal. But you get to play Danny Sullivan. Traffic drives me crazy."

When they arrived at Stonehaven, Riley experienced the same wrench she had the first time she'd met Tyson. She caught a glimmer of confusion in his eyes when she walked in with Michael, but she made it clear that he'd brought her out because Walker was away. Michael left them alone for a couple of hours, and because of what the agent had told her about Tyson and the videos, she picked up where they'd left off on Sunday, telling him about every single thing she could think of that had happened to his city-slicker brother while he was at the ranch. And every time he laughed, she wanted to cry, because it was so evident that whether Walker Manley realized it or not, he was the most important person in his brother's life.

By the time Michael returned to pick her up, Tyson's reserve of strength was clearly spent, but even as exhausted as he was, he still hung on to her hand. Thrown into emotional overload yet again, she couldn't bring herself to unclasp his fingers from around hers, so as Michael waited, she sat on the edge of the bed and rubbed Tyson's back until he fell asleep. And when she left, she knew exactly what Walker experienced every time he had to leave him there. It was like leaving a large chunk of her heart behind.

After that, she went out to visit him often. It was during the third visit that she realized Tyson was beginning to assume she was a permanent fixture in Walker's life. And she knew she couldn't let him nurture any false expectations or become too dependent on her visits. Every time she thought about how little time she had left, she experienced an insidious kind of panic—the kind that would have her up in the middle of the night, her insides churning, her heart pounding, the kind that made her feel helpless and desperate.

And as much as she tried to avoid thinking about it, there were a few realities she had to face: her leave of absence was nearly up, and she had a limited amount of cash in her checking account. The hard cold truth was that her time was running out. She knew it, Michael knew it, and she tried to make it clear to Walker's brother that she was going to have to go back to Canada soon.

The day that Michael took her over to Priscella Cosmetics to see the layouts for the ad campaign and she saw the absolute artistry in the photographs Walker had taken of her, it was all she could do to keep it together. Intimate, sensual—he had captured little pieces of her life and imbued them with a richness of mood and texture. Nor was she prepared for what it did to her when she found out Walker had made the final selections the same morning he'd left the note and airline ticket on the table for her. But the worst was when George gave her the check for "services rendered," and she suddenly felt as if her time with Walker had been reduced to a single piece of paper.

Standing in George's plush office, the check in her hand, she realized one very stark truth. She had stayed for the wrong reasons. She had stayed because she wanted to make Walker see, to make him understand—but she couldn't *give* him that. He had to find that understanding within himself. And until he did, there was nothing she could say or do that would change how he felt. Staying assured her of nothing. Leaving was a risk she was going to have to take. And if he ever came to terms with the past, he knew where to find her. It was as simple—and as terrifying—as that. As soon as she got back to his apartment, she finally dealt with the inevitable and booked her return flight.

But Riley couldn't bring herself to book a ticket on the first one available. There was Tyson. And saying goodbye to him was going to be hard enough as it was, but it would be even harder if she left, feeling that she had somehow abandoned him, as well. She remembered Walker, standing on the hill just before he left, telling her that he would never say goodbye, and the memory crowded in on her, especially in the dark of night. Uncertainty followed, and the panic moved in, leaving her faced with another sleepless night.

As she pulled into the parking lot at Stonehaven the next afternoon, Riley experienced a flash of amusement. At least some things stayed the same—like the things she'd never acquire a taste for: big cities, small-minded people and cooked peas. But one thing she had acquired a taste for, and that was high-powered, high-performance cars. She'd driven Michael's Jag a couple of times, but mostly she used the Porsche. Liberated the Porsche, as Michael had put it. And it was, she thought with a grin, a liberating car.

She picked up her handbag and the parcel from the passenger seat and slid out, checking to make sure the door was locked. The gift was for Tyson. She'd taken him outside in his wheelchair a couple of times, and she'd discovered he had a fascination with birds. She knew he didn't have enough strength or coordination in his left hand to manage a regular set of binoculars, but she'd found an excellent set of opera glasses in a pawn shop, and she was sure they were light enough and small enough for him to handle on his own. And, Lord only knew, there were enough birds around Stonehaven to keep him amused for hours, and there were always some in the berry shrubs right outside his window.

She was so preoccupied with Tyson that she was halfway across the drive before it registered that there was a car with rental plates parked along the opposite curb. She stopped dead in her tracks, her heart lurching into double time, the box with the opera glasses cutting sharply into her ribs. A rental car... Closing her eyes, she corralled that thought before it even had time to completely take shape. She was not going to do that to herself. When she had started coming to see Tyson on her own, she had entertained a desperate hope that she would run into Walker on one of her visits.

But that was before. Before she realized that what he'd said was true—her being there for him only made it worst.

She forced herself to relax her hold on the items she was clutching against her and, taking a deep, steadying breath, started toward the doors. She was here to see Tyson, to tell him she was going home the day after tomorrow.

Her pulse had almost, *almost,* returned to normal by the time she turned down the corridor to Tyson's room, but there was still a peculiar little flutter high in her chest. Hope, she was beginning to realize, was a tenacious thing. It didn't die easily.

The door to his room was ajar and she had her hand on the knob to push it completely open, but a quietly spoken comment drilled through her equilibrium. Her heart stopped, and her stomach dropped away with such a sickening rush that the rest of her body felt almost weightless. No. She didn't need this now. Needing something solid to connect with, she leaned back against the wall and closed her eyes, the sudden frenzy in her chest echoing in her head. Now what? Now what was she supposed to do? Leave? Go in? Wait until he left?

Riley opened her eyes and stared at the opposite wall as a second shock wave hit. Tyson knew she was coming. She'd promised him that she would be out this afternoon. Was this one of his good days, when he could communicate enough to let Walker know he was expecting her? Or was it one of his bad days, when speech was almost impossible? And if it was a good day, would he say anything? Tyson was severely disabled physically and he had a pronounced speech impairment, but there was no doubt in her mind that his thought processes were still very much intact. The expression in his eyes indicated he comprehended far more than most people gave him credit for. And maybe, she realized with a jolt, he, more than anyone else, was aware of the burden his brother carried.

She closed her eyes again, waiting for the frantic churning around her heart to ease. Walker. He was here, and he was safe, and he was so close. So close. She couldn't go to him; she knew that. But the thought of having to watch him walk away filled her with such a sense of loss it nearly crippled her, and tears slipped out from beneath her lashes. *Be kind to yourself, love. And please know that I love you.* Trying to hold back the ache that was unfolding in her, she clenched her jaws, the sound of his voice pulling her in deeper and deeper. The sound took shape, and she heard the words—and she heard the anguish, crystal clear.

"... and after the accident, I stopped talking for a lot of reasons, but mostly because I felt so damned guilty, I couldn't talk to anyone. But God, I need to talk to you now."

"About—the accident."

"Yeah, about the accident." Walker's voice caught, and there was a long pause before he continued. "I need you to know how sorry I am. And I need you to know that every day of my life I regret what happened."

"I know. And I'm—sorry—too. For you—Walker."

Riley swallowed hard, fighting against the building pressure in her chest. The years of anguish in this room were more than anyone should ever have to bear. She heard the sound of a chair being shifted; then there was a long pause. When Walker started to speak again, his voice was even more strained than before. "But it's more than just the accident, Ty. There are other things."

"With Riley."

Riley's eyes flew open, and her heart started to pound again, only this time it was different. She waited, her whole body tensed, prepared for denial, praying for a revelation. It seemed like an eternity before he finally answered.

"Yeah, with Riley."

His quietly spoken answer set off an uncontrollable reaction in her as hope and fear twisted together. She began to tremble, and she covered her face with her hand, the anguish in his voice tearing at her. So much pain...

"Talk to me—Walker."

Drawn by the torment in his voice, driven by the need to see him, Riley shifted so she could see into the room. Her arms locked around her middle, she rested her head against the door frame, her vision so blurred she could barely see. He was sitting hunched over in the chair by Tyson's bed, his head bent, his hands clasped between his knees. His back was partially turned toward the door, but even in profile she could see what his self-punishment had done to him. He looked as if he hadn't slept or eaten for days, his unshaven face scored with a haggardness that wrenched at her. His leaving had cost him—cost him dearly.

And when he started to speak, that cost him, too, and his voice wavered. "I couldn't handle the guilt over her, so I sent her away. I've been sitting out on that damned boat for days, trying to sort out my life, but it got to the point where I couldn't stand the loneliness any longer. I hit rock bottom out there. I'd watch the sunset, I'd smell the sunshine—and she'd be there. I felt like I was dying without her. She brought sunshine back to my life, Tyson. All the good things I thought I'd lost, she's given back to me—and I felt so damned guilty, because I'd cheated you out of ever having those things for yourself."

Tyson reached out with his functioning hand and touched Walker's shoulder, the tears in his eyes clearly evident. "Don't pay—for me—Walker. I was—to blame—too."

"But the guilt is mine, Tyson. And it's always going to be there. I know I can't give you your life back, but I learned something sitting out on that damned boat." He hauled in a deep breath. "Love isn't just what happens physically between a man and a woman. Riley put her hands on the real guts of who I am, touched everything inside. I'm whole with her, Ty, and I need her. We both need her."

"Yes. Sunshine—for both—of us."

Moved beyond words, Riley closed her eyes tight, tears slipping relentlessly down her face, humbled and touched beyond belief by these two men. God, a little sunshine—surely she could give them that. And a whole lot of love.

"I hurt her pretty bad, Ty. And I'm scared as hell she won't talk to me, but I've got to go see her. I've got a flight booked...."

The awful wad of emotion around her heart shifted and changed, and Riley wasn't sure if she was laughing or crying when she straightened. Her voice was very unsteady and thick with tears when she was finally able to speak. "Lucky for you, you aren't going to have to go very far."

The long shadows of the early evening spilled across the floor, and a light breeze eddied in through the open window.

Riley was aware of both the shadows and the breeze, but the first real sensation that penetrated her sated haze was a soft stroking at her temple. The second sensation was the slick surface of the gym mat clinging to her back. Heavy with contentment, she smiled and smoothed her hand up his back, not wanting to move for the next hundred years. There was something to be said for a gym mat on the living room floor.

When she opened her eyes, Walker was watching her, a softness in his face she'd never seen before, an intensity in his eyes that touched her heart. He cupped her face with one hand, and, lifting her chin, he kissed her, his mouth soft and warm and infinitely gentle as he brushed his lips against hers. His voice was very husky when he spoke. "Are you okay?"

She caressed his back, her voice just as husky as his. "I'm so high right now, I can't tell."

She felt him smile against her mouth, and she tightened her hold on him, loving him so much she felt as if her chest couldn't contain it all.

He kissed her again, then cradled her more securely beneath him as he cupped the back of her head, tucking her face against his neck. And he held her as if she was his whole life.

Struggling with the ache his tenderness aroused, she ran her hand up his spine, wanting to erase the shadows in his eyes. Flattening her hand against his back, she kissed the curve of his neck, then tipped her head back to look at him. She smiled again, then spoke, her voice soft. "Try to kick me out now, Manley, and see where it gets you."

Avoiding her gaze, he carefully brushed some loose tendrils of hair back from her face, his hand not quite steady as he tucked the strands behind her ear. "I wouldn't let you go even if you tried," he whispered gruffly. "I love you, sunshine."

Struggling to get her arms free from beneath his, she caught his face and made him look at her, afraid to believe he'd finally said the words. But the confirmation was there in his eyes, and feeling as though she'd just been set free, she closed her eyes and hugged him hard. Her voice broke. "I didn't think I was ever going get that out of you."

He slid one hand beneath her neck and nestled his head against hers, the weight of his body molding her tightly against him. "God, you'll never know how I felt when I saw you standing in that damned door."

She could hear the ragged catch in his voice, and she stroked his head, determined to ease the strain. She pressed a kiss against his shoulder. "I thought I must have made some sort of impression, the way the chair went flying across the room—and the way you grabbed me."

Walker raised his head and gazed down at her, not a trace of humor in his eyes. He toyed with her hair, the muscles in his throat working; then he finally spoke, his voice gruff. "I'm always going struggle with the guilt, Riley. Every time I look at him, I'm going to have to face it."

She gazed at him, her vision blurred by tears, her voice trembling with intensity. "I know that, Walker," she whispered. "Just let me share the burden."

"It's been mine for so long, I don't know if I can do that."

She raised her head and brushed his mouth with a soft kiss, her voice husky as she whispered, "Then I'll teach you."

He stared down at her a moment, then finally—finally— he smiled. That lopsided, endearing grin that turned her bones to jelly and her insides to mush. "So," he said softly, "what else are you going to teach me, McCormick?"

She smiled back, then pulled his head down, her mouth brushing against his. "I'll think of something, Manley. You can be damned sure of that."

Epilogue

Riley shivered slightly in the shelter of Walker's upraised knees, and he tightened his arms around her middle. Pulling her back against his chest, he enfolded her deeper in his embrace, his breath warm against her ear. "Cold?"

She locked her arms over his, the wide band of gold on her hand catching the sun. She shook her head. "Nope. Just happy." Which was an understatement if ever there was one.

They were sitting out on the hill behind the barn, hiding out, doing nothing except soaking up the colors and smells of a late Canadian autumn. Actually, what they were doing was celebrating one of their anniversaries...one that no one in Walton, Alberta, knew anything about. Eight weeks ago they'd been married in Connecticut in a quiet ceremony in Tyson's room, with only Michael and Tyson present. Walker didn't want the McCormicks to feel badly because their eldest daughter got married without them being there, so they'd come back up here and done it all over again two weeks later. Michael said it was all a ruse to get two wedding presents out of him—which they did. A third gift was presented to them at the open house of the ranch, a beautifully gift-wrapped present, inside an equally beautiful leather engraved case. Inside was *his* key for Walker's apartment, which was bad enough, but the little speech he made along with the presentation was double-edged, to say the least. Riley didn't think she'd ever seen her mother's eyes sparkle the way they had then. There was no doubt about it; her mother could certainly put two and two together.

But that was only part of the craziest eight weeks she'd ever spent. George Nicholson and his wife came for what Walker termed "the Canadian affair." And by the time George left four days later, he'd bought the ranch adjacent to Wayne's, Walker and Michael had slapped down hard cold cash for another, smaller ranch, and George, Walker, Michael and her big brother had incorporated as Silverado Enterprises, in honor, of course, of the Silverado Saloon. Wayne McCormick, who was no dummy, either, was now the manager of one of the biggest spreads in this part of the country, and he hadn't quit smiling since.

As a wedding gift to the groom, her father had presented Walker with one dog—Max, to be exact—a gift that she'd despaired over, but which had delighted her husband to no end. Riley had told Walker—and told him and told him—she didn't want an engagement ring, but he bought one anyway and gave it to her mother—a whopper that Molly McCormick flashed at every opportunity. He said it was really a medal of valor for putting up with the woman he'd married for as long as she had. That amused her father to no end, and he chuckled about it for days.

The day after "the Canadian affair," with only a little persuasion from George and Michael, and a whole lot of help from a rum punch her father was famous for, Walker got them all down in the back pasture and taught them the rudiments, the most elementary rudiments, of polo, using a soccer ball and anything that was long enough for a mallet. The polo set in Newport would have died from mortification. Molly and Mrs. Nicholson sat on the sidelines in lawn chairs, Molly flashing her diamond, Barbara Nicholson laughing so hard she fell over backwards in her chair. But the highlight was Walker. Lord, the look on his face when he first mounted up was something Riley would never forget.

Her eyes suddenly misted, and a huge lump formed in her throat. God, but she loved this man. She loved him for the nonsense, but most of all she loved him for his consideration. Like what he had done for her mother. Five days after the wedding, John and Molly McCormick were on a plane to Houston, Texas, all expenses paid, partly for a long overdue vacation, but mostly for a thorough checkup for her mother by the top cancer specialists in the country. And when her parents stopped in New York eight days later, John McCormick looked ten years younger. The prognosis looked good. While her parents were there, they took them to meet Tyson, and Walker had to leave the room when her mother hugged Tyson with the same maternal warmth all the McCormick kids and grandkids took for granted. They brought pictures of the wedding and a video George had taken, and the sparkle in Tyson's eyes had both Walker and Riley in a panic. But he didn't blow their secret. All he did was grin and say, "Nice wedding."

And then there was Tyson. Riley swallowed hard and slid her hand across the back of Walker's. It was so hard. There were countless times when the only thing that kept her tears back was the look on Walker's face. They had told Tyson about California. The solution should have been simple— Riley wanted to find someplace where they could have him with them, but it was Tyson who dug in his heels. No. Plain and simple, unequivocally no. He wanted to be close, but he did not want to feel dependent upon them.

As far as California went, support had come from an unexpected source—and that was Walker's mother. She also dug in her heels, and the outcome was that they had found a truly wonderful place in a little town in Connecticut that dealt exclusively with disabled patients. And two weeks ago

Walker had given Riley his wedding gift to her—a marvelous old rambling farmhouse on twenty acres of land just on the outskirts of that same little town. The house was now in the process of being renovated, and the very first thing to be installed had been a ramp for a wheelchair. The second priority—turning the huge sun porch into a room for Tyson. And on special occasions, weekends and rainy Mondays, they would bring him home.

"What are you thinking?"

She shifted her hand so their wedding rings aligned, then laced her fingers through his. She turned her head on his shoulder and kissed him under the chin, then grinned. "I was thinking about you giving my mother my engagement ring. I was thinking about my father giving you my mother's dog. I was thinking about Michael giving us *your* key. I was also thinking about three grown men who don't know one end of a branding iron from another, and who were full of rum punch at the time, going into the cow business. I'm no authority, mind you, but I'm almost positive this isn't exactly normal behavior, Walker."

He chuckled and hugged her hard. "Mild cases of insanity. It's not contagious." He kissed her neck and made her shiver again. "Remember when some little snot gave me hell? Told me to dump my New York attitude, buy a case of beer, smoke some cheap cigars and chase some loose women? And, as I recall, the closing shot was that I was to get a life."

She grinned and snuggled back against him. "Wrong. You were told to join the human race."

"Ah, yes. The human race." He pulled one arm free, and, holding her firmly against him, he twisted around, hauling out something stashed beside the rock. He set it in her lap. It was a six-pack of beer and two cigars.

Laughter burst from her, and she dropped her head back against his shoulder, hugging his arms against her. God, but she loved his silly little surprises. He was grinning as he tucked his head alongside hers. "The New York attitude was kicked all to hell by the same little snot, we've got the beer and cigars—and I think I can safely say that I've joined the human race. So all I need now is a loose woman." He tucked his head down deeper, his breath warm and sensual against her ear. "So tell me, what's in the loft in the barn, Mrs. Manley?"

Still grinning, Riley shifted her head a little. "Mostly mice."

"So what do you say, sunshine? Wanna check it out?"

Her grin broadened. "Check what out?"

He caught her earlobe between his teeth, then thoroughly moistened the hollow just below her ear. "Come to the loft and I'll show you."

And he most certainly did.

*   *   *   *   *

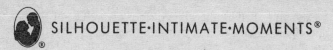

COMING
NEXT MONTH

#401 DESERT SHADOWS—Emilie Richards

Private investigator Felice Christy's latest assignment was driving her crazy! Stuck in a convent pretending to be a nun in order to protect a *real* sister, she had to deal with new handyman Josiah Gallagher, too. His drifter act didn't fool her for a moment. But did he spell trouble for her mission . . . or her heart?

#402 STEVIE'S CHASE—Justine Davis

Chase Sullivan's shadowed past made him a loner by necessity, *not* by choice. Then sweet Stevie Holt stepped into his life, and he dared to dream that things could be different. Suddenly he realized that he'd placed Stevie's life in danger, and unless he did something—quickly— they would *both* be dead.

#403 FORBIDDEN—Catherine Palmer

Federal narcotics agent Ridge Gordon's cover as a college football player didn't stop him from making a pass at sexy English professor Adair Reade. But when new evidence pointed to her involvement in the very drug ring he'd been sent to bust, he fumbled. Was he falling in love with a drug runner?

#404 SIR FLYNN AND LADY CONSTANCE— Maura Seger

When Constance Lehane's brush with date rape ended in tragedy, she hired criminal lawyer Flynn Corbett to defend her against a possible murder charge. Instinctively she knew that his passion for the law would save her, yet the flames that burned between them hinted at a different sort of passion altogether. . . .

AVAILABLE THIS MONTH:

SILHOUETTE®
OFFICIAL SWEEPSTAKES
RULES

NO PURCHASE NECESSARY

1. To enter, complete an Official Entry Form or 3"× 5" index card by hand-printing, in plain block letters, your complete name, address, phone number and age, and mailing it to: Silhouette Fashion A Whole New You Sweepstakes, P.O. Box 9056, Buffalo, NY 14269-9056.

   No responsibility is assumed for lost, late or misdirected mail. Entries must be sent separately with first class postage affixed, and be received no later than December 31, 1991 for eligibility.

2. Winners will be selected by D.L. Blair, Inc., an independent judging organization whose decisions are final, in random drawings to be held on January 30, 1992 in Blair, NE at 10:00 a.m. from among all eligible entries received.

3. The prizes to be awarded and their approximate retail values are as follows: Grand Prize — A brand-new Ford Explorer 4×4 plus a trip for two (2) to Hawaii, including round-trip air transportation, six (6) nights hotel accommodation, a $1,400 meal/spending money stipend and $2,000 cash toward a new fashion wardrobe (approximate value: $28,000) or $15,000 cash; two (2) Second Prizes — A trip to Hawaii, including round-trip air transportation, six (6) nights hotel accommodation, a $1,400 meal/spending money stipend and $2,000 cash toward a new fashion wardrobe (approximate value: $11,000) or $5,000 cash; three (3) Third Prizes — $2,000 cash toward a new fashion wardrobe. All prizes are valued in U.S. currency. Travel award air transportation is from the commercial airport nearest winner's home. Travel is subject to space and accommodation availability, and must be completed by June 30, 1993. Sweepstakes offer is open to residents of the U.S. and Canada who are 21 years of age or older as of December 31, 1991, except residents of Puerto Rico, employees and immediate family members of Torstar Corp., its affiliates, subsidiaries, and all agencies, entities and persons connected with the use, marketing, or conduct of this sweepstakes. All federal, state, provincial, municipal and local laws apply. Offer void wherever prohibited by law. Taxes and/or duties, applicable registration and licensing fees, are the sole responsibility of the winners. Any litigation within the province of Quebec respecting the conduct and awarding of a prize may be submitted to the Régie des loteries et courses du Québec. All prizes will be awarded; winners will be notified by mail. No substitution of prizes is permitted.

4. Potential winners must sign and return any required Affidavit of Eligibility/Release of Liability within 30 days of notification. In the event of noncompliance within this time period, the prize may be awarded to an alternate winner. Any prize or prize notification returned as undeliverable may result in the awarding of that prize to an alternate winner. By acceptance of their prize, winners consent to use of their names, photographs or their likenesses for purposes of advertising, trade and promotion on behalf of Torstar Corp. without further compensation. Canadian winners must correctly answer a time-limited arithmetical question in order to be awarded a prize.

5. For a list of winners (available after 3/31/92), send a separate stamped, self-addressed envelope to: Silhouette Fashion A Whole New You Sweepstakes, P.O. Box 4665, Blair, NE 68009.

PREMIUM OFFER TERMS

To receive your gift, complete the Offer Certificate according to directions. Be certain to enclose the required number of "Fashion A Whole New You" proofs of product purchase (which are found on the last page of every specially marked "Fashion A Whole New You" Silhouette or Harlequin romance novel). Requests must be received no later than December 31, 1991. Limit: four (4) gifts per name, family, group, organization or address. Items depicted are for illustrative purposes only and may not be exactly as shown. Please allow 6 to 8 weeks for receipt of order. Offer good while quantities of gifts last. In the event an ordered gift is no longer available, you will receive a free, previously unpublished Silhouette or Harlequin book for every proof of purchase you have submitted with your request, plus a refund of the postage and handling charge you have included. Offer good in the U.S. and Canada only.

SLFW-SWPR

SILHOUETTE® OFFICIAL SWEEPSTAKES ENTRY FORM

4-FWSIS-2

Complete and return this Entry Form immediately – the more entries you submit, the better your chances of winning!

- Entries must be received by **December 31, 1991.**
- A Random draw will take place on **January 30, 1992.**
- No purchase necessary.

Yes, I want to win a FASHION A WHOLE NEW YOU Sensuous and Adventurous prize from Silhouette:

Name _____ Telephone _____ Age _____

Address _____

City _____ State _____ Zip _____

Return Entries to: **Silhouette FASHION A WHOLE NEW YOU,**
P.O. Box 9056, Buffalo, NY 14269-9056   © 1991 Harlequin Enterprises Limited

PREMIUM OFFER

To receive your free gift, send us the required number of proofs-of-purchase from any specially marked FASHION A WHOLE NEW YOU Silhouette or Harlequin Book with the Offer Certificate properly completed, plus a check or money order (do not send cash) to cover postage and handling payable to Silhouette FASHION A WHOLE NEW YOU Offer. We will send you the specified gift.

OFFER CERTIFICATE

Item	A. SENSUAL DESIGNER VANITY BOX COLLECTION (set of 4) (Suggested Retail Price $60.00)	B. ADVENTUROUS TRAVEL COSMETIC CASE SET (set of 3) (Suggested Retail Price $25.00)
# of proofs-of-purchase	18	12
Postage and Handling	$3.50	$2.95
Check one	☐	☐

Name _____

Address _____

City _____ State _____ Zip _____

Mail this certificate, designated number of proofs-of-purchase and check or money order for postage and handling to: **Silhouette FASHION A WHOLE NEW YOU Gift Offer,** P.O. Box 9057, Buffalo, NY 14269-9057. Requests must be received by December 31, 1991.

ONE PROOF-OF-PURCHASE

4-FWSIP-2

To collect your fabulous free gift you must include the necessary number of proofs-of-purchase with a properly completed Offer Certificate.

© 1991 Harlequin Enterprises Limited

See previous page for details.